I0589965

HEAR ME OUT

CAROLINE SPRINGS CHARTER

LILA ROSE

Hear Me Out Copyright © 2017 by Lila Rose

Hawks MC: Caroline Springs Charter: Book 5

Editing: Hot Tree Editing
Interior Design: Rogena Mitchell-Jones

All rights reserved. No part of this eBook may be used or reproduced in any written, electronic, recorded, or photo-copied format without the permission from the author as allowed under the terms and conditions with which it was purchased or as strictly permitted by applicable copyright law. Any unauthorized distribution, circulation or use of this text may be a direct infringement of the author's rights, and those responsible may be liable in law accordingly. Thank you for respecting the work of this author.

Hear Me Out is a work of fiction. All names, characters, events and places found in this book are either from the author's imagination or used fictitiously. Any similarity to persons live or dead, actual events, locations, or organizations is entirely coincidental and not intended by the author.

Second Edition 2019
ISBN: 978-0648483571

PROLOGUE

BEAST

*R*age and fear boiled up inside of me as I punched the door open. The room was full of people, but I couldn't find it in me to care who saw me losing my shit. It wasn't every fucking day when a person woke and couldn't hear shit, and I knew it wasn't just a blocked ear or some crap like that. It was serious. When my head had been spinning earlier, I'd thought a quick nap would make it better like all the other times. Then bam. Nothing but silence when I woke.

My heart thundered in my chest. I rubbed the back of my neck while stalking through the common room at the compound. I needed out. I had to get away to seek help.

Fuck. I was scared.

What if the doctor says I won't hear anymore?

Jesus. I couldn't even go there. I was out the door to the compound and heading towards my ride when a hand landed on my shoulder causing me to jump like a damn pussy. I spun around to find Dallas, Dive, and Vicious in my personal space.

Christ.

Shit. Fuck me.

Their mouths moved, but I couldn't hear shit.

My gut churned. My heart beat so goddamn hard I laid a hand over my chest.

With wide eyes, I backed up a step. My eyes caught Mena coming up beside her man Dive. She grabbed his arm and said something to him. All men looked down at her, and Dive replied with something.

Fuck. I couldn't hear.

Clenching my jaw tightly, so I didn't cry like a little girl, I swiftly turned and bolted for my ride. If they were yelling for me, I didn't have a bloody clue nor did I care. I wanted answers. Needed them.

Riding towards the hospital, worry seeped into my veins, consuming me. If I couldn't hear, I'd be useless. I wouldn't be able to help out my brothers.

Fuck me.

Fuck.

My whole life I'd kept quiet for one main reason. I hadn't liked how I talked. But it was more than that. More than the sound and nothing to do with my accent. Things with my brain didn't connect right with my mouth, and sometimes I'd say shit but meant it as something else. It didn't bother me being silent. My brothers accepted it, but already I was wishing I had talked more.

Shit, even with all the teasing I got as a kid, I wished I'd talked more. Life could be bloody cruel. Not only could kids be ruthless, but so could adults. My dad didn't beat me, but he was a dick about the way I spoke. A dick day in and out when I'd stuff up what I wanted to say or stutter over shit when I tried to get it right. My mum was a gem, but my dad… fucking arsehole. Lost count of the times he'd smack me in the back of the head and yell, "Spit it out right!"

I shouldn't have let them get to me.

Christ, I should have talked more.

After finding a parking spot, I climbed off my ride and found a car pulling in beside me. My glare turned to it, and Mena clambered out of Dive's vehicle. Her lips moved, her eyes shone with panic, and her hands moved all over the place. I pulled my brows down and shook my head at her.

She stopped just in front of me. Her hands and fingers did some shit in front of her, but I didn't have a clue what, and then I saw her sigh. She lay a single palm on my arm. I didn't need her worry. Shrugging off her hold, I started towards the doors. Then a hand grabbed me with a force I didn't expect her to have. She pulled me around to face her, drew her hand up and tapped her mouth. I looked there. Slowly, she mouthed, "Let me help."

My heart did a double beat that hurt.

Did she know I couldn't hear?

Pulling my phone from my pocket, I looked up her number and realised I didn't have it. She slid my phone from my hand and pressed her fingers over it for a few moments before turning it to show me.

In a text, she wrote out: **You can't hear, can you?**

Slowly, I closed my eyes, pain slicing my chest. Opening them, I looked up at her and shook my head.

Her smile was sad as she nodded and typed something else

into the phone. When she passed it back over, I read it. **Let's go in and find out why.**

Fucking hell.

She needed to leave. I was good at dealing with shit on my own. I didn't need a brother's old lady tagging along trying to fix me.

The phone was thrust back in front of my face. **I'm not leaving. Deal with it.**

I found myself snorting. Mena was finally growing into her biker babe status. She'd first been meek and mild. Since then, it seemed she was becoming stubborn as shit.

With a frustrated groan, one I couldn't hear myself, I nodded and started for the doors once again, with Mena matching my strides beside me.

MENA

Ever since Beast had come home from Sydney, after helping Dallas and Melissa, I had noticed there was something wrong. He'd acted the same, smiling when he was with his brothers, working out in the mechanical business when he had to, but staying his silent self. However, I'd also noticed times when dizziness would overcome him. He'd find something to hold on to until it passed. He wasn't a man a woman could get to know; he kept to himself a lot, except with his brothers, especially Knife, but even with that bond something had changed. Since they'd been back, I hardly saw them together. I wondered if something had happened between the two of them. Only what, I didn't know.

Kalen had seen me one day watching Beast. Stupidly, and kind of jokingly, he'd asked if I had a crush on Beast and if I did, he would beat the man black and blue. Of course I told him how ridiculous he was being. I also told him that I had a feeling something was going on with Beast. He'd smiled and said, "Sunshine, love you. But leave the brother alone."

I couldn't do as my man had asked though. Beast was dealing with things he didn't need to on his own, and I wanted to help him.

When Beast had stormed from the bedroom area at the compound earlier, I knew, knew something bad had happened. And as I watched his fast pace through the room, he took no notice of his brothers, nor some of the women calling him. Then it was as if something clicked; I got up and raced after him. When I found him and his brothers outside, I saw Beast's puzzled expression as his brothers tried to talk to him.

When I had been working in childcare, there had been a little girl who had been deaf. She was timid but sweet, so I'd made an effort to learn sign language so I could talk with her.

Why she popped into my mind as I watched Beast leave didn't register immediately, not until I saw her expressions of confusion and frustration mirrored on Beast's face.

I realised then, as he stormed off from his brothers, that he couldn't hear a single word said.

Grabbing Kalen's arm, I whispered in a rushed voice, "Let me follow him. He doesn't need a brother right now."

"I don't think—"

"Please, Kalen. Please trust me in this."

He searched my face and finally nodded. Knowing his keys had been in his pocket, I grabbed them quickly and ran for his

LILA ROSE

car. I was surprised I'd made it to the hospital car park just after Beast. At first, I thought he would have told me to get lost, even when I demanded to go in with him. So I was shocked when he nodded. Then again, the fear in his eyes was palpable.

While we waited, I sat beside Beast as he bounced his leg up and down, biting his thumbnail again and again while his eyes flicked wildly around the room.

Knowing him... actually, knowing he was a Hawks member, there was no doubt he was searching for potential threats. Despite my need to reassure him that nothing could harm us in there, I didn't, thinking at least his search kept his mind occupied.

"Maddox Lawson?"

Since I'd seen the paperwork Beast had filled out, I knew that was his name. Glancing at him, I saw he had his eyes over at the front door. Reaching out, I tapped his arm. He spun his gaze to me, and I gestured to the doctor. We both walked into the emergency room.

"Hi, I'm Doctor Spencer." The doctor smiled as we entered, his hand flying out to the bed. He eyed Beast in his biker gear as Beast sat on the bed. I stood behind it while the doctor sat in the swivel chair opposite the bed. "What seems to be the problem?"

Beast's brows dipped low, so I shifted forward and said, "Be—Maddox is having trouble hearing."

"Hmm." The doctor flipped open whatever file he had for Beast. "Says here he was in an accident nearly five weeks ago and had a bad head injury." He looked up. "Has there been any other problems?"

"I've seen him get dizzy a few times," I offered.

I jumped when Beast slapped a hand to the bed. Blushing, since we were talking about him like he wasn't there, I typed into his phone: **Sorry. The doctor said you were in an accident and asked if anything else was going on. I told him I've noticed that you've been getting dizzy.** I quickly handed it to him.

After he had read it, he nodded and then deleted what I had and wrote back.

Taking the phone, I read it out to the doctor: **Headaches.** I looked up, concerned.

Doctor Spencer nodded and wrote a few things down before he suddenly stood and said, "I just have to speak with another doctor, and we'll need to run some tests. I'll be back."

I typed into the phone what the doctor said and handed it to Beast. He read it, dropped the phone to the bed, and then ran a hand over his face.

Without thinking, I signed that everything would be okay. His eyes narrowed on my hands. Biting my bottom lip, I cringed and picked up the phone again. **Sorry, I was using sign language. You don't know it?**

After he had read it, he shook his head, but then typed something back. I read it as he did. **I never needed it. I could hear and talk.**

My eyes widened. I grabbed the phone. **You can talk?**

Pain darkened his eyes, he nodded. "I talk don't right." His face screwed up in frustration. He couldn't hear himself, yet he knew he'd said it wrong. He snapped the phone from me and typed out: **I don't talk right. My words get mixed up. I know what I want to say, but it comes out wrong.**

I typed: **Is it all the time?**

He shook his head, clenching his jaw. I could tell he didn't

7

like talking about it, so even though I wanted to ask a million questions, I didn't. He had enough to worry about.

With the phone in my hand, I thought about what I wanted to say. He needed to know that everyone around him who was important wouldn't care how he spoke. If his hearing loss was forever, he should feel comfortable to still speak.

Standing from the chair, I paced the room and typed into the phone. **No matter the outcome today, you have people who will support you. Even if you don't feel you could talk to them (though, I think they wouldn't care how you spoke), there are other ways to communicate. Like sign language. These are just thoughts for now. We don't know anything yet. But I want you to know, we all care.**

A nurse came through the curtain. She smiled at me, and when she spotted Beast, the big, brooding man on the bed, her eyes widened.

"Um." She started and then licked her lips as her gaze travelled over him. "I came to take your blood." When I glanced to Beast, I saw he sat glaring at her.

Smiling, I nodded to the nurse and added, "It's fine." While she went about it, I handed the phone back to Beast.

His jaw clenched a few times, and after he had finished reading, he placed the phone on the bed. When he pulled his head up to meet my gaze with his own, I saw moisture in them. My heart clenched for the large man. As soon as the nurse moved away, I was at his side in seconds, and without a thought, I wrapped my arms around his waist. It took a few beats until I felt his arms wind around my shoulders.

BEAST

Heart of gold. My brother was fucking lucky to have a woman like Mena. Christ, to have her there with me meant a lot, and I wasn't sure I could ever repay her. However, I wasn't certain I could let her words in. My brothers may not care how I spoke, but I did. I sounded like a dick. She tried to give me hope to hold on to, but I knew I was fucked.

Never would I hear again.

Fucking hell.

It hurt. Christ, did it hurt.

When the doctors came back in hours later, and after a heap more tests, some from different doctors, I had Mena write down everything they said, with me watching over her shoulder. I wasn't surprised when she wrote I wouldn't hear again. It'd been due to the bike accident I'd had before I went to Sydney. Due to the head injury, they called it a sensorineural hearing loss. As they handed Mena some pamphlet shit about it all, I sat there with no thought running through my mind.

I was finally numb.

CHAPTER ONE

BEAST

There was a knock at my door once again. Hell, I couldn't hear it, but I could feel the pounding against it since my living room wasn't far from the door. Whoever it was wanted my attention, but there was no way I was getting my arse up off the couch and away from the drink of straight whisky in my hand.

It'd been a few weeks since the hospital visit, and I'd hidden away feeling sorry for myself. And I didn't give a fuck who knew it. I hadn't left my house except to buy booze. I ordered food in, kept an eye out for it since I couldn't motherfucking hear the door unless they were being dicks like the person currently still at the front. The fucker must have been stomping their feet to make that much vibration in the wooden floor.

My phone vibrated in my pocket. I dragged it out and

looked at the screen; it was a little blurry with the amount I'd drunk, but I could work out it was from Dodge, president of the Hawks MC, Caroline Springs charter. **Open your fuckin' door or I'm gonna kick it in.**

Shit.

I had a mind to ignore the fucker. Then again, no one ignored the president and got away with it. Lifting myself off the couch, I set my drink on the side table and stumbled over to the door and opened it. Without looking at him, I turned back around and made my way back to the couch. My spot was still warm as I sank down into it. I felt the front door being slammed shut and too soon, Dodge stood in front of me with his arms crossed over his chest, glaring.

My chin lifted in greeting, just before I picked up my glass and took another sip. His jaw clenched. He was pissed, but I could also see concern splashed across his face. Hell, why else would he be at my place?

Dodge shifted, and when he did, it was to pull a piece of paper out of his back pocket and hand it to me.

Slowly, I took it and just looked at it. I didn't have a fucking clue what it said, but since my emotions were shot to shit, a thought flashed through my head about the note saying I was cut from the club since I was a deaf, dumb dick.

My body jerked when Dodge planted his boot into my shin. "Fucker," I mouthed. His head gestured to the paper. Sighing, I opened it.

We're worried, brother.

So worried we got Dive to talk to his old lady and her being also concerned, she confessed shit to him.

Fuck, brother. Why didn't you come tell us yourself? No brother in the club deals with huge shit on his own. We got

each other's backs, no matter the goddamn situation. You don't want all to know, fine. But Dive and I know, and we're here to help you get through this shit and get you back to us.

Mena will be here soon. Knew you'd be in a shit way wallowing in pity. Get cleaned up. She's gonna take you to a class in an hour where you'll learn sign language. Know you, so I know you won't want your brothers there, so Mena's gonna teach me and Dive until and IF you want the others to know. But I'm tellin' you now, brother, you got nothin' to fear from us knowing. We're family.

So go deal with Dive and me knowin', but do it showering.

And when Mena gets here, do not give her shit about spillin', or Dive will have your balls.

Fuck me. My throat felt thick. I'd finished reading, but I couldn't drag my eyes away from the paper.

We're family.

Mena had talked, and it didn't surprise me, but she didn't just blab to anyone. She told her man, who told our prez, and he was now standing in front of me.

He'd come to sort my shit out and get me clean to move the fuck on.

Didn't he see I'd be useless to Hawks? I couldn't hear if trouble came our way. I couldn't stake shit out. Christ, even in a fight I wasn't sure I could best a man again.

Still, he was there calling me a brother and stating we were family.

Maybe he had more confidence in me than I had in myself. Or maybe he just didn't see what I saw, how useless I was to them all.

Another jolt of pain to my shin and he thrust his phone in my face. **Stop thinkin' and just do. You'll always be a part of Hawks, and there will always be a place for you. Now get the fuck up and get showered.**

Hell, was the guy a mind reader?

Didn't matter. The depressing-as-shit emotions of "what if" were dragging me down. Dodge was there, he was the president, so I did what I had to. I got up from the couch, gave Dodge the finger, which caused him to smile, and walked from the room to the bathroom.

When they'd figure it all out, about how I was no good for the club, I'd deal with it then.

Then again, my brothers were good guys. They'd probably let me work in the garage. At least I damn hoped.

Goddamn Dodge showing and taking me out of my own pity party, giving me hope. I just prayed it wasn't false hope.

Hell, knowing my luck, it was.

I'd felt false hope before, during one night in a hotel room in Sydney.

Dumb cunt I was thought things would change, that a relationship could have been possible with a certain person. Shaking my head as I got undressed, I realised once more how bloody stupid I'd been to think things could be different. I'd barked up the wrong tree, and it'd cost me.

Cost me fucking huge.

After turning on the water, I waited for it to heat up and caught my own gaze in the mirror.

Haunted and dead would be the best way I could describe what I saw staring back. My eyes were bloodshot and tired. My skin pale and looking lifeless. Shit, it looked as if I'd lost weight in the last few weeks, something that pissed me off.

Snorting to myself, I shifted into the shower and slipped the shower curtain closed. The water ran over my body, the hot water stinging my skin. Still, I welcomed the pain.

Pain was something I was used to.

Not only physical, from being the best and fastest I could, but mental pain. Both showed up in my life like we were old friends.

My dad was good with mental pain. I'd lost count of the times he'd called me stupid or told me I wasn't worth shit. Even the kids through school taunted me, that was until I got stronger and they became scared to say crap like that to me. I'd moved out of home as soon as I could to get away from my dad's vicious words. Moved out of home and found myself a new family with the Hawks MC. They took me as I came: silent, but a person who could be deadly. There I met Knife.

He'd already been a prospect at Hawks for a month before I showed. I'd seen Hawks MC around and liked what I saw. I wanted it for myself, so I joined. Knife and I, being around the same age, connected, and our friendship lasted over a decade, until I messed it all up.

We'd spent most of our time together. That was if he wasn't off fucking all the pussy he could get. Hell, even before Dodge showed and took over as president, we'd been on the same way of thinking how Hawks was going to shit. We were going to chance a meeting with the big boss, Talon, just before Dodge showed and things changed once again for the good.

Dealing in shit was something a lot of the members didn't want, so when we got clean, we breathed easier, and it'd been the best fucking feeling.

One month, though, and everything had gone down the shitter.

If I thought my life sucked back in the day, I'd been wrong.

I was at my lowest, and I wasn't sure I could pull myself out, even with help.

Running a hand through my hair one last time, I turned off the shower and got out. Drawing in a deep breath, I found my balls and sucked in all the emotional crap. All I could do was see how things went. Drowning in my sorrows wouldn't get me anywhere, but shit, it was something I wanted to keep doing for a little while longer.

Knife would tell me to get the fuck over everything. I wasn't dead, so I shouldn't act like it.

Fuck, I missed the dickhead.

The dickhead I'd been in love with for, Christ, too long to count. He never knew, never suspected I was gay. Shit, I hid it well by taking women to my bed. It was all a cover because I was scared about how the brothers would react. Then Pick and Billy showed, and after dealing with the woman they both loved, they fell for one another as well, and it surprised the hell out of me the brothers didn't care.

The thing was, they had a woman in the middle to defuse other shit. Then there was Julian and Mattie, but they were in Ballarat, and I'd seen some of the brothers looking at them like they were freaks.

I didn't want that. I'd played up to my image so well no one suspected a thing. From the way I was built, looked, I shouldn't want to fuck some guy. Shouldn't want to date, love, marry, have kids with a man.

But I did.

I wanted it all. But I wanted it with a man who'd freaked

after what we'd done in a hotel room in Sydney. He freaked so much, he got on a plane before any of us and took off home. He hadn't spoken to me since.

I'd fucked it all up, screwed our friendship over me wanting something I couldn't have with him.

I was to blame, and it damn crushed me.

We'd seen each other around but avoided one another.

Actually, that wasn't right. He avoided me. I'd tried to get his attention, sent him texts, gone to walk his way. All failed.

He wanted me gone from his life.

The sting from it all still zapped me in the chest every goddamn day.

So it didn't surprise me he was a no-show when I hadn't been at the compound for three fucking weeks. I got messages from most, except him. The person I wanted one from.

He didn't care.

It was time I didn't either.

After getting dressed in black jeans and tee, I pulled on my boots and left my club vest sitting on my bed. I didn't have a right to wear it.

Not until I sorted myself out... if I could.

DODGE

My brother was fucking.... Shit, I didn't even know what he was feeling, but I knew it wasn't any good. His place was a mess. He'd been sitting in a dark room alone and drinking. His head was in turmoil about being deaf and where that left him with the brotherhood. I knew it was, because if it had been me, I'd be thinking the same goddamn thing.

It was time to help the brother out. But in doing it, we'd have to go slow.

Christ, when Dive came and told me Beast, a brother, could no longer hear, I felt it deep.

He thought he could fight this shit on his own. He was wrong.

A soft knock came to the front door. I stalked there and opened it, finding Mena shuffling from one foot to the other. Looking over her shoulder, I spotted Dive in his pickup. I gave him a chin lift, and he took off. Not that he wanted to; he would have come in and talked to Beast, but Mena had suggested things would be better if the words came from his prez and her since she went to the hospital with him.

She'd been right. The way I found him, he wasn't ready for anything, but I'd force things on him because I refused to lose him as a brother.

"How is he?" Mena asked as I stepped back and she entered. A frown marred her face as she took in the place. I went to the blinds in the living room and spread them wide. "Not good," Mena answered her own question.

"Babe, all we can do is be there for him. Still, it's also good to give the fucker some tough lovin'. He's showering and going with you to the class."

She nodded. "Good. Um, have you, ah… Knife, has he been to see Beast?"

"Darlin', it's best we leave that shit alone."

"Do you know what's—"

"Mena, babe. No, and it ain't my business unless one of them comes to me."

"But they were so close."

"Yeah, and something happened. It's for them to sort that shit out."

"What do you think—"

"Sorry, darlin' but I ain't talkin' about this with you."

She nodded and huffed out her breath. Good to see a woman of a brother worrying about another brother. But the women needed to learn the men didn't gossip about each fucking other. Whatever the issue was between Beast and Knife, was with them. Even if I had an idea of what it was, I had to tell my own woman to stay the fuck out of it. If it caused the club trouble in any way, it was then I'd wade in. Until then, it was their problem to sort the fuck out.

It just sucked it was this way because they'd been close.

Closest brother Beast had ever had. He'd been one to keep to himself, and I was sure he'd had past shit to deal with, but I didn't push myself on him.

Not until now.

How-fucking-ever, I wasn't risking losing him to something like being deaf.

Life went on, and he'd soon see it.

CHAPTER TWO

KNIFE

I was 100 percent fucked. I could only wish it was literally. Instead, it was my head that was all fucked up. Where it should have been thinking and dreaming of pussy, pussy, pussy, nice tight, wet snatches, it wasn't. My traitorous mind was being fucking hateful and throwing at me, both day and bloody night, cock, cock, and more goddamn motherfucking cock.

Ever since that night in Sydney.

I'd gone to bed before Beast, not knowing where the man, who I had to share a tiny double bed with, was. However, in the middle of the night, I'd soon found myself wide awake and hornier than a teenage boy with his first stiffy. I'd also found myself curled into Beast's back, my hand on his hip as I'd thrust my dick into the seam of his arse. At first, as I fully woke up, I thought I was home and had a woman in bed with me; it wasn't until I opened my eyes and saw his naked back that I realised just who I was rubbing up against. I froze. My dick throbbed for release so I must have been at it for some time before I'd woken.

Freaked, I shifted back and would have tugged one out, even with Beast lying next to me. Only that didn't happen. When I started to move my hand from his hip, his hand came down on it, and he jerked his arse back on my dick.

"Beast," I warned low, because shit, I was close to blowing.

He didn't listen. If anything, the sound of my voice got to him since he jerked his arse back again, then shifted up and down on it.

Lost.

I was fucking lost in the feeling.

It was wrong, the whole scene, but my dick led me to do shit I'd never thought I'd do. Gripping his hip, I'd glided my cock up and down his seam. He'd grunted through a groan, hitting me right in the dick and left me exploding right into my boxers.

It should have stopped there.

It didn't.

His hand on mine pulled forward. I'd fallen against his back more, my eyes wide, my fuckin' heart just about beat right out of my chest when he'd wrapped my palm around his huge, hard cock. With his hand over mine wound around himself, he'd ran them up and down his dick.

Even though I'd been riding the high after coming hard, I should of pulled back. I should have shoved him away. I didn't. I put it down to the fact my mind wasn't functioning right. Which was how I ended up tugging him until he groaned low and squirted his release over my hand and floor.

Then it had all kicked in.

What we'd done.

Wide awake, I'd flopped to my back and wiped my hand on the sheet.

Hell, it was then I freaked. After all, I'd just ground against my mate's arse and come, then held his dick in my hand while he'd gotten off.

The bed dipped as Beast shifted around, and my pulse had ticked higher. When I saw his hand rising as if he were going to touch me intimately, I'd scrambled out of bed and went to hide in the bathroom.

Wasn't sure how long I stayed in there. I sat on the toilet with the seat down and ran through my head what went down in that bed. In a way, I was kind of disgusted with myself. What scared me the most was thinking of how we'd go on from there.

He was Beast.

My friend.

My closest friend.

Christ, I hadn't even known he was into that shit.

Was he gay?

He couldn't have been. I knew the man got pussy.

With not knowing what to do, I'd showered and then crept into the room. I wasn't sure if he was asleep or faking it. I didn't care. I'd been too freaked. I'd grabbed my shit and flew out of there like my socks were on fire.

From that night on, I'd been a dick.

It'd been too many weeks since I'd spoken, made eye contact, or stayed in the same room as Beast. I couldn't explain why, maybe I was a coward, but that shit scared the fuck out of me. What we did wasn't us…. At least I didn't think it was.

The day I saw him race from the compound in a furious mood a few weeks back, I knew something bad had happened, yet I couldn't bring myself to see if he wanted or needed my help. I sucked at being a friend, all because of what happened in that room.

Something was going down with Beast though. Everything inside of me wanted to know what. However, like the pansy I was, I didn't find out.

And as each day passed, it got harder to restrain myself from getting some answers. Hell, I even tried bringing it up with Dodge after I knew he'd been to see him a week back. He'd glared and told me, "Find out your fuckin' self."

Which was what I was going to do.

I was sick and tired of missing the big fucker.

I had to put what happened behind me. Shit, I'd freaked for a good time; it was time to move forward and get back the friendship we'd had.

That was if I could forget I had his *dick* in my *hand*.

There lay the bigger problem.

I couldn't forget.

Night after night, I woke hard from dreaming I had him.

As in I *had* him.

Taken his arse instead of grinding against it, and he fuckin' loved it as much as I did.

It all confused me.

Fuckin' confused me to a goddamn point I wasn't sure I knew myself any longer.

I'd never thought about a man's arse. Never looked at my

hand, like I was doing then, and thought about having another guy's dick in it while I jacked him off.

I wasn't gay.

Pussy was my best friend, and I fucking loved it.

But since that bloody night, my mind threw thoughts of cock at me.

Most importantly, Beast's cock and arse.

"Fuck," I whispered harshly into my empty room at the compound.

I'm not gay.

But I needed my friend back.

For him to be away from his brothers, something big had gone down, and I was an arsehole for not being there for him like all the other brothers.

Standing from my bed, I made my way out of my room and down the hall, to the back of the compound where the kitchen was.

Thank fuck it was deserted. I wasn't in the mood to deal with anyone. Low must have been in there recently; the place was clean. Nary was also present with the fruit and cupcakes on the huge-arse table. I grabbed a banana from the basket and peeled it, throwing the peel into the bin beside the counter. Leaning against the table, I took a bite, chewed, and swallowed, then froze.

My mind was my own, but it was a dirty fucker.

Seeing the banana in my hand, my mind took me to the hotel room where I held Beast's dick in my hand. It wasn't even the goddamn same size; Beast was bigger.

Aw, shit, now I'm comparing a banana to a man's cock.

Then my mind went ahead and fucked me up royally because it placed a picture in there of a person giving head.

23

Was it something I could do?

Screwing my face up at the thought, I shook my head and went to take another bite, only to pause and slide my mouth down slowly on the banana. Wasn't bad. I could handle it. *Why in the fuck am I thinking I could handle a dick in my mouth?*

It touched the back of my throat, and I gagged, only to choke when Mena and Dive suddenly appeared in the doorway.

Dive's eyes widened. Then he smirked and asked, "What in the fuck you doin'?"

I tore the banana out of my mouth, only it was still down the back of my throat, so I retched a little, breathing heavily through my nose. Quickly chewing and swallowing what I could, I shook my head and gave him the middle finger.

Mena shifted into the room and over to the coffee maker. Finally finishing what was in my mouth, I shot daggers to my brother and replied darkly, "Eatin' a fuckin' banana. What in the hell you think I was doin'?"

He'd better think of his life before he answered.

He shrugged, his eyes dancing with humour. "It kinda looked like you were giving it a blow—"

"Kalen," Mena cried. She must have seen the way I tensed and stood slowly. "Um, honey, let's have that coffee before I go."

Ignoring the grinning brother, I asked Mena, "Where you off to, darlin'?"

Her cheeks heated, and she glanced to Dive, to me, to her man and then back to me. "Um…."

"She's goin' to see Beast."

My body tensed for a new reason.

Mena was hanging with Beast?

Why?

Clenching my jaw, I bit out, "Didn't know they were close."

The humour died from Dive's expression. His eyes narrowed as he crossed his arms over his chest and stated, "Guess you don't know a lot of things these days."

Crossing my arms also, I braced my feet apart and asked on a snarl, "What's that supposed to mean, brother?"

Dive's upper body kind of came forward when he gruffly said back, "Means maybe you need to get your head outta your arse and open your eyes."

"Kalen," Mena called.

"You got no idea what you're talkin' about."

He straightened. "No, I don't. But what I do know is that I had two brothers who were close, so close they never went a day apart from each other, then something went down, and now a brother in need doesn't have the support from his so-called close brother."

"Then tell me what in the fuck is happenin'," I demanded.

"Ain't mine to tell."

Shaking my head, I clenched my teeth together. I turned my gaze to his woman, "Mena—"

Her eyes widened. "I have to go," she announced before placing her half-full coffee on the counter, going to her man, giving him a kiss, and running from the room.

"Do not ask my woman," Dive clipped. "Grow a pair, Knife, and do it soon." He stalked from the room.

"Fuck," I muttered, running a hand over my face.

Since it wasn't that long ago I'd decided to do something about Beast, I guessed it was lucky Mena and Dive came into the kitchen when I was blowing a banana or else I wouldn't have known to follow Mena. See if she was heading to his place or meeting him somewhere.

I sure wasn't happy with their little friendship.

In fact, it pissed me off.

Answers were what I needed, and in finding them, I had to get my arse out of there.

CHAPTER THREE

KNIFE

Thank fuck I caught Parker on the way in as I headed out. Parker was a brother, only he didn't carry the club's cut since he was a detective, much like his cop partner, Lan, who was also Stoke's cousin. Stoke being a brother in the Ballarat charter. So even though he didn't wear the cut, I knew as soon as I got in his face and said I needed a lift somewhere, he'd do it, and he did. Turning back around, he walked out of the compound and straight to his GEN-F HSV GTS Maloo 1. If I wasn't in a hurry, I would have taken the time to appreciate the beauty, even though nothing, and I mean *nothing*, could best my baby, my Harley Dyna.

"Where we headin'?" Parker asked after we were both situated in the vehicle.

Pointing to Mena in Dive's truck, I said, "Follow her."

"Mena?"

"Yes!" I yelled and gestured for him to go with a wave of my hand.

"Why?"

"Jesus, just go, and I'll tell you on the way."

His brows rose at me, but he started the car and pulled out of the compound car park. More luck, Mena was a cautious driver, which meant she was slow. In no time, we were a couple of cars behind her.

"Right. You gonna talk?"

Fuck. I really didn't want to, but I also didn't want to take my ride to follow Mena. She would've heard it, and her not knowing was the perfect opportunity for me to find out what the situation was with her and Beast.

Sighing, I sat back into the seat and relaxed my body a little. Hadn't realised I'd been holding it so tense. "Something is happenin' with Beast, and no one is sayin' shit to me. Mena's goin' to meet with him now."

"But aren't you and Beast close?"

"Yes. But, look, some shit happened. We haven't talked for a while, so I don't have a clue what's happenin' with him now."

"So," he drew out. "Why not go and ask *him*?"

Why not go and ask him? He made it sound so simple.

Christ.

It was so simple, and it was what I should have done. Not that day, it should have been when Beast stormed out of the compound.

"Shut the fuck up and just drive," I told him.

"Damn, I love pointing out the obvious and gettin' abused for it. Sits right in me just here." He tapped his chest. I rolled my eyes and gave him the middle finger. I was famous for using it all the goddamn time. "You gonna go talk to him with Mena?"

Was I?

No, not yet, not when I wanted to find out how and why those two had become close.

"We'll see," I offered.

"Hmm."

"Hmm what?" I asked.

"She just pulled off."

I threw my hands up in the air. "And you're driving by, why?"

"I thought we were still hiding. Didn't want her to see me pull in after her. She'd spot us."

"Okay." I nodded and then looked out the back window, to the side window. "Where'd she pull in?"

Parker had done a U-turn before he answered and when he did, his voice was quiet. "An Auslan centre."

"What kinda place is that?" Some kinky place? Were they gonna get their freak on? Hell, that was highly doubtful since Dive was a possessive fucker.

"Knife."

"What?" I questioned, my eyes running all over the building and people walking in and out of it while Parker pulled into a parking space.

"It's where people go to learn sign language."

I stiffened, then slowly turned to Parker. "What?" Was sure I heard him wrong.

"Mate, I don't know what's gone on with Beast, but with Mena being here to meet him, tells me, fuck, mate, he's here to learn sign language. Never heard the bloke talk. Has he always been deaf?"

Beast, deaf?

Deaf?

Shit. Fuck.

I'd cut people's throats, slit their wrists. Taken down, beaten, and killed many. Each and every time, not once was I scared about doing any of it. Nothing had scared me. Until then.

My chest hurt, my stomach turned. Sweat broke out on my skin while the back of my neck itched.

Beast was deaf?

But how in the fuck did that happen?

It couldn't be.

Fuck.

Motherfucking Christ.

I hadn't been there for him.

No. It couldn't be that.

Shaking my head, I said, "No, maybe they're there to learn for another reason."

"Yeah, could be," Parker replied, but he didn't sound convinced.

Shifting back to look out the window, I squeezed my eyes closed and prayed they were there for another reason. "Wait here for me," I ordered, and not waiting for a reply, I had the door open and was out stalking my way to the entrance in seconds.

My footsteps ate up the pavement quickly. I had the door open before I stopped. There was a main office and then hallways down each side. Had Beast already been here waiting for Mena? Must have been or else I'd see Mena standing there, and she was none of the few standing around talking.

A woman in her late fifties started towards me. Her gaze

raked over my body and stopped on my club vest for a second before smiling. "Hi, are you a friend of Maddox?"

Maddox. Beast's real name.

Clearing my throat, I said, "Ah, yeah. Is he about?"

"Already in class. Come this way." She turned about and started down the hall to the left. "Are you joining the class? If you are, there's a fee you have to pay."

"No, I, ah, just wanted to have a word with him."

"Okay. But you should really think about joining. Having friends who are willing to learn with him helps a lot."

"Right." I nodded.

So he was deaf.

Fuck me.

Pain pinched at my chest.

"He's just in here. I can call him out?" Her hand went to the doorknob.

"Wait." Fuck. "Shit, I mean, sorry, could, can I, just, uh… I can talk to him after, but could I just see for a bit?" There were no windows in the room except for the one in the door.

The woman studied me for a moment before she nodded. "Sure." She gave me a sad smile and then patted my arm for some fucked-up reason. "Take your time."

"Thanks," I said and then watched her walk back down the hall.

Christ.

Beast was deaf and there learning how to communicate. And Mena was there to support him. How'd she known? Why did he open up to her?

Because you weren't there for him, fucker.

Shuffling forward, I ducked a bit to glance through the window. There were about ten people at the other end of the room away from the door with one man up the front waving his hands around. I found Beast first. He was a big fucker, and next to him was Mena. She looked up to him and smiled, then laughed. Beast grinned down at her, then turned his gaze back to the screen the dude up the front was pointing at.

He was there learning.

Mena was with him learning as well.

Bloody hell.

I felt like the biggest piece of shit out there.

Spinning around, I walked out to the front desk to see the same lady as before sitting behind it. "I gotta get shit, I mean, stuff done. Don't tell him someone was here for him."

Her brows dipped. "But—"

"Not a word. *Please.*"

As soon as I had her nod, I turned and made my way out to Parker's car. Opening the door, I climbed in and sat. My eyes to my knees, thoughts running through my head.

"You okay?" Parker asked.

"Not even a little." I thumped my head back against the headrest and sighed. "He's deaf."

"Thought as much. No one knows?"

Snorting, I said, "Maybe Dodge and Dive. That's it."

"Sounds like he's only coming to terms with it himself. Doesn't seem he's ready for others to know. Fuckin' sucks."

It more than fucking sucked. It was crushing.

"Can we get outta here?"

"Yeah, mate." He started his car. "Compound?"

"Yeah, need a drink or twenty."

"What you gonna do?"

What was I gonna do?

I didn't have a fuckin' clue.

32

"Not sure." Shaking my head, I knew I needed to process it all. Let it sink in and then deal with what I knew. First, I needed to take my mind away from it all. I'd process when I was alone. "Anyway, what were you coming to the compound for?"

"Needed to talk to Dodge. A strip club just outta your territory has had some trouble."

"What kinda trouble?"

"Robberies. A girl found another in the car park beaten."

"Raped?"

"Nope."

"You think it'll drift over to our side?"

"Learnt in the past month that hadn't been the only strip joint dealing with things similar to that. Another had a fire started in the dumpster out back. Another had a woman taken, beaten, and then dropped back."

"The women know who?"

"If they do, they ain't talkin'."

"You know if it comes our way, to our clubs, we'll sort it out ourselves, yeah?"

"Course, just wanted to give you all a heads-up."

"Appreciate it, brother."

Maybe the distraction of something happening in our area was what I needed. Then again, maybe not. Christ, I needed a drink, to mellow and to think. Let me just pray my mind stayed on task and didn't drift off to dirty land in that time.

CHAPTER FOUR

BEAST

*I*t'd been a month of going to Auslan, and I was still learning new shit every time. The instructor was a good bloke, a few years older than myself, so a few weeks back, after class had finished for the day, I'd approached him with Mena. What I wanted to learn was how to sign curse words. When Mena blushed through asking, since Ben, the instructor, could hear, he threw his head back and laughed. Apparently he'd been wondering how long it would take me to ask such a thing. We got to talking. He'd signed that he thought it good my girlfriend came with me to every class. I told him Mena wasn't my girlfriend, but my brother's woman. Mena, understanding it all, blushed once again, something she did a lot. She also didn't miss the way Ben's eyes looked me over with a new interest lighting in them. Not that he knew I liked dudes, and not that I'd go there with him when I was still stuck on a certain prick who wanted nothing to do with me. A prick I was sure I'd seen standing out the door at the Auslan class. Then again, it could have been my mind messing with me.

If it weren't for Knife, Ben could have been a man I'd be interested in. He was big and good-looking. I even liked the tats covering his hands and arms. Had to wonder how he got into the business of teaching sign language when he wasn't deaf himself.

When I'd asked just the other day, he smiled and said, "Grab dinner with me one night, and I'll tell you all about it." He'd used his mouth and hands to get his question across. Telling me it was good to watch the lips move, another way to learn what people were saying was to read their lips. I'd caught some of the words, but lip reading wasn't as easy as sign language; it was going to take me longer to grasp.

I'd glanced down at Mena to see she was looking everywhere but at us. Did she know I was gay? I wasn't sure, but I didn't feel comfortable accepting his offer with her around. Ben, seeing me glancing to Mena, tapped my arm and said, "I'll give you my number. Text me if you want."

Searching his face, I realised his offer could also mean he wanted to just talk and it wasn't an actual date he was asking me on. So I nodded and gave over my phone.

It wasn't until two nights later I texted him. **Gonna head out to eat.**

Ben: **Is that an offer to join you?**

My teeth bit into my bottom lip. Me: **Suppose.**

Ben: **Lol. Sure. Where?**

Me: **Burger joint down from Auslan?**

Ben: **See you there in ten.**

Me: **Right.**

Just as I was heading out the door, I got a text from Mena:
Hi, Beast. Would you like to come for dinner at Kalen's?

Shit.

I could say I'd already eaten, then I thought why in the hell was I hiding getting dinner with the guy who was teaching us sign language? I replied with: **Thanks for the offer, but headin' out to talk with Ben.**

Mena: **Okay, have fun!**

What did that mean? Have fun in what way?

Goddamn, I was going to have to sit Mena down and talk with her. We'd become close over time. In fact, she was a woman I'd call a close friend. I enjoyed her company and sharing time with her. If it wasn't for her and Dodge, I'd still be holed up in my house drinking my sorrows away. Since I was coming to terms with shit, I knew my life wasn't as dark as I thought it would be. With Mena having my back, I decided she deserved to know more about me. Everything.

As I WALKED into the burger joint, I couldn't help but want it to be walking in there to see my brothers. However, I'd told Dodge I wasn't ready to come back to the club or see the brothers in person yet. He understood, and still he popped in when he could. Dive also messaged me, along with a heap of other brothers. Only there was one who hadn't done shit, and he would have known from my absence there was something going on, yet I still got nothing from him. Guess I'd scared him stupid.

It fucking sucked. What was worse was how much I missed the dickhead.

Hell, I missed all their company.

But mostly Knife.

However, I couldn't go back in time. I couldn't change what I forced on him. If I could, I would, so I was stuck with knowing I fucked it all up because I'd been hell'a turned on after waking and finding him rubbing up against my arse.

I'd lost count of the times I'd tugged one out thinking about that moment and when I'd wrapped his hand around my cock, and he hadn't pulled away. My thoughts too regularly turned to when my hand guided his, and I'd all too quickly finished myself off. It hadn't taken long either because I'd always wanted that. A scene like that with Knife. Jay Conger.

He was the one man who consumed my mind day in and out, who played in every fucking fucked-up fantasy I'd had since that night. I wished my feelings hadn't grown towards him.

It should have stayed as a friendship.

Fuck, I still wanted a friendship with the dick, but I'd scared him off.

Regret burned through my veins. There was no escaping it.

Ben waving across the shop brought me away from my thoughts. I sent him a chin lift, which he smiled at, and made my way over. He was seated in a booth, so I slid into the other side of it and signed "Hi." He signed it back, and I also saw his mouth move over the word.

Pulling the menu my way, I took a look at it, suddenly feeling weird about being there with him. I wasn't sure how long I glanced at it, but then I felt fingers tap my arm. Meeting his gaze, he signed. *Are you going to ignore me the whole time?*

Shit, I felt my cheeks heat. I gave him a smile. *No, but I am starved.*

His body moved as he chuckled. *I can understand that. You're a big guy.*

My hands flew before I could stop myself. *Are you gay?*

Yes. Are you?

No. Yes. And then I added a nod to go with it.

He raised his brows. *No one knows you are?*

No. How did you?

He smiled. *It was more hoped.*

Fuck me.

He was into me.

I'm not here for that.

He shrugged. *All good. You're catching on quick to signing.*

You teach well. I also had Mena over when I could since the classes we went to were only refreshing her mind to what she already knew.

He winked, and I felt that in my cock. Instead of signing, he spoke, "I'm glad to help." At least that was what I thought he said, if I was reading his lips right.

I signed. *Did you say, I'm glad to help?*

He grinned. *Yes. You've been practicing reading lips?*

Yeah. YouTube helps.

He threw his head back and laughed just as a waitress came to stand beside the table. Hell, I hadn't even thought of how I was going to get across what I wanted. I guessed pointing at them would be the best. I slid the menu her way and pointed to something. A hand came down on my arm.

Ben shook his head and signed. *Tell me what you want and I'll let her know.*

Nodding, I told him I wanted the burger and fries with a Coke. He relayed it with his own order.

Once she'd left, Ben looked back to me. *Don't ever be afraid to sign in front of people. You never know who knows ASL. Give them a chance first or if you have someone who understands it with you and can speak, ask them to help.* I gave him a chin lift. *Can I ask something?*

That's what we're here for. Questions and shit. I signed with a roll of my eyes.

He smirked. *Why don't you talk?*

How do you know I can?

Because you snort or scoff, you have your vocal cords.

Damn, he was smart. *There are people who can't talk even if they have vocal cords.*

There are, but I think you can.

I glanced around the place. I wasn't sure if I was fuckin' comfortable sharing stuff like that with him.

Meeting his gaze, I shook my head. *Next question.*

He studied me, then finally nodded. *Do you have other family besides your brother's wife?*

My head jerked back. *My brother's wife?*

Mena. He spelt out since there wasn't a singular word for her name.

It dawned on me. I'd said Mena wasn't my girl but my brother's. *I don't have any siblings.*

What? But—

I held up my hand. *He's my brother in a sense of an MC club. I'm a part of the Hawks MC, so I have many brothers.*

His eyes widened. *Really?*

Chuckling, I nodded.

Do they know?

About what? Me being deaf? No, well, besides Mena, her man, and my president.

Why?

Why, was the question. I just didn't think I was ready for their pity. Poor Beast, the one who never spoke and was now deaf. How would he bring help in a situation? Shit, I was probably overreacting, and Dodge would have my balls if he heard that crap, but I'd deal with it eventually. I wasn't going to hide forever. I think what I was waiting for was for me to be back to the person I was. If I was fluent in ASL and lip reading, I'd feel confident then.

Ignoring his question, I asked one of my own. *How did you get into teaching when you can talk and hear?*

He sighed at my obvious evasion of answering him. Before he could answer though, the waitress was back with our drinks and food. After Ben had thanked her, she left, and he answered while I dug into my food.

My mum is deaf. She taught me all I know, and I enjoy teaching others.

I nodded and then asked. *The ink?*

Teen rebellion. He smiled. *Yours?*

Because I like them.

They look good on you.

My pulse picked up. *Same to you.* Damn, I really shouldn't have said that. Things were steering in a way I wasn't wanting. I quickly changed the subject. *How long it take you to learn lip reading?*

"A few months."

Raising my brow, I asked. *Just once?*

He grinned and shook his head, putting his burger in one hand to sign with the other. *A few months. Don't worry, I stuffed up all the time when I was learning. At least you'll be a professional at ASL very soon.*

I shrugged and admitted. *I understand mostly everything. If I don't, I can get the gist of it from the other words being said. And add that to a lot of practice.*

That's good. It'll be like a second skin to you soon. Natural and normal.

Hell, was I ever really going to feel normal? I didn't think so.

CHAPTER FIVE

KNIFE

*O*bsessed.

It was the best way to describe my actions recently. I was obsessed with learning sign language over the net. I was also obsessed with knowing who in the fuck that Ben guy was who taught the class to Beast and the others.

It was lucky I'd made friends with Mary at the counter, and she'd let me slip by to watch the class through the door. Told me how good of a teacher Ben was. *Yeah, right.* I'd been there the day Beast and Mena went to the front of the class to talk to fuckface. I'd seen the way he eyed Beast up and down like he wanted to goddamn eat him alive.

Why did I care so much about that look? I didn't have a clue, not until I'd found myself following Beast to a burger place where he met up with dickhead. Was it a date? If it was, why did that thought burn my gut?

As I sat in my car out the front, I put my feeling's down to the fact I was worried Beast had found a new friend who'd understand him better and what he was going through. I'd left shit too long, and now he was moving on to find newer friends.

Ones who looked like he wanted to take a bite out of Beast's cock.

Fuck me.

Why in the hell did I care who took a bite from his cock? I shouldn't have been even thinking about his dick.

The bastard had messed with my mind with that incident at the hotel. Never in my life had I thought about a dude in that way. Hell, I wasn't gay.

I wasn't.

Women were it for me. Their sweet bodies, their warm mouths, and their tight, wet snatches.

What I needed was to get laid. It'd been a while since the last club slut I took to my bed because my head had been messed up.

Wait a fuckin' second. Beast and the dude walked out of the food joint smiling and talking with their hands. I hadn't seen Beast smile in a long time and he was wasting them all on him.

Jesus. I wanted my friend back.

Usually, it'd be me and my antics that brought a smile from Beast's usually sober expression.

Christ. What was wrong with me?

Thinking of Beast smiling, watching Beast on a date… if it was a date.

I clenched my jaw at the sight of the cunt reaching out to touch Beast's arm. *That hand would sure look good shoved down his throat.*

Fuck it. I had to do something. It was obvious the absence of not having Beast around was making me think of him in more ways than I should when I wasn't into dudes.

It was time to gain back what we'd lost before that night.

Throwing my door open, I climbed out of my Jeep and slammed the door shut. Beast, of course, didn't hear it, but Ben did. Meant he could hear. So why was he teaching a class to deaf people? Maybe he did it so he could pick up men? He wasn't anything special, so he could be hard up to find a date. Instead, he preyed on his students.

When the dick's eyes landed on me across the road, they widened. Beast, seeing his reaction, turned his gaze my way and then narrowed. Still, I gave him a chin lift before I started my way over.

Ben signed something to Beast who nodded. "Hey," Ben said as I stopped just in front of them.

"S'up?"

"I'm Ben. Maddox says he knows you."

My jaw clenched. My nostrils flared from hatred raging inside of me.

Maddox.

He called him Maddox.

"Knife."

Ben's head jerked back before he asked, "Sorry?"

"Name's Knife, and his"—I pointed to Beast—"is Beast. You don't get to call him Maddox. Did he tell you he's a part of a MC?"

"Yes."

My eyes narrowed on Ben's lips when I saw them twitch. "You findin' somethin' fuckin' funny?"

Beast reached between us and clicked his fingers. When he had Ben's attention, he signed something. If I caught it right, he'd asked what I was saying. Ben replied, but I didn't watch what he said. I was eyeing Beast as he followed Ben's hands. Only maybe I should have been watching Ben because the way Beast's eyes widened and swung his gaze to me was suspicious.

Beast started to sign, his hands flying like a pro, so I missed most of it, but lucky *Benny wenny* was there. He translated. "He's saying, what gives you the right to come at us like you are? Who in the fuck do you think you are by stating I call him Beast instead of Maddox? Who does this shit? As far as he knew you were out of his life."

My eyes stayed glued to Beast as he ranted at me. He was pissed, and I couldn't blame him. I had no right to even be there saying the crap I did, but I was fuming, and when that happened I went with it without a coherent thought.

I'd fucked up. Again.

Still, before I left them to whatever was happening between them, I lifted my hands. *Never out of your life.*

Before I turned and made my way back to my car, I caught Beast's eyes widen.

BEAST

Hadn't seen the fucker in nearly two months and then suddenly he appeared when I was out with Ben and knew, *fuckin' knew*, I was deaf.

He'd signed.

How in the fuck did he know?

Was it Mena, Dive, or Dodge?

Shit. Fuck me.

The way he walked over like his anger was hanging on by a thread; but why was he angry in the first fucking place? He had no right. He didn't.

As I watched him stalk back to his car, I couldn't help but want to run after him and yell some more. Seeing him after so long... Christ, it was like my eyes wanted to drink the sight of him in. My body hummed and wanted to reach out and touch him, make sure I hadn't imagined he was standing in front of us spouting the bullshit he had been.

What in the hell was he going on about?

Jesus. What a goddamn fuck-up.

Glancing to Ben, I signed I was sorry for my brother.

He shrugged. *I thought he was an old boyfriend.*

My head jerked back, and then I threw it back and laughed. Shit, if Knife heard that, he would have kicked Ben's arse. I shook my head as my laughter died. *No, hell no. We were friends. Shit went down, and we're not so close now.*

His brows rose. *You sure?*

Nodding, I also moved my fist up and down for the sign yes. *Anyway, see you at the next class.*

He grinned. *Looking forward to it.*

As Ben walked off, I sighed in relief he didn't try any shit on me. I wasn't in the mood. In fact, it had darkened when Knife showed up. I had an urge to drive to the compound and confront the idiot about how he showed, said shit, and left. Acting as though he had my back and it hadn't been two months since I'd seen him.

Maybe it was time to move shit up, see my brothers and

explain what had happened. Besides, even though I had some savings, didn't mean I didn't need to get back to work.

Shit, seeing Knife had me thinking things with the rest of my brothers wouldn't be so bad. How he found out, I didn't know, but I would find out. However, the fact he'd obviously found out and then went out and learnt sign language somehow meant a shit-ton to me.

Meant he'd accepted it, and me like that.

My phone vibrated in my pocket on the way to my car. It'd been too cold to ride my baby. I pulled my phone out and stared down at the screen.

Knife.

I didn't open it until I was seated behind the steering wheel.

Look. Didn't know who that guy was. Thought he was hassling you. I snorted. That was the biggest load of bullshit I'd heard. Still, I read on. **Sorry if I fucked anything up with you and him.** He thought I was on a date. So he had come to the conclusion I was gay from that night in the hotel room. At least it was out there, not that I was ready to tell the whole fucking brotherhood. **Just want things to go back to how they were. Gonna be the biggest pussy here and say I miss your ugly mug around the compound. Yeah, I know you can't hear. No one told me. I saw you go into that place one time. But why you haven't come back to the compound is fucked up. No one will care. You're still a brother, always will be.**

I acted like a dick after... I shouldn't have been that way. I just didn't expect, you know, that to happen. You flying that way doesn't change anything either. Just look at the

brothers with Pick and Billy. They won't give a fuck. Just like I don't.

I was a dick. I'm always a dick, and you know this. Now, you're gonna get over it and we can get back to what we had?

Christ, trust the fucker to end the message like that. Like I had to get over the way he was because he apologised. He didn't know how hard it would be for me. Not only to forget the way he acted but to be around him. The brothers I could handle.

Knife I couldn't because I was in love with him.

Had been since in our twenties.

A decade and a half in love with a man who would never see me that way.

I was fucked no matter what. But I knew not having Knife in my life would be harder.

Throwing my phone to the seat next to me, I started the car, watching the gauges kick to life. Then I rested my head on the steering wheel.

Fucking hell.

Leaning back, I picked up my phone and typed in six words back to Knife. **Over it. See you next week.** There was no chance I would mention that night to him. He wanted to forget, fine. I could live with that since it freaked him the hell out so much. It was a night we'd have to put behind us. It was going to be hard every time I saw him not to think of it and the way he kept it going. The way he didn't run until after we'd both finished. But I'd deal. I wasn't losing the club over it and him. And there was no way I was letting the club lose me. Fuck anyone who says shit about me. Seeing Knife did one good thing, and that was fill me with strength. It was time to get on with life.

I sent off another text, one to Dodge asking for church when I came back, but how I also wanted Mena there so she could translate what I wanted to say.

Dodge's response was quick. **Glad to have you back, brother.**

I pulled my car out of the park and drove home calm and smiling.

To start with, finding out I was deaf had been scary as fuck. Not a day or night went by when the demons didn't feed my fears. Shit, for a while I wanted to end my life.

However, with time, I learned it wasn't so bad. Hell, I wasn't dead. I was still living, breathing, and feeling.

It took time to deal with it, but I wouldn't be the only one going through shit like that, and I wouldn't let it beat me down.

I had support.

Brothers.

They'd trusted me in so many situations. It was time I trusted them.

CHAPTER SIX

BEAST

*D*odge sent me a text stating the main brothers were in church waiting for me to arrive with instructions that after I was done, they'd spread the word about what had gone down. Mena had stood beside me before we entered, and I hadn't thought I'd be worried, but I was. Shit, it was like going to school knowing you have to get up the front of the class and share your project. Not that I ever did. I refused to do a lot of shit in school, but I still saw the fear in other kids back then, so I reckoned I was finally feeling what they had been.

But I knew the worry would all be for nothing.

They were my brothers.

"You ready?" Mena asked, signing at the same time.

Thank you for, fuck, everything.

"Not a problem. We're family, right?" she signed and said.

My lips tipped up. *Yeah, family.*

I walked into the compound. Immediately, brothers who were hanging around greeted me. I gave a nod and chin lift, but kept on walking and stopped just outside the room I knew Dodge, Dive, Pick, Billy, and Knife were in. Taking a breath, I opened the door and entered with Mena right behind me. I saw their smiles, and the ones who didn't know I was deaf, their greetings.

I stood tall at the end of the table, Mena beside me. I let my hands do the talking while Mena translated, "Some already know, to those who don't, about a month or so ago I lost my hearing. It took me time to deal with it all, but I have, and now I ask that things go back to what they were. I'll always be a brother and help when I'm needed. Being deaf doesn't mean I can't do shit. I can. You all know I don't talk and yet I've still communicated fine with you all before. I still got hands to text if you don't know what I'm saying. So learning sign language doesn't mean you all have to learn it."

The room was silent like my ears. I watched them all take it in and look to one another. Pick was the first to stand. Mena shifted forward so I could see both of them. "Being deaf doesn't change anything. You'll always be a brother. Good to see you here."

My jaw ached from how hard I was clenching it.

Dodge stood. "If anyone can't deal, they're out. I don't give a fuck who it is. Welcome home, brother."

Goddamn shit.

They had my back.

Knew they would, but hearing it, seeing it… it meant a fucking lot.

Yep, I'd been crazy to think things would be different with

my brothers. Fucking loco. It was going to be hard. People would have to get used to me not hearing, but it'd be cool.

My eyes caught on Mena's hands. "I'd like to offer lessons on sign language if any, um… brothers would like to learn."

Jesus.

That woman.

If she wasn't already my brother's and if I wasn't gay, I'd be snapping her up in seconds. Pure gold with the biggest heart out.

She smiled and signed, *Dive's already learning. Dodge just said he wants to, so do Pick and Billy.*

My heart lurched in a fierce beat.

As she looked to Knife, her brows drew down. I glanced there also. He shrugged and said while he signed, *Already learning, but it'd go quicker if I had a beautiful babe to teach me. Maybe private lessons.*

He'd stumbled over some words, but what he said was Knife through and through. A fucking flirt no matter who he was doing it with. The room vibrated with a fist pounding into the table.

Dive stood and leaned over. "I saw enough of what you said. You say shit to my woman like that once more, you and I will have problems."

Knife's hands came up in front of him. "No harm, brother. No harm."

"No harm my arse. Where'd you learn to sign anyway?"

A question I wanted to know also.

I suddenly realised as Dive and Knife spoke, they also signed what they were saying.

Shit and damn.

"Learned from the Internet."

His words hit me in the gut. He'd learnt. For me.

And just when I knew I'd have to cut my love loose for the guy, he went and did shit like that. Fucking prick was making it hard for me.

All eyes shifted to the door, so mine did also. Jason had poked his head in. "Hi." He smiled. "There's a lady here who wants to speak with Knife."

Tension filled the room. Not sure why, could be just one of Knife's hook-ups.

"You know who?" I saw Dodge ask our brother.

Knife shook his head, but got up from the table and started for the door. We followed behind, wanting to know what type of situation he was walking into and seeing if he needed our backs. Jason had led a woman into the common room. The woman, who was in her early forties, dressed in jeans and a blouse, looked our way. I could sense her fear. It came off her in waves. What probably didn't help were the other brothers standing around glaring at her.

Mena stayed beside me to sign. I didn't bother reading lips. I wanted to make sure I caught everything being said.

The woman licked her lips and said, "I'm after Jay Conger. My name is Sana."

"That's me." Knife replied, stepping up front.

"C-can we have a private word?"

"Nope." Knife shook his head, his arms crossing over his chest.

Her gaze swung around the room. "Please, it's important."

"Can't see how it's important when I don't know you."

Mena signed, and my eyes went wide as surprise flickered through them. She wasn't one of his hook-ups, so her being there may have brought trouble in.

Her arms went around her middle, and she pulled in a breath through her nose. "I wasn't asking for privacy for myself. I thought you'd want it when I tell you what I have to."

"Don't need it, so tell me."

"Fine. You may remember my friend Stacey Montgomery?"

Knife shook his head.

Sana sighed, and it was a big one from the way her body moved. "She didn't think you would either. Look, ah, she came to me the other day, told me you were a part of Hawks MC and that I had to find you to deliver something to you."

His head jerked back. "What?"

"It's, um, outside in the car."

Knife sneered at the woman. "You think I'm that stupid? I don't know you, lady. I ain't following you outside. Just tell me now."

Her eyes flicked around the room again. She may have noticed all brothers were on alert. Sana nodded. "Fine—"

I caught Mena's hands moving, telling me Muff had just entered and said, "Yo, why is there a baby in the car outside?" Then Muff appeared in the doorway.

Knife tensed. Shit, the whole room did, and we looked to our brother, only his eyes were glued to the woman. I glanced at her in time to see her nod. "She's your daughter."

Knife shook his head. "Can't be."

Mena tapped my arm. I met her gaze, and she signed, *Kalen's sending me outside to the baby.*

Nodding, I mouthed, "Go." She quickly ran out of the room.

Knife took some steps towards the woman, his arm thrown out wide. I knew he was yelling something, but I couldn't see his face any longer to know what it was and since he was in Sana's face, I didn't catch her response.

Dodge got close, placed a hand on Knife's shoulder, but he shrugged it off.

The situation was one where I wished to Christ I knew what was going on. It sucked watching and missing shit when I couldn't read the words on their lips when they faced away. Knew my brothers would fill me in, but it still goddamn sucked.

My eyes went to the doorway. Mena stood in it holding a girl, who looked not even one, in her arms. I flicked my eyes around to see the whole room had gone still, and all eyes were on the girl. Knife ran a hand through his hair once, twice. His body turned towards the doorway, the woman now forgotten.

Christ.

Anyone could see she was his girl. She had his eyes, his hair colour, and his mouth. I knew, hell, *I knew*, it was his mouth because I'd looked at it enough.

Knife had a child.

Slowly, he stepped over to Mena. She smiled up at him and I caught on her lips, "She just woke up, so she's a little out of it."

He nodded and stared down at his girl. Looking over his shoulder, he asked, "Her name?"

I shifted forward so I could see Sana's lips clearly. "Nevaeh."

Knife's jaw clenched. He also knew, without a doubt, she was his. He glanced back to his girl. Mena asked, "Want to hold her?"

Knife's shoulders lifted in a shrug, yet his hands came out in front of him. His girl looked at Knife like she wasn't too sure of him. Still, she went into his arms. He turned with her, his eyes staying on her face as she studied her dad. She must have liked what she saw because she smiled and lifted her little fist to punch him on the jaw. Knife grinned, then chuckled, then blinked. His jaw clenched before he glanced back to Sana and I saw him ask, "What happened to the mother?"

Sana gave him a sad smile. Mena got close and signed what she said. "Stacey came to me in the middle of the night. I hadn't seen her in months, and when I opened the door, she barged right in talking a mile a minute. Finally got her to slow down. She was ecstatic. The man she'd been after finally got a taste of her, but he didn't like kids."

"You're fuckin' kiddin' me?" Knife bit out.

Sana shook her head. "No. She left Nevaeh with me stating I had to find you since you're her daddy. Your name is on the birth certificate and all. Stacey said she never wanted kids because she knew her parents wouldn't be happy about it. She's always been a wild one, and her parents kicked her out for it. If they knew about Nevaeh... I'm not sure what they'll do."

"She left her girl for a piece of arse?" Knife asked.

"Yes."

Disgust was written all over Knife's face, his brows drawn and upper lip raised. "Fuck me."

"She was sure you'd take Nevaeh in. I, um... I have three children of my own, so I can't—"

"She's mine." Knife cut in. "But if you ever see Stacey again, tell her I better not see her fuckin' face. It won't be pretty if she even tries to pull shit for this girl. She gave me Nevaeh. She's mine, and now I goddamn know about her, I won't give her up for fuckin' anything."

Nevaeh took the break in him talking to smack him in the mouth again. Knife smiled and tipped his chin down. "Yeah, baby girl, you're mine and Hawks. We take care of our own."

Motherfucking Christ.

I thought the man couldn't get better. He just did.

Without too much thought, he'd claimed his girl, and I knew he'd fight through the thickness of hell to keep her. Only he wouldn't be fighting alone.

We'd have his back.

CHAPTER SEVEN

KNIFE

*E*ven as Sana left, leaving her number in case I needed help, and a bag of baby stuff, my new reality had yet to sink in. Still, I knew enough I wanted that little girl under Hawks protection. Especially if her slut of a mother took off for a man.

Fucking twat.

As the brothers surrounded me and Nevaeh—a pretty name for a pretty girl—my mind was catching up with my actions.

I had a kid. A seven-month-old kid. A precious little girl.

I wanted to scream my joy to the room for the gorgeous little bundle. Then again, I also wanted to shit my pants in panic.

I had a *kid*.

A little girl.

What in the hell was I supposed to do with a baby?

Not sure if Dodge saw the fear on my face, but the room soon cleared except for Dodge, Mena, Dive, and Beast. "You doin' okay, brother?" Dive asked, his lips twitching, and I wanted to punch him for it.

"I have a kid." I stated the obvious and stared down at Nevaeh in my arms. She looked back and mumbled some baby talk before grabbing onto my ear and pulling it. "What am I supposed to do with you?" I asked her like she had all the answers I needed. Glancing up, I asked the people left, "What am I supposed to do with her?"

Mena stepped up, and as she spoke, her hands moved for Beast's sake. "Just take care of her."

My head tilted to the side. "How?"

She smiled. "I'll help."

Some of the fear settled inside of me. Mena was good with kids. Hell, so were all the old ladies. I knew they'd rally behind me, but fuck, she was my little girl. I'd accept the help, but I needed to do a lot of it on my own.

Where that grown-up thought had come from, I didn't have a clue.

I ran from kids. They scared the fuck out of me, yet there I was claiming one and wanting to be the father she could look up to as she grew. I wanted to be a good dad.

Hell, I still acted like a teen myself, but all of a sudden, since I held Nevaeh in my arms... no, it was before that, since I saw my eyes and mouth on her cute little face, I wanted to grow up.

At least I wasn't alone. If I fucked up, I'd have the old women advising me, and I knew, the brothers who understood kids because they had their own, would also help me out.

I wasn't alone.

"You need a place of your own. Can't have her around here all the time," Dodge suggested.

"Shit, yeah, of course." Wouldn't want her growing up thinking it was normal to see club sluts going at it in the common room. Shit, they wore next to nothing for clothing. There was no way in hell Nevaeh would do the same. She'd be clothed top to toe, right down to her wrists.

But where would we go? I didn't have a home to call my own. I enjoyed living in the clubhouse. I couldn't go to anyone's place that already had kids, it'd be too packed, and then Nevaeh wouldn't get the attention she needed. I couldn't ask Vicious and Nary to put me up. They were just starting out, and Dallas was out since his woman was moving our way soon and he'd choked up about the word relationship in the first place. Throwing a kid on his doorstep with me would probably send him into a mental hospital.

My eyes sought out one person I thought could help. "You mind if we crash at your place?" He saw it. He read the question from my lips, not even glancing to Mena's hands.

But shit, as soon as I asked, I knew I should of thought it out more. We'd just gotten our friendship back and there I was asking if my daughter and I could move in. By the look of shock that passed over his face, Beast wasn't sure he was the best choice either but still, he lifted his chin at me.

Nodding, I said, "Right. So, now all I gotta do is learn how to take care of a baby girl."

"Mena and I'll give you a lift to Beast's since we got Koda's car seat. I'll leave Mena there and take off to grab some shit for Nevaeh while Mena guides you through some things. Sound good?" Dive asked.

"Perfect." I nodded.

"Do you even remember Stacey, the mother?"

"Fuck yeah, just said I didn't. She had the biggest titties… shit, sorry, baby girl." I covered her ear and placed her other against my chest. "She was good in the sack. I always remember the good ones, but she was a nut. Liked snortin' shit and feeling free and wild. Only had her a coupl'a times, but enough I knew I had to get rid of her."

Nevaeh squirmed in my arms. I uncovered her ears, and she beat my chest, obviously hating I did that to her in the first place. Tough cookie.

Hell, a thought occurred to me. She liked me enough then, but would she always like me? Fuck me, could I actually take care of a kid? There was no other option anyway; she was mine. I had to man up and ignore the anxiety eating my gut.

She'd been dealt with a dumb-fuck mother.

I wouldn't be a dumb-fuck father and pass up the opportunity of getting to know and love my girl. She was a part of me.

Christ.

She was a part of me.

Even had my genes.

And she'd grow up.

She'd grow and be a looker like her papa…. I was totally screwed.

No, I wasn't screwed; all the men would be if they tried shit with her.

WE'D BEEN at Beast's, who was in the kitchen, for two hours and I was already thinking I was totally out of my depth on anything to do with having a baby. She cried, I freaked. She made a noise, I freaked. She pooped, I freaked. She'd had a bottle, I freaked because I wanted to make sure she got the right amount of formula and then Mena went ahead and said she'd get wind from it which could cause her pain until she got it up.

Knowing my girl could get pain from having what she needed scared the fuck out of me.

Which was how I ended up pacing the floor with a screaming Nevaeh in my arms, patting her back trying to get the motherfucking wind out so she'd be in peace again. I was near in tears when suddenly she let out the biggest burp I'd heard from any girl. If I hadn't changed her diaper before, as Mena instructed, I could have sworn she was a dude just from that burp.

Then, the crying stopped. She stopped her restless moving in my arms and looked up at me like she'd just defeated a monster, and she was proud. Hell, I was as well.

"Good girl." I smiled down at her and kissed her forehead.

Christ, she'd been in my life just over two hours and I was already a goner for my baby girl. A big soppy goner.

"Having a baby is scary all on its own, but I think you're going to be okay, Knife," Mena offered from her position on the couch.

"I'm seeing the scary part, and maybe I'll believe the being okay part in a year or two. When I'm not freakin' out over every little thing."

Mena giggled. "You've been thrown into this, and you've never been a man who... how should I put it, liked children? I

have noticed you run from the room every time the children are around, but look at you now. You're doing amazing, and I'm very proud of you for claiming Nevaeh."

"Can't miss she's my girl."

"No, you can't, and still, even though you knew she was yours, you didn't have to claim her. You could have found other places for her, another family, you didn't. You saw her and took to her straight away. You're an amazing man, Knife."

I had no words. What she was saying happened, but I didn't see it was being amazing for doing it. She was my daughter. She needed me more than I needed anything. To me, I had no choice, and I didn't care that my choice was taken from me.

The front door came open, and Dive walked through first with his arms full of shit, followed by Pick and Billy.

"Did you buy out the store? Why in the fuck do we need all this?" I asked.

Dive chuckled. "You don't know it yet, but kids need a lot of crap." He placed some boxes on the floor beside Mena and then leaned in to kiss her.

"Which room we setting up the crib in?" Billy asked, then smirked at me. "Hell, never thought I'd see the day of Knife being tamed by a baby."

Rolling my eyes, I replied, "Fuck off. Beast gave her the middle spare room. Dump the shit in there, and I'll get to it soon."

"All good, brother. You got your hands full. We'll get this started," Pick offered and then took off down the hall with Billy following.

"No sexual shit happenin' in that room," I called after them.

Billy barked out a laugh and Pick scoffed. "We can restrain ourselves, dickhead."

I snorted. "Sure."

"Anyway, we'd better hit the road, gotta get Koda off Low," Dive said with a clap of his hands.

My gut clenched. I wasn't sure I was ready for Mena to leave me alone with my girl when I hardly knew shit about a baby, and she was the most experienced considering the rest of us in the house. "Yeah, ah, thanks for helpin'."

Mena must have seen my fear. She smiled and got up from the couch. When she was in front of me, with a hand on my arm that held Nevaeh's butt to me, she leaned in and said, "Stick to the schedule I wrote out and you'll be fine. Don't worry, Knife. You won't break her."

"Yeah, I got this." Fuck, I hoped I had this.

"You do." She nodded. "At least Beast is here to help."

"It's like the blind leading the fuckin' blind. Neither of us have dealt with a kid before."

"Then it will be good to learn together."

Why did I have a feeling her eyes were trying to portray a different meaning than the one she'd said?

"Look, do you reckon you could drop in tomorrow?"

She grinned. "I'd love to, and I'll bring Koda with me."

"Good. Great." I just had to survive around eighteen hours with my baby girl without fuckin' anything up. "Also, you reckon you could teach me a few things in sign language?"

Her eyes warmed. She knew I was only asking because Beast was a mate, right? Hell, the other brothers were wanting to learn also.

"I'd like that. You seem to know the basics already, and I think it's amazing you taught yourself."

"Yeah, it is," Dive commented with a smirk. My eyes moved into slits. Why was the guy smirking? In fact, I'd forgotten he was even in the room since my girl had curled her head against my chest and was content to just sit in my arms.

"It's nothing," I stated. Because it wasn't.

"Sunshine, we gotta get gone."

"Right." She nodded. "If you need anything, Beast has my number, program it into your phone. But I'm sure you'll be fine."

Fuck. I seriously hoped so.

After a quick goodbye, I looked around the empty room and felt the weight start to drown me. In a matter of hours, my life had changed. I knew it'd be for the better. Just glancing at my girl, I could see it would be. Still, it was fucking freaky shit.

CHAPTER EIGHT

BEAST

*F*uck me. Motherfucking hell.

How was this new situation going to help me get over the fucker in the living room since he was living under my goddamn roof?

Christ, the way he took on his girl without a thought was powerful. Wasn't sure if it'd sunk in how much his life would change since he was a father. There'd be no club pussy when he wanted it, or drinking and hanging with the brothers. His time patrolling our territory would be cut right down, so would the time he'd be called into a situation. Then again, there were enough old ladies to help him out, and hell, I wouldn't just stand back and not assist him. Babies didn't freak me out like I knew they did him, yet there he was taking one on without hesitation.

Rubbing the back of my neck, I knew for certain falling out of love for the dick had just been made harder.

Why in God's name did I agree to him staying here until he had his feet under him and knew what he was doing with a baby? Crap, I hoped he knew the living situation was just temporary. That was something we'd have to talk about.

Knife had a kid.

Just a wee baby girl.

And they were staying in my house. Under my roof.

Christ.

Shaking my head, I reread over the schedule Mena had written out. She'd just had her bottle, so it was playtime before she had a nap. Mena had suggested to hold off the nap for another hour, so then she wouldn't get tired and cranky before dinner.

Taking the sheet with me, I walked back into the living room and stopped. Knife had just set Nevaeh down on the couch, and she was already sleeping. He looked over at me and grinned like he'd just done the best thing in the world. I shook the sheet out in front of me. Knife's brows dipped together. I waved the sheet again and stalked over to him. I pointed out the problem.

His eyes widened, and his lips moved in a curse. *What do I do?* He signed.

That still shocked the hell out of me; he'd taken the time out to learn. Then again, we'd been pretty close before....

I shrugged. *Wake her?*

"*Walk her?*" he mouthed.

Snorting, I shook my head and spelt it out slowly. *Wake her.*

But she's asleep. He sighed and then tapped his mouth. I

watched his mouth move. "What happens if I wake her and she starts screaming?"

Groaning, I took my phone out and typed out a text. **I can only follow so much. Did you say.... What happens if I wake her and she starts a scrimmage? She's a bit young for that.**

At least the worry from his eyes left, when after reading my text, he threw his head back and laughed. Only to abruptly stop and glance down at his girl to make sure she was still asleep.

I'll ring Mena and ask her what to do.

I jerked my chin up in reply. It was then I noticed shit around the room. The brothers must have come and gone already. Which had me wondering if there were things I needed to put together.

Leaving Knife to his phone call, I made my way down the hall and stopped in the doorway to see, not only a hell'va mess, but Pick and Billy putting the finishing touches on a baby crib. Billy saw me first and tipped his head. Fucking hated I couldn't just say shit, but I didn't want to sound stupid.

Instead, I sent off a text to Billy. **Need help?**

He paused what he was doing and took out his phone. After a glance, he typed back. **We're good here, but there's a change table in the living room that needs to be put together.**

Me: **On it.**

How could one tiny person need so much? The room looked like a tornado had ripped through it. Not that I cared; it'd be good to have people in the house besides just myself. Would have been better if it were anyone else besides the man

I loved, but I wouldn't throw Knife and his girl out. When Knife had mentioned my place, I was sure my heart was going to detonate in my chest, but I'd seen the fear building in his eyes. I couldn't have said no.

He was one person I could never say no to.

Which was how we got into so much shit when we were younger. Speeding, drunk driving, indecent behaviour when caught in the park fucking. Actually, Knife had been pounding the woman hard while I'd been watching him and waiting for my turn. It wouldn't have taken me long to blow my load into the woman's snatch, even if I hated the thought of a woman under me, but watching Knife and fantasizing it was me he was laying into had me near coming in my jeans. That was until the cops showed and put a stop to it all.

Damn. I'd been in love with the idiot for far too long. I needed to get over it instead of wanting him under me, or shit, over me.

Maybe another date with Ben, or any guy where I could just fuck him, was in order.

As I walked back into the living room, I saw Knife sitting on the couch staring down at his girl, but his hands were moving over some signs. Fuck, he was practicing. He must have heard me because he looked up. *Mena said it was okay. We just have to put up with her being upset later.*

He was slow at it, but spot on with what he'd said.

Wait a fucking second.

We?

He'd said we.

As in *we* had to put up with her later.

I knew I'd assist him when I could, but I didn't expect.... Fuck, I didn't know. I just thought he'd come here to stay with her and he'd do mostly everything for her while I was a bystander and helped out when I could. Never expected to be placed in the same parenting role as him.

Shit, I'd leave it and see how things played out. He could have just slipped up and said we. Instead, I gestured to the box containing the change table. *Putting it together.*

He nodded and smiled. *Thanks, brother. Have to keep an eye on her. Mena said she wasn't safe sleeping on the couch.* Again, he signed slowly but had all the words right.

After a chin lift, I got down to work on the change table. A motor I could put together with my eyes closed. A change table was another goddamn story. It took me longer than I thought it would, and then I moved on to unpacking diapers, wipes, creams, and everything else in the bags. The clothes I found were tiny. I'd pack them in her room when Pick and Billy were done. Then again, maybe it was best they were washed before she wore them. With that thought, I took them into the laundry room off the kitchen and set about doing just that.

HOURS LATER, my place was starting to look back to normal. Only there was a shit-ton of girly things laying around. Toys, pink blankets, a bath, only that was in the bathroom with Knife as he gave Nevaeh a wash down. There had been pink, purple, hell, all bright coloured clothes that were washed, dried, and folded. In her room, I organised the crib to the window, the change table beside it, and a goddam ugly yellow rug on the floor. I'd even moved the living room around so I could place the overflowing tub of toys in the corner and a device a baby sat in to help them walk, plus a stroller. I did all that while Knife dealt with Nevaeh after she woke. He seemed to have been doing a good job. Before he'd taken her for a walk, I'd caught a few smiles and laughs on her face. She looked happy enough to be in the house.

Thank fuck I'd cleaned the whole place just the previous day. I'd felt content when I saw her playing on the living room floor earlier.

By the time the sun set, Pick and Billy were long gone with a wish of luck. Fina-fucking-lly, I was sitting on the couch doing nothing, but was exhausted. Too tired to even cook. Thank fuck the pizza places had the online option since I couldn't have rang an order through.

Just after I finished ordering, my phone vibrated with a text.

Ben: **How's your day been?**

I found myself smiling. Me: **Busy. Yours?**

Ben: **Good, since you replied.**

Shit. I liked what he'd said; it showed me he was interested. Also meant he'd let me have his arse. But... Knife walked into the room with Nevaeh in his arms. Christ, he looked good holding a baby, his own baby. Though he looked good no matter.

I was done for.

I needed a distraction from the man, so could Ben be one?

My phone vibrated. Ben: **Too soon? :)**

Was it?

We'd known each other a little while, but could there be more between us?

Me: **Not sure.**

Ben: **All good. I'll keep trying. You coming to class tomorrow?**

Me: **Yeah.**

Knife's bare feet stopped in front of me, I glanced up. "Who you talkin' to?" I read from his lips.

Ben. I waited for anything from him, but got nothing. Actually, what I got was a shrug. Then he turned back around and went over to the space on the floor to place his girl down. I pulled my attention back to my phone when it vibrated again.

Ben: **Great, I'll see you then and ask if you want to catch dinner tomorrow night.**

Snorting, I grinned. Me: **You're not asking now?**

Ben: **Nope. Give you more time to think. Because after dinner, I'd like to kiss you.**

My eyes widened. I looked up and caught Knife shifting his gaze from me back to Nevaeh sitting on the floor playing with something.

Holy fuck.

He wanted to kiss me. He was telling me so.

Did I want him to? Hell, did I want to go to dinner with him again? I enjoyed his company, but could I find myself lip locking with him after it?

Fuck it.

I'd never get what I wanted from the man sitting in my living room, so why the hell not get what I could from Ben? He was being straight with me, so I could with him.

Me: **'Kay, see you tomorrow, and when you ask me, I'll say yes. As long as you know I ain't lookin' for anything permanent.**

My heart raced in my chest. I chanced a glance to Knife,

and nearly jumped when I saw his eyes already on me. His hands lifted. *Dinner?*

Got pizza on the way.

Right. I'll feed Nevaeh. He paused to study me. *You cool?*

Yes.

His gaze searched my face once more. *Right.* He stood, picked Nevaeh up, and dragged her high chair into the kitchen.

My phone vibrated.

Ben: **Sounds fine to me :) See you tomorrow.**

CHAPTER NINE

KNIFE

*S*omething was up with Beast, and it had to do with that cockhead Ben. I wanted to know what they were talking about. Why Beast smiled the way he did, and shit, why his cheeks heated when he read something on his goddamn motherfucking phone?

As I was just finishing up with Nevaeh's dinner, Beast walked into the kitchen. *Going to wait out front for pizza, should be here soon.*

Nodding, I watched him spin back around and walk out of the room. I guessed the texting to Ben had stopped.

"Stupid fuckin' loser. Ben, what kinda name is boring Ben?" I asked my girl as I cleaned down her face. She started giggling. Smiling, I pulled her out of her seat and took her back into the living room. Only once my eyes landed on something, my feet came to a halt.

Beast's phone sat on the couch.

Before I could control my body, not that I was trying real hard, my feet took me to the couch where I sat next to his phone with Nevaeh on my lap. She cooed and then started to get testy about something. Leaning over, I picked up the toy she'd thrown earlier and handed it to her.

I was distracted from my girl, and I hated that I was. It was the tool out the front's fault. It'd be his fault I went through his phone.

Shit. I was invading his privacy.

But he'd just left it lying around.

It wasn't my problem I found his phone out in the open and knew his password.

That was if the password was still the same.

Picking up the phone, I prayed the password was still the same and smiled when I pressed in the numbers and it lit to life. Only to motherfucking frown when their messages popped right up; he mustn't have got out of messenger.

Then my frown turned into a hiss. My hand clenched around the phone.

Dickface wanted to kiss Beast.

Wanted to eat dinner with him.

Kiss him.

Fuck. *Kiss.* Him.

Why didn't the thought of that sit well with me? Maybe what I read off the guy the other night was right? There was something about him I didn't like. He could be into shit we didn't know about. I had to get Parker to do a background check on the dick.

Nodding to myself, I scrolled down to see Beast's reply and froze.

What the ever lovin' fuck?

Beast was going to have dinner with the cockhead.

He didn't want anything permanent. What in Christ did that mean? Did Beast want to screw him? Kiss him, dip in him and then dump him?

Fucking hell.

I didn't like it.

Beast could do better. Shit, I had to put that crap off in one way or another. Then I'd get the background check done and if the results came back saying he was an outstanding citizen, then Beast could—I screwed my nose up—go to dinner with twatface.

The front door came open. I jumped and nearly lost the phone in my hand. Instead, I quickly placed it down between the couch cushions.

Standing, I took Nevaeh over to her walking machine, taking my furious thoughts off Beast and that dude, and onto my girl. God, I hoped she was going to be okay being in a new place. At least she seemed to be taking to it. Still, Mena did warn me she could fuss that night.

How her cunt of a mother could leave her I didn't know. Christ, I didn't think I'd ever know. My girl was sweet. She was practically with a stranger and was coping okay. What did that woman put my girl through before she dropped her off to Sana?

I never wanted to see that woman's face again.

Leaving her own kid to a man she hardly knew, even though I was the daddy. The bitch made me sick with disgust.

76

PIZZA CONSUMED, while Nevaeh had played and we'd eaten and watched football, I'd then sorted her a bottle and made sure she got her wind up. Shit, I was even proud I hadn't collapsed in a heap when she'd started crying. It had me thinking I could handle about anything.

I was wrong.

So very fucking wrong.

Staying up late was the wrong move to start with, but I wanted time with just sitting with Beast. We'd watched football while he showed me some signs for curse words. Before he'd headed to bed, I thanked him for everything he'd done that day. His house had been a disaster, but he got it under control while I'd spent some time with my girl. It was what Nevaeh and I needed, and I reckon he knew it as well.

It felt like I'd just gotten my eyes closed when she'd woke crying. I rushed in there naked, reminding myself to wear clothes to bed in the future. When I picked her up, I found her PJs soaked. She'd peed through the nappy. Then I discovered it'd been my fault because I hadn't done the diaper up properly. After a change of clothes, blankets, and nappy, I eventually got her back to sleep. With my eyes half open, I stumbled into my room and slipped on a pair of boxers before I face-planted the bed. I was sure it was only seconds I was down when I heard her crying again. I got up, ran to Nevaeh's room and picked her up. As soon as she was in my arms, she settled her head against my chest. I rocked her a few times and set her back down.

Another wrong move was walking over floorboards. I was fucking certain I stepped on every goddamn squeaky board as I tried to sneak out of her room. I'd just made it into the hall when she started bawling again.

Ten more times, where a few I'd made it to my room, I concluded I wasn't made out to have a child because lack of sleep and I weren't friends.

So, to make sure I wouldn't be the biggest bitch in the world the next day, I walked down the hall with my girl in my arms and opened Beast's bedroom door. Switching the light on caused Beast to come to life. He was out of his bed blinking sleep from his eyes in seconds.

He was also naked.

As in *naked*.

His dick swung from the movement, and it was as though it had tranced me to watch it move.

Huh, I thought, *so that's his dick. He's big. Bigger than me.*

Suddenly a click to the quiet room had me snapping my head up to meet his gaze. I knew my cheeks were heating, so I glared, covered my daughter's eyes and clipped, "Cover it up. My girl doesn't need to see it."

His eyes watched my mouth before he snorted and picked up the boxers beside his bed, slipping them on.

Making sure I kept my eyes on his face and not his hypnotising body, which obviously could trance a man who was all about pussy, I walked towards him and deposited Nevaeh in his arms. "I'm beat, brother. She won't sleep. Been crying for the last four hours. Just need a nap and I'll be right."

His eyes widened. It was a low blow, but I knew he couldn't say shit when his arms were full. I climbed into his bed, on the other side he'd been sleeping in and landed on my back. It took effort, but I lifted my tired arms and signed. *Just five. Please.*

I opened my eyes enough to catch Beast nod down at me.

Then I was out.

BEAST

That was a wake-up call I didn't need. The light flashing behind my eyelids scared the fuck out of me, and I thought someone was coming in to attack. Which was how I was out of bed so fast ready to fight. Only to find Knife standing there looking like death.

Then reality crashed in.

Knife had seen me naked.

Hell, I was being a freak because I was watching him sleep in my bed as I rocked his girl in my arms standing next to it. I was also doing it smiling.

He'd seen my junk, and he fucking *watched* it for a good amount of time.

What was up with that?

Shit, that was something I couldn't think about. There was no way in hell I'd get my hopes up. Not after he freaked the way he had with the hotel incident.

But damn, he looked good sleeping in my bed.

Shaking my head, I strolled from the room with a sleeping Nevaeh in my arms. Knife looked like rat shit. He needed some sleep, so I'd stay with Nevaeh in her room. It was only a few hours before I had to wake anyway.

I *had* to get out of my room and away from the image I liked a hell of a lot.

KNIFE

My eyes were speared with white light. I cringed and pulled the blanket up over my head. Only it was snatched away too quickly and then I was kicked in the leg.

Rolling from my stomach over, I shielded my eyes from the sun streaming in through the window and asked my brother standing beside my bed, "What the fuck?"

Then I remembered the previous night and glanced around the room to see I was still in Beast's bed.

Sitting, I threw my legs over the side of the bed. *Nevaeh?* I signed slowly through her name and then took Beast in.

Living room. She's good. Got to shower and head to the garage.

Standing, I stretched and caught Beast watching my body. *Thanks for last night. Needed that sleep. You working today?*

No worries. Yeah, a few hours.

Crap, I then remembered he was going to head out on a date with Ben. *Look, make it up to you for minding my girl. I'll cook dinner tonight.*

He stiffened, looked to the door and then back to me. *Got something on.*

That would not fucking do. *Come on, brother. I make an awesome lasagne. You can't miss that.*

He ran a hand through his hair before responding, *Sorry, this thing's already organised. Can't back out. I'm going to shower.*

I nodded.

Shit, fuck, shit ran through my mind.

I had to think of something else to get him out of his date. Why it was important, I didn't know, but I felt it deep in my bones that Beast should not go anywhere with Ben.

I was a brother looking out for a brother.

Knew I wouldn't be able to get him out of attending the signing class, but the date I could do something about... and keep putting Beast off Ben until I found out more about the fucker.

Their names together sounded like shit. Beast and Ben. B1 and B2.

Rolling my eyes, I started for the door to find my girl and to start some planning.

CHAPTER TEN

KNIFE

Fucking bastard. Parker refused to do a background check on Ben. It didn't help I had no clue of his last name, but I told him I could find out. All I had to do was call up the centre where he worked and ask. Still, he refused and… I still could not believe he said it to me, but he told me to man the fuck up.

What in the Christ did that mean?

Man the fuck up about what?

I'd asked what he meant, and he'd laughed, goddamn laughed in my ear over the phone, and I guessed it was lucky he was over the phone or I'd have had my hand around his throat choking the life out of him and doing it smiling because he then said, "Mate. You're into him."

After I'd coughed and spluttered over my clogged saliva

because I was so pissed, I then asked him what drug he was on before hanging up.

I was not into Beast that way.

Fuck no.

And if I didn't have my Nevaeh to take care of, I would have gone to the compound and screwed a club slut to prove it.

"Um, Knife?" Mena called hesitantly. "Are you just about done scoffing over your thoughts?"

"What? Ah, shit, yeah. Sorry, babe. What was the next word?"

"Are you okay?" she asked, instead of continuing with the lesson.

"Wait, shouldn't you be at the class with Beast?"

"He's comfortable going on his own now, and I've become busy teaching Kalen's brothers."

Great. Just fuckin' great. Beast was alone with the grabby Ben.

"Knife, are you sure you're okay?"

"Yeah, babe. Why?" I asked, picking up the mugs on the table and taking them to the sink. The kids were in the living room where we could see them playing. Koda and Nevaeh had taken a liking to each other right away, which was great to see.

"You seem... stressed. Is it about Nevaeh? Are you regretting taking her in?"

Turning, I leaned my butt against the counter and crossed my arms over my chest. "No. I'd never regret it, even after only getting a few hours of sleep last night."

"Good." Mena smiled.

"You know Beast is gay, right?" Why in the fuck did that pop out?

Her cheeks pinked. She was a shy sweetheart. "Um, yes."

"What's your take on that Ben guy?"

She brushed her hands down her skirt, looking everywhere but at me.

"Mena?"

"He's nice."

"Nice?"

"Yes, and friendly."

I snorted. "Yeah, figured."

Mena sighed. It was cute and quiet, but I still heard it. "He could be good for Beast, Knife. And I think Beast needs good right now, especially after everything he's been through."

The sincerity in her voice hit me hard. She was right. I knew she was, yet I still fucking hated hearing it for some reason.

Shit.

Fuck me.

I had to step back.

Beast deserved happiness, and if dickwad could bring it, then I had to let him try. For Beast's sake.

Besides, I couldn't give Beast what he wanted. Not saying I was what he wanted, but I didn't see myself in that type of relationship.

Still...

No, I couldn't.

Then there was Nevaeh. My girl should come first. I had to stop thinking of myself and my worries when I had a little girl to take care of.

So, I'd try my goddamn best to support Beast while we lived there and went on with our lives.

TRYING COULD FLY RIGHT out the motherfucking window. I was fuming mad. Jesus, Beast hardly knew the guy, and there he was getting in late from his date with fuckface. When the front door came open, I was sitting in the living room with Nevaeh in my arms. She was having another rough night due to, as Mena figured out, teething. My girl's tooth was ripping apart her gums, and she was in pain. Hell, that night I felt like crying with her.

Beast came into the room. I was already looking his way so I caught the shock crossing his features before he rearranged them to a calm look and gave me a chin lift.

Bad night again? He signed.

My jaw ached from all the times I'd clenched it. Standing, I readjusted the seat in Nevaeh's stroller and lay her in it, since she liked to be rocked in it. I then straightened. *Have a good night?*

My eyes narrowed further when his lips twitched. He nodded. *Yeah, was okay.*

Since I was pushing the stroller back and forth, I asked instead of signing, "Where did you go?"

Dinner and back to a friend's place.

Fury burned in my gut. "Really?"

He tilted his head to the side, then righted it and nodded, crossing his arms over his chest.

Did he put out? My eyes widened along with his when I

finished signing that question. What was wrong with me? Why in the hell did I ask that?

What are you talking about?

Seriously, he was going to play dumb? "Your date with Ben."

His eyes narrowed. *You read my messages.* His hands fisted down at his sides after signing that.

Fuck.

Shrugging, I said, "So what? You never used to care if I was on your phone."

Stay out of this.

I rolled my eyes. "Why? He not playing nice with you? Not giving you what you want?"

Oh no. He gives me what I want. After all, he just sucked me off good and proper. That what you want to hear?

Christ. No. No, I didn't want to hear that. My anger turned up a notch, to where I wanted to punch him. But I couldn't because I'd brought it all on myself.

Clearing my throat, I shifted from one foot to another. "Maybe next time you want to be out late to get off, you can think about messaging me telling me you'll be late." Fuck me. I sounded like a whiny old maid. "Shit, ignore that. I'm tired," I added. I waved him off and bent to pick up Nevaeh. She was sound asleep, so I prayed when I took her to her room, she'd stay that way. I needed to bury myself in my bed and try to get some much-needed sleep, while ignoring the fact I just acted like a total pussy.

My eyes met Beast's when I stood with my girl. He nodded down to my daughter. *Want me to take her for a bit?*

Since I couldn't sign, I shook my head and left the room.

Maybe living with Beast wasn't a good idea after all.

Then again, I really had to take it back to when we were just friends. If it was back, then I wouldn't have given a fuck if he were out. Shit, I would have shaken his hand about getting some.

So why in the hell did I feel like I wanted to be sick over the thought of Ben…. Goddamn, I couldn't even think the word without wanting to bash some walls in.

Maybe what I really needed was to talk to someone.

Fuck, first I had to admit to myself I couldn't stop thinking about that night. As I climbed into bed after putting Nevaeh down, I found my cock twitching at just thinkin' of that night. Thinking of rubbing my dick against his arse. How his cock felt in my hand and how'd he come all over it.

Confusion at how I couldn't feel disgusted over it swirled in my head. But I wasn't. If anything, I was turned the hell on and thought about his body more.

Shit, if I wasn't so tired I'd have my hand in my boxers rubbing one out.

Yeah. I needed to talk to someone. Maybe they could punch some sense into me.

Only, who could I talk to?

Julian was totally out. He annoyed the shit out of me too much to have an actual conversation with him.

Mattie was also out. He was a decent guy, but he'd no doubt tell Julian since they were partners, and then Julian would tell the pussy posse. After that happened, my life would no longer be the same because everyone would know about it.

Hell, I'd be sure my parents would somehow find out too, and that'd be just bloody brilliant. They already hated me for turning my back on them when I was in my teens. But there was no way in hell I wanted to take over Mr Frank Conger's, also known as my schmuck father's accountant firm. Not only was he corrupt with his accounting, which one day would blow his arse wide open, but he was a lying, cheating, arrogant arsehole. He hated I wanted nothing to do with his business, so he'd hate me even more if he found out I was even thinking of turning gay.

Holy fuck.

Was I thinking of turning gay? Was that even a thing?

Christ, I needed to shut my brain down and get some sleep. I didn't really know what I was thinking.

Still, maybe once I talked to someone about what was in my head, it would get sorted out more, and I'd quit being a idiot.

God, I was probably just thinking the way I was because I hadn't been laid in a while.

So who could I talk to? I needed someone who'd understand what was in my head without judging. There was Pick and Billy, but then I didn't think they were the right brothers to talk to. They had Josie, and I knew they weren't into what I was thinking of. They might give each other head, but they didn't fuck each other. That was what I'd heard anyway.

I had a feeling *if* I was going to change, I'd need to talk to someone who'd gone through what I was. A dude who wasn't gay, but had happened to have switched teams for some reason.

Hell, I knew no one like that, so I was fucked.

My body stilled.

There could be someone.

I'd heard Pick and Billy talking about some customers in their new bar. I'd have to investigate, see who they were and what they were like. Then maybe they could shed some light on things.

What I needed right then was for my brain to shut off.

Exhaustion and my brain didn't get along; it made me think too much.

Like Beast.

His swinging dick.

My hand wrapped around it.

Rubbing against him.

Bloody goddamn hell, once again I grew hard.

CHAPTER ELEVEN

BEAST

*E*ven though a month had passed, I was still confused by Knife's words when I'd gotten home from being on a date with Ben. Hell, it was like he was either acting like a mother hen or a jilted lover. He was neither. Maybe it was like he said, he was just tired, so things in his head were weird.

Since that night, he'd been okay. Things weren't like we used to be, but he hadn't got in my face like he had that night.

We'd hung out, shared our home time with Nevaeh, who was thankfully settling after two teeth finally popped. Some nights we cooked together. The company, having him in my house, felt good. But I also knew there was something missing. It was as if he didn't know how to act around me, and I couldn't understand why. Actually, that wasn't right. I'd put it down to the fact he knew I was gay, which made him feel uncomfortable. The banter we used to have was gone. We were mates, and that was it. The closeness we once had, where we shared everything with each other, was lost, and it fuckin' sucked.

Admittedly, I didn't think he'd appreciate knowing about what Ben and I got up to. I hadn't been lying about him giving me head that night. He did, only I couldn't blow my load. Something was holding me back, embarrassing the fuck out of me.

Ben, being the cool guy he was, told me not to worry about it, suggested we'd work up to that part. We'd been seeing each other on and off for the past month. It got heated when we kissed, so I jacked him off in his car. He tried with me since I was rocking an erection and was into it all, but in the end, I pushed his hand away.

There was something seriously wrong with me when I couldn't find release.

How-fucking-ever, I wasn't one to give up. I'd try again when I saw Ben next out of class. He helped distract from Knife. Having Knife in the house all the time.... Shit, it was hard to separate my feelings for him when he was constantly in my personal space.

At least Nevaeh helped. She was a beauty. Seeing her laugh or just enjoying things like her food, was something special to watch.

Never thought Knife would have it in him, but he'd proved me wrong. He was a good father.

Even though he was managing, I knew he needed a break, which was why I was going to offer to have Nevaeh for the night. He needed to chill, hang with the brothers. Destress a little and start fresh the next day.

Even if the thought of him picking up a slut for a rough

time churned my gut, I had to let it pass because it'd be unfair if I was... Christ, I couldn't even say getting a bit since I wasn't coming. But I was enjoying my time with Ben, so Knife should enjoy his time away from the house.

Fuck. It killed me to even think about Knife out on the town with women around him. Still, it was the least I could do for him since he was the one who suggested I get a dog.

Apparently Knife had been doing some research and came across a site about dogs who helped in all types of situations, and one was for deaf people. At first, I thought the suggestion was a dick move on his part, saying I needed help. It wasn't until Knife showed me a video on just what the dog could do that I saw the merit.

The dog could let its owner know if someone was at the door, being called by someone, an alarm clock went off or if a baby cried. They helped in public situations like sirens or when dicks honked their horns.

In fact, the more I thought about it, the more having a dog appealed to me. Which was why I was at home waiting for the trainer to arrive with my dog. The training took three to five days, where the trainer would come back each day to help us get used to one another and to teach us everything we needed to know.

Movement caught my eye. I glanced up to see Knife, with Nevaeh in his arms, point towards the door. He went back down the hall, no doubt putting his girl down for a sleep, and I got up to answer.

Opening the door, I was greeted by a smiling man who looked a few years younger than me. *Hi, I'm Mitch, and this is Kevin, your hearing dog.* The guy greeted, then pointed down to the German Shepherd sitting beside him. The dog looked up at me with his head tilted to its side, and fuck, that look alone won me over.

A smile turned up my lips, and I glanced back to Mitch. *I'm Maddox. Come on in.* Stepping back, Mitch entered with Kevin, an unusual name for a dog, right beside him. I shut the front door and went into the living room to find them standing in the middle.

Not sure how this works. I admitted.

His smile widened, and I saw his gaze sweep over me just as Knife stopped at my side. *I'll help you through it. Hi,*—he faced Knife—*I'm Mitch, and this is Kevin.*

Knife. Was Knife's only reply.

Mitch's smile faltered a little. *Do you live here?*

"Yeah, with my daughter."

"Oh, you speak and hear," Mitch said while continuing to sign.

"Sure do."

Ignoring Knife, I stepped further into the room and stopped beside Kevin. *Can I pat him?*

Mitch's grin was back. Turning away from Knife, he gave me his whole attention. *Yes. Get to know him, let him get to know you. We'll have a coffee and a chat about it all. I have some supplies in the car for him. A dog bed and such. It's best if he never sleeps on the bed or couch else they could tend to get lazy. But we'll talk about it more soon.*

Nodding, I bent and ran my hand over Kevin's head then down his back. His tail wagged, and I felt the vibration from hard hits to the floor.

Yeah, I could see myself easily getting along with Kevin. Vin, for short, was much better though. When I'd looked at the site, I'd seen all small dogs and was worried

I'd get a miniature poodle or some shit. Guess I lucked out.

IT WASN'T until dinner time when I remembered to offer Knife the night off. Most of the afternoon was spent with Mitch as he taught me some commands and all things I needed to know for Vin. Hopefully the week would fly by so I didn't have to see Mitch again after the full week of training. He kind of annoyed me. I found out more about him than I should have. Where he lived, what he liked, how he liked to date men older than him. The last part was said with a glint in his eyes. I wasn't interested though. The guy was tall and lanky, not my type at all. To me he had one purpose, to integrate Vin into my life and me into his.

Walking from my room down the hall, I watched Vin stride next to me. He was a happy dog, a smart one too. When Nevaeh had woken from her nap earlier that day, Vin had come to my side and nudged his nose into my leg, which Mitch told me was a command for me to follow him. I did, and Vin led me right into Nevaeh's room.

There were all types of commands, something I was going to write down, until Mitch again mentioned he was there all week for assistance. But the commands I got quickly used to were when a phone rang and when someone knocked at the front door. Shit, that was only the start of what Vin could do.

Making my way into the kitchen, I found Knife sitting and feeding Nevaeh. She looked over, her hands reaching out for Vin. That afternoon they seemed to have bonded when she played on the floor. I stopped beside the table and waited for

Knife's eyes. It didn't take long until he was looking at me since his daughter's attention had been pulled away.

Only, before I could say anything, he said, "Don't like that dog training guy."

My brows dipped. *Why?*

"He gives you more attention than what he does training."

Rolling my eyes, I then shook my head. *He'll only be around for a week.*

His chest rose quickly, so I knew he'd grunted. He then turned back to his girl and smiled.

Fuck. That smile went right to my cock.

Running a hand over my face, I was tired of how my body reacted to him since I knew it wouldn't go anywhere.

Clicking my fingers, Knife's eyes went right to me before I signed, *I'll mind Nevaeh tonight. You need a break. Go check out Pick and Billy's bar. Have a drink, catch up with some of the brothers.*

His eyes widened. "You sure?"

With a chin lift, I also signed. *Yes.*

He looked to his girl, biting his bottom lip, thinking it over. Goddamn, he didn't make shit fair. I would give my right nut to have my teeth sink into his bottom lip.

Hell, I shouldn't even be thinking like that when I had Ben. Not that we were dating, but we were... something.

Over the last month, though, I still couldn't get the man before me out of my head. I'd lost count of the times I took my cock in hand and thought of that night in the hotel. The way he'd handled my cock until I came caused me to squirt my release all over the tiles in the shower near every morning.

Life wasn't fucking fair.

While he thought it over, I made myself a mug of coffee, knowing my dinner was in the fridge for later, something that Knife had prepared earlier. He found it easier to cook while Nevaeh was down for her afternoon sleep. Yet another thing I loved. He cooked and liked to do it; plus, he was goddamn amazing at it. He didn't ask if he should cook for me while making his; he just did it.

Knife came to stand beside me at the counter just as I poured the milk into the mug. Catching my eyes, he said, "I'd fuckin' love a night with the brothers."

Offering a small smile, I nodded. *Have at it then, brother. Enjoy. Now I got Vin, and he's already alerting me to Nevaeh crying, you shouldn't have anything to worry about.* I signed slower than normal so he caught everything. He was so much better at sign language though. What helped was us practising every time we were around one another, mainly at night in the living room.

He rolled his eyes. "True, she already adores you."

I smiled because she did seem comfortable with me, would even reach out for me if Knife and I were close and talking and she was in his arms. *Course she does. So take it easy. She'll be fine.* I wanted to reassure him.

"Thanks for this."

Don't mention it. This is what friends are for.

He nodded, but what puzzled me was his eyes lost some life and his jaw clenched along with that nod. He signed as he told me, "Going to go get ready. She's eaten, so she'll play for a while and then have a bottle later right before bed. Don't forget to change her diaper. Her PJs are in the top draw—"

My palm came up in front of his face to shut him the fuck up.

You been here a month. I know the routine, and I know where things are. Don't freak about her with me. I can deal. Vin and I can deal. It'll be all good.

He ran a hand over his scalp. "Yeah, okay. I... shit, no, you're right. You know it." His punch to my arm was light. "Thanks again. I'll go get changed and head out."

Right. Have fun.

What I wanted to add was "just not too much fun."

Christ. There went my stomach.

CHAPTER TWELVE

KNIFE

*W*hen Beast offered to have Nevaeh for the night, I felt guilty to start with. She was my daughter and had only been with me a month, but like he'd said, I needed the night to destress. How he'd known that I didn't have a clue, but I was glad he did.

Sitting at the bar, I thought of the last month and how the time had flown by. My girl was turning one in four months. I'd found her birth certificate in the bag Sana had dropped off with Nevaeh. She was born November fourteenth. Nearly a Christmas baby. Finding it made me realise how much I'd missed out on, though. Her stupid fuckin' mother should have told me right from the start, and I couldn't help but wonder why she hadn't.

"Want another?" Muff asked from across the bar. Pick and Billy had a good idea buying a bar for the club. Once word got out the bar was owned by Hawks MC, the place boomed with customers. A lot were wannabe bikers. Then there were women who wanted a thrill for one night with a Hawks biker. Not that I was taking notice of any of the women, which was crazy because there were a lot to pick from. Shit, I reckoned I could just snap my fingers and a woman would come runnin', wantin' to suck my cock.

However, my cock had other ideas. He wasn't even hard with the amount of skin walkin' around the joint. It was like he was snoozing, waiting for the right person to get hard for, and that person was at home.

Yeah, he took notice every time Beast was in the goddamn room. Perking up to say hi whenever Beast did anything. Only he didn't simply perk up when Beast bent over. No, he went raging hard when that happened.

After sending Muff a chin lift requesting another beer, I looked down at my cock and glared. The stupid appendage was confused. It was like he was playin' me, causing my mind to get pissed every time Beast left for an ASL meeting or when I knew he was goin' out to see fuckwad Ben. Never had I felt jealous over anything, until those times.

Hell, I hadn't even had time to look into the people I'd heard Pick and Billy speak about. Nevaeh had most of my time, not that I minded one second of it. Then again, maybe I was puttin' it off for other reasons. Like even thinkin' I could change was weird as fuck since I'd never thought of a guy's body or junk before in my life.

"Yo, Knife. You finally gracing us with your presence." Billy grinned as he took the stool next to me. "How's your girl?"

A true big smile lit my face. "She's good, brother. Real

good. All settled in and everything." Which was true, after her two front teeth came through to join with the bottom ones she already had. Those nights had been hell. They seemed to play on her more when she was trying to get some shut-eye. Still, I knew there were more to come and 'cause I knew she'd be in pain, I wasn't lookin' forward to those days.

"Still can't believe you've got a girl."

Snorting, I said, "Me either. Never thought I'd want one until she showed in my life. How're things with the club?" I worked when I could at the garage, while Mena minded Nevaeh, but I hadn't been involved in anything more than that. I missed it.

"Things are good for once. But that could change at any given time. Then there's also strippers gettin' beat at other establishments. None of Hawks."

"Yet?" I questioned when his brows dipped in concern.

"Yeah. Yet. We're just waiting for it to happen. Dodge has our places covered pretty tight, though."

"He good for brothers to cover all the places?" We had five strip joints in our territory. With the garage, plus the one that opened a while ago, and the bar, brothers could be doing overtime on everything.

"It's good. Nothin' for you to worry about. Just get sorted with your girl."

"Beast and I can take turns patrolling," I said before taking a pull of my beer.

"All good, seriously. We're taking on more prospects soon. It'll be sorted." He bumped his shoulder into mine and looked over to the corner where Josie was with Pick and some other people I didn't know.

"Who're they?"

Billy turned back and grinned. "New friends. The black dude is a lawyer named Liam. His girl next to Josie is Liberty, and their other bed partner is Damien."

My brows shot up. "The three of them?"

"Yep." He nodded.

They'd been the ones. Apparently Damien never had experience with a dude, not until Liam. While Billy was talking to Muff about some supplies, I studied the new group. Liam was sitting with Pick, and they were talkin'. Damien sat with the women. He constantly smiled, and while he made the women laugh about something, his eyes flicked over to Liam, who caught his look and winked.

Shit, could I really talk to someone I didn't know about what was in my head?

"So," Billy started, "how's living with Beast going?"

My body tensed. "Fine." And fuckin' hell my voice sounded higher than normal, like I'd lost my balls.

Billy, who hadn't been lookin' at me, slowly turned my way and searched my face. Only I wasn't lookin' at him, but across the bar at the drinks sitting along the wall, wondering which one would be best to get me smashed. "Right," he drew out.

"What?" I questioned, and then hardened my expression, glaring at him.

"Nothin' at all." He spun on his seat and yelled across the place. "Yo, Damien. Come meet a brother."

Fuck.

What the hell was up with that? Why would Billy call Damien over? Did he have a sixth sense where he knew shit without even being told anything?

As Damien walked over grinning, which seemed to be

his norm, I grabbed my beer and downed it in one go, knowing there was no way I could talk to him about anything.

"YOU KNOW WHAT?" I asked Damien after taking a shot of whisky, and wished to Christ I wasn't so drunk where I'd just spout any shit from my mouth.

"What?" Damien asked. We sat at the bar after shooting the shit for a good two hours while drinking, and I was fuckin' drunk as a skunk. Damien seemed just as drunk, so in a way, I knew I would say shit and considered it wouldn't matter because we were both drunk. Hell, he'd probably forget anything I'd said by morning.

"You're an okay dude, even knowing you suck cock."

Damien's shot sprayed the bar as it flew outta his mouth. I cheered and then laughed.

After he had got himself under control, he said, "Thanks. I think." He eyed me. "You got something against people finding their happily ever after with whoever they want?"

"Nope," I said, popping the p outta my mouth. "How'd, you know, like it?"

"What?" he asked.

Rolling my eyes, I said, "Givin' head? Heard you'd never noticed guys before."

He chuckled. "I hadn't until Liam, and it's the best fuckin' feeling giving and takin'. By both of them."

"Yeah, but, you know. He's a dude." I shook my head, still unsure how a person could change like that. Like me, I think. "And you," I yelled as Billy went to pass us. "How'd you end up likin' head with a dude?" I busted a gut laughin' when Billy's eyes widened.

He then glanced around, so I did also and noticed the place had quieted down a bit. I glared at the people close to us, some fuckers I didn't know. Billy stepped up and clipped, "Fuck off from here."

Vamoose. People disappeared.

Shit. Billy was a wizard.

Billy then pulled up a stool in front of Damien and me. "Why you askin', brother?"

My shoulders lifted on their own, though they were part of me. Which meant I probably lifted them, like my cock was a part of me. So really, it was my fault I liked lookin' at Beast and got hard from it. Fuck, I was drunk.

"Just wonderin'," I mumbled.

Damien cleared his throat. I glanced there to see him watchin' me. "Never in my life had I thought I'd like a guy. So when it all changed, when Liam caught my attention, I thought there was something wrong with me. It wasn't until a mate of mine made me realise I wasn't into guys. It was only *one* guy. It only took Liam and him to open my eyes and see what I was missing with a certain special someone. Yes, we have Liberty, but it's still different. I'm in a relationship with Liberty, and I'm also in a separate relationship with Liam. The times we come together, do things with each other, the two of us, then it's our relationship." Damien snorted. "I may be dribbling shit because my head is spinning, but what I'm asking is are you thinking of getting involved with a woman and a man?"

My head was shaking before I knew it. "Nah. Not like that."

"Beast?" Billy voiced.

My jaw clenched, and then I nodded. Lifting my head, I glared at my brother. "If you say shit to anyone, I will slice your throat while you sleep."

"That threat actually seemed real," Damien commented.

Billy snorted. "It was."

Damien blew out a breath. "You bikers don't do things half-arsed."

"You have my word, I won't say shit, Knife."

I was sure even through my drunken haze, which was fading quickly, his words rang true. Nodding, I asked, "What made you say him anyway?"

Billy shrugged. "Always seen the way he looked at you." I straightened hearing that. Billy laughed. "You were blind to it, like every other fuckin' brother, except maybe Pick. But we haven't talked about it. I only said Beast's name 'cause I noticed something between the two of you had gone down after you both got back from Sydney. I was surprised you moved in with him. Didn't think you two were talkin', but you were both close, so I guessed you got over whatever it was."

"Somethin' like that."

"Billy, can you let us talk for a second?" Damien asked.

My brother glanced from Damien to me and then back. He nodded, slapped me on the shoulder and said, "It'll all work out. And no matter what, brother, no one will give a flyin' fuck." He went back over to Pick and Liam. Liam's eyes were already on us, and they were narrowed. Billy said something, which had Liam nodding and moving his gaze from us.

"Your guy's protective," I commented.

Damien smiled. Yeah, the dude was always happy. "I know.

I'm the same with him. Look, I asked Billy to leave because I sensed you didn't really want to talk around him."

"Shit, now I'm sobering, I guess it doesn't matter since I've already said so much."

"Okay." Damien nodded. "Then I also asked him to leave to talk to you more. No offense, but when you walked in here, it looked like you had the weight of the world on your shoulders."

Winking, I asked, "You noticed when I walked in?"

Damien let out a surprised laugh. "Only because you seemed like you wanted to hurt someone. I didn't want that someone to be me."

"Good call. Though I was more agitated than anything."

"Are you into women?"

"Fuck yeah, love me some pussy."

Damien chuckled and nodded. "You sound like me. Then what are you confused about?"

With a sigh, I rubbed the back of my neck. "Something did happen between Beast and me, and since then, it's like he switched something in me, and now I can't stop... but I've never been like that. I wasn't, you know... I didn't think of guys like that."

"Not until him?"

"Fuck. Yes, but I can't... it just ain't right when I never.... Hell, I'm all about pussy."

Damien shrugged. "Why not go over to the woman who's been eyeing you off like a new candy bar then and take her home? If what you feel for this other guy isn't right, then it'll be easy to pick up some random pussy and screw her."

Looking over my shoulder, I noticed a nice pair of legs, a sweet-as-fuck body, and a good-sized rack. Goddamn, she licked her lips like I was a new candy bar. I waited for the thrill, for blood to travel south and pump my cock hard.

Only it never happened.

"What I thought," Damien said. I turned back to him and raised a brow. He shook his head and instead came out with a question. "You ever kissed a guy before?"

I jerked back a little, my hand slapping down to the bar before I fell off my seat. I hadn't kissed a guy, but I'd thought about pressing my mouth against a certain someone's, which freaked me out. "Ah, no."

"Oh, I'm not offering, but that was how Liam got me to thinking. I never thought of kissing a guy, never thought I would want to touch a guy, not until him. If you can picture yourself kissing this Beast, touching him, wanting him, then I don't see a problem. Not like the one in your pants right now when you see a stunning fuckable woman right in front of you and he"—he pointed to my junk—"doesn't even want to sniff her out. Do you get hard around him?"

"Jesus Christ, you say anything."

"Yes." He grinned. "So do you?"

I shrugged.

Damien laughed. "That means a yes. What do you have to lose if you take a chance on him?"

"Our friendship."

"From what Billy said it already seems strained."

Shit. He was right.

"Beast already has someone."

"How does that make you feel?"

"Fuck, you want me to lie on the counter while you question me, Doc?"

Damien snorted. "No, but I want you to answer."

"It burns."

"Then change it."

"It ain't fuckin easy to."

"It is. Take a risk, a chance. If you want him, make it happen." He glanced over to his people. "A risk is worth taking when it ends well."

"And when it doesn't?"

His eyes met mine. "If it can bring peace within yourself, then it's still worth risking."

Fuck. I went to a bar and I ended up gettin' Dr Philled.

Still, it was worth it. Damien patted my arm and went back over to his man and woman. I watched, realising I could be missin' out on something special. They seemed to have found it, so why couldn't I?

My somethin' special could be with Beast, and even if it wasn't, I reckon I'd enjoy the figuring out part.

Only how in the hell did I go about changing shit?

Then a thought popped into my head. Maybe it was time to see if I liked my mouth on Beast's.

CHAPTER THIRTEEN

BEAST

Knife came outta his room earlier than I thought he would. When Vin woke lettin' me know Nevaeh was crying, I could smell the alcohol in the house. Thought Knife wouldn't be faring well in the morning and couldn't believe I was wrong. He strolled into the living room smiling. Actually, he looked refreshed so the night out must have been good to him.

Jesus, motherfuckin' Christ.

Did he have sex? Was that why he seemed in such a good mood as he swung Nevaeh up in his arms and kissed her?

I wanted to punch him in the nose for being so sickly happy.

Glaring, I signed, once I had his eyes. *Have a good night?*

He shrugged and tickled his girl's belly. I watched as her mouth opened and she giggled. He gave her one last kiss before he stuck her back in her walker. *Wasn't bad. Good to catch up with everyone.*

Yeah, I'm sure it was.

Christ. I had no right to feel like there was a hole in my heart.

No right what so fuckin' ever.

He claimed a seat next to me on the couch. *Thinking of watching that new alien movie I bought tonight. You in for it?*

Alone time with Knife while my mind festered over what he got up to the night before? No, thank you.

Busy. Not that I was. I had no plans. Still, I could find something to do. I was sure the brothers could use extra eyes for patrolling. I shifted my eyes to Vin, who lay on the floor next to the couch near me. He was watching Nevaeh scoot around in her walker.

What the fuck? My head jerked sideways as my hair was tugged on. Clenching my jaw, I looked to Knife, who was grinning. *Come on. Don't be busy. Watch it with me. We watched all the others together.*

Shit, we had.

Still, I wasn't in the mood to be around happy Knife. The way he used to be before...

Can't, sorry.

Some of the cheer left his face. *If you change your mind, I'll have it on at eight, after Nevaeh is down for the night.*

My brows rose at him. *Thought you'd want an earlier night after having such a late one?"*

He answered immediately. "Wasn't that late. Home by one."

Nevaeh had slept through the night, like Knife had told me she'd been doing for the last couple'a weeks, so I couldn't tell if he was lying or not. That hadn't left him much time to catch up with the brothers and fuck a woman since he'd left the house at nine.

Jesus. I had to remember who I was talkin' about.

It was Knife.

He could fuck in the bathroom for all he cared. He didn't need a private place. If someone caught him, he just kept at it until he was finished. I knew that from experience when we'd been out clubbin' in our younger years, and I'd caught him in the male toilet with some bird.

Many out? I queried.

"Packed."

So being the good-looking prick he was, he would have had a pick of any woman he wanted. Hell, I'd seen them throw themselves at him, and with just a look from a woman, he was eager and ready.

Fuck me. I had to stop thinking about it.

Glad you had a good night, but now you're up, I've got to get to the garage.

He nodded and then smiled, his normal old smile at me. The dick. *See you later.*

Not if I could help it he wouldn't, or else I would punch him in the mouth if he kept smiling like that. Hell, he must have gotten a lotta pussy to make him act like himself again.

Motherfucker.

My mind jacked me around all goddamn day. One second I was thinkin' I should go and watch the movie with him, then next I was tellin' myself it was a bloody stupid idea. All the conflicted thoughts caused me to be in a fuckin' foul mood. Brothers steered clear of me, and I didn't blame them. Even though I couldn't hear it, I knew I was banging loudly around the garage while fixing up the cars I had. Even had Vin flinching a few times. Mitch had already been by to see how we were going and showed me more commands to use, even at work.

There'd been only one brother in there brave enough to approach me. Pick walked up, matching my glare with his own. *What's crawled up your arse?*

Hell, seein' him sign got me in the chest every fuckin' time. He hadn't been the only one to attend Mena's class. All the brothers had. As in *all* of them. Some I wasn't even close to took time out to learn. Then again, they could have done it so they'd know if I was talkin' about them. I would have done the same.

Still, the fuckin' thought to do it, in case they wanted to communicate with me, even when they knew I had it nearly down to read lips, got me to feel shit I shouldn't've been in a biker compound.

Nothin'. I signed back to Pick.

Bullshit. You're making everyone on edge. Either get over whatever it is or go the fuck home. Not real sure you're gettin' much work done anyway. Then he bent, patted Vin, and walked off.

There lay the problem. I wasn't sure if I should go home. Nodding, I leaned back under the hood of the car and realised I'd fixed the fan belt twice.

Pick was right. I was useless at work. Hell, what was a movie among friends? I'd just have to give up obsessing over what Knife got up to at the bar. Then again, I could just text Ben. I was sure he'd be interested in seeing me.

Not that I really wanted to see him.

Not when Knife was on my mind. Fuck, it wouldn't be fair to him.

Wiping my hands on a rag, I pulled my phone out and texted: **I'll grab pizza on the way home. Just about finished here.**

Saying home and thinkin' of Knife being in that home was dangerous. I liked it way too much. Fuckin' hell, I had to get over him.

Knife: **Awesome. You know what I like.**

Yeah, I did. I knew too much about the guy.

The car I was fixing took longer than I thought it would. Mainly because I checked over what I'd already done before making the decision to watch a movie with him.

Anyway, it *was* only a movie.

At least watching it could fill my mind instead of him and the bar and club sluts.

Fuck.

It was around eight by the time Vin and I got outta there, and then I had to grab the pizza before I made it home, which had me showing at ten to nine. I should have left earlier. At least then Nevaeh would have occupied my mind. Poor Vin was no doubt starvin' too. He eyed the pizza from the back seat the whole drive home.

Walkin' through the front door, with Vin at my side, I found Knife on the couch as his eyes met mine. Stupidly I raised the pizza, as if he hadn't already seen it, then placed it on the coffee table he'd got the other day. *I'm gonna shower. Leave some pizza for me.*

He smiled wide. *I'll try.*

There went my dick. Why couldn't it be so responsive for Ben?

Fucking stupid cock.

The shower was quick because I wanted the night over. Vin lay on the floor in the bathroom and then in the bedroom while I dressed in a tank and track pants. The house was warm since the heater was on and I always ran hot anyway.

Entering the living room, Knife already had the pizza box open and had eaten half of it. Bloody lucky I'd bought a family-sized one.

How was work? Knife asked as I sat on the couch next to him, too close for comfort despite being as far away from him as possible.

Good. I signed, then picked up a slice and bit into it. With my free hand, I gestured to the TV.

Knife nodded and did some shit to the remotes to get the movie started. As I ate, I watched the movie, read the captions and also glanced at Knife every now and then because the fucker wouldn't stop fidgeting.

About halfway through the movie, I finally turned to him and asked. *What the fuck?*

His head jerked back. "What?" he voiced and signed.

First, you don't need to sign, I can read your lips. At least I could mostly. *Second, can you sit the fuck still? You got ants in your pants or something?*

"No, I... ah, can't get comfortable, that's all."

Rolling my eyes, I said back. *Well, find a way because you're getting on my nerves.*

"Can I ask you somethin'?" he blurted quickly, nearly making it hard for me to catch.

Yes.

My eyes flicked to his neck to watch him swallow. It was then I noticed a slight gleam on his forehead and how his eyes wandered the room and didn't stay on me long. He was nervous about something. My eyes narrowed when he didn't answer, I leaned in and shoved his leg. *What?*

"Right. You and Ben, you two, you know, serious?"

It was my turn for my head to jerk back as shock radiated through my body. For a beat there I sat dumbfounded. Rolling my shoulders, I shook it off. *You seriously asking me about this?*

He nodded. "Yes."

Why?

He waved a hand around. "Just want to know."

Not sure we should talk about this.

"Okay then. Why didn't you tell me you were gay?"

Fuck me.

What I wanted to say was, because I was in love with my best friend and I didn't want to freak you out, but I knew that'd have him running from the room screaming. So I shrugged instead and turned my attention back to the TV.

When the couch dipped, I glanced back to find Knife closer. "Answer one question at least," he asked, and I saw his jaw tick.

My heart beat like a base drum in my chest. I wasn't fuckin' sure if it had to do with the awkward subject or the fact Knife moved closer. His knee hit against mine. I flicked my eyes down to it and then back up at him.

"Talk to me."

Why?

"Because I want you to."

Snorting, I shook my head. *You want to talk now while we're watchin' a movie?*

"I'll pause the movie if you'll answer my questions."

Sighing, I ran a hand over my face, frustrated with how persistent he was being. *Fine. I'll answer only one. Ben and I aren't serious. Now can we watch the movie in peace?*

He grinned. "No." He shook his head.

Groaning, I asked. *Why?*

"Because I want to try something."

What was he going on about? *What?*

"Kiss me."

My body froze. I had to have read his lips wrong. What in the hell? Had he said kiss me or was it piss me, or shit, hiss me? *What?*

He smirked. His gaze ran over my face before he said, "Fuck it."

CHAPTER FOURTEEN

KNIFE

"Fuck it," I muttered, more to myself than Beast and leaned in to touch my lips to his. He was statue still, and I worried I'd broke him from shock. I was also scared shitless that he'd throw me away and storm from the room yelling he didn't want to mess around like that with a man who didn't know shit about being with a guy. Because clearly I didn't. I held my lips against his and had no clue what to do next. Usually women melted against me, and we'd be making out like pros. However, Beast was still frozen, with his hands down at his sides. They certainly weren't on me, groping me, but at least they weren't pushing me away. I had one arm along the back of the couch and the other splayed on the couch cushion at my side.

As my heart bottomed out in my gut from fear, I took another leap and brought my tongue out to lick Beast's lips.

It was then he came unstuck.

He moaned against my mouth as his hands landed on my sides and he dragged me closer to him.

I smiled against his lips and thought, *Well, there you have it, folks. I'm enjoying kissing a dude.*

I wasn't grossed out by it. I didn't want to throw up in his mouth.

In fact, I fuckin' liked it.

Moving closer still, my hand on the back of the couch came to his shoulder, and I lifted the other to the side of his neck and gripped while tilting my head to the side. Our tongues touched, tasted, and teased.

We groaned, and the kiss turned harder, and hotter. It was different than kissing a woman. His whiskers grazed me, but I even liked that.

Jesus Christ.

Jesus fuckin' Christ.

My gut was in a swirl of feelings. My heart wanted to break free of my chest, and when I slid my hands over him, I realised they shook. My cock pulsated in my jeans, and as I ran my hand down to rest against the side of his chest, I found he was breathing as heavily as I was.

Breakin' the kiss, I moved only inches away to see his eyes smouldering with... hell, desire. I wondered if my eyes said the same. His hands left me, and I knew he was going to sign some question. Only I didn't let him.

Leaning back in, I touched my mouth to his, once, twice and then linked our lips together in another wild kiss.

This was Beast.

A man.

My friend.

And yet, I wanted more from him.

I wanted to touch him and him to do the same to me.

Was he as hard as I was?

The need to find out overcame me. I slid my hand from his chest slowly. His stomach quivered under my hand from my touch. I smiled against his mouth, and he knew it. He growled against my lips and gripped me tighter.

Shit. This was what I was missing.

Should never have run. Freaked.

I fuckin' loved what I was feeling at that moment and wanted it to last forever.

Only it didn't.

Beast flung me aside. I bounced on the couch cushion and saw him swivel his head down to the floor. I spotted Vin bouncing around, jumping at Beast and then back facing the hall. Beast was up off his seat in seconds and running for the hall. I knew it wasn't Nevaeh. I couldn't hear her cry and I'd come accustomed to even hearing her grizzle. Yet something was wrong.

Standing quickly, I bolted after Vin and Beast. He was in her room and then, fuck, I heard a crash, barking from Vin, and screaming from my girl.

Fear bombarded my senses. I ran, slipping, but got to the door in time to see Beast take a man to the ground and sit on him. Vin, down on all fours, growled low. Beast's wild, angry eyes looked to me and lifted his chin to Nevaeh. Stalkin' in, I scooped her up in my arms and hugged her close.

"It's okay, baby. Daddy's here. It's okay," I cooed, gently pressing her head into my chest. My eyes flicked to the window to see it open. The fucker had broken in. Why? What in the hell did he want? "Who are you?" I questioned, my voice filled with steel.

The man grunted but said nothing.

Stepping up, I kicked his head. "Who are you? What you think you're doin' breakin' in here?" Nevaeh started crying again. She didn't like her dad's tone. I had to get her outta that room. Meeting Beast's eyes, I ordered, "Stay here. I'll call in the brothers." After I had got a nod from him, I walked outta the room, found my phone and called in some help.

Fury built higher and higher inside of me.

If the skinny motherfucker thought he could fuck with my girl, he was dead wrong, and he was going to find out how much trouble he was in soon.

MENA SHOWED WITH DIVE. She took Nevaeh back to their place, with Dallas following. Low was already at Mena's minding Koda while he slept. I paced the living room just after she'd left with my girl, while my brothers stood around me.

"This is fucked up," I said.

"It is," Dodge agreed.

"No one breaks into Hawks and gets away with it."

"Agreed," Pick replied.

"He pays after we get what we need," I demanded.

"Yes," Billy agreed.

"Bring him to the shed out back. Beast made it sound-proof." Billy took off to tell Beast, who'd been stuck with the motherfucker while I took care of getting Nevaeh outta there and the brothers in. As I walked through the house and then out the back, I knew I didn't have to look behind me to see my brothers were there. They'd be in this because it was Hawks' business. We took care of our business as one.

Dodge, Pick, and I stood to the back of the small shed and waited. I only knew it was soundproof because I'd helped Beast install the stuff myself, so he could play the drums, which were off to the side, without annoyin' the neighbours.

The door crashed open. Billy and Beast entered with a struggling man. It was then I noticed Beast had a red mark on the side of his face and he also had his tank off. The man had obviously tried to fight when I'd left the room, but Beast had the better of him. Still, the dickhead would pay for marking Beast.

What was also in the back of my head, which was fucked up in that type of situation, was the need to find a top for Beast. No one had the right to look over his body. Hell, even if they weren't, I still wanted to cover him. That shit would be for my eyes only.

Running a hand at the back of my neck, I asked, "He said anything yet?"

Beast shook his head and Billy said, "Nope."

My smile was gleeful. "Good. Means I get to work it out of him." Glancing to Dodge, I jutted my chin up and ordered, "Get the shears off the wall. Both of them." Dodge moved off to do as I asked. "Lay him out," I ordered Billy and Beast.

Billy smiled. Beast, when in business mode, or most of the time actually, expressed nothing on his face. They threw the guy to the floor and each brother kneeled on an arm after they'd flattened his limbs out at his sides. The man kicked out and up, trying to throw them off, until Pick came forward and stood on each of his shins.

Dodge came back over and handed me the first shear. Tapping it in my hand, I stood behind the guy's head and looked down at his red face. "You got somethin' to say?"

"Fuck you," he yelled.

Scoffing, I snarled. "You'll talk soon." Raising the shear over my head, I forced it down, straight through his right wrist and into the dirt ground. Blood squirted out as the guy screamed and thrashed, only he soon realised the more he moved, the more pain he received. Billy climbed to his feet since he didn't have to hold the arm down due to the shears spearing it in place on the ground.

Standing, I held out my hand. Dodge slapped the other shears into my palm, and as I strolled slowly around the man's head whistling, I noticed he'd quieted and kept his eyes glued to me.

Leaning in, I asked, "Huh? What's that? You got somethin' to say?"

"Can't...," he muttered, voice filled with agony. He wouldn't be using his hand anytime soon. Well, that was if he was gonna live through the night.

"Can't what?" I asked, stopping beside Beast, who still held his other arm down, leaving enough room for me to get to the guy's wrist. "Can't tell me what you were doin' in my girl's room?"

The man's eyes flared for a second.

What was that about?

"Shit, man. I'd tell him before he loses it completely," Billy taunted.

The dick shook his head side to side. My eyes flicked to Beast, and again, I saw the red mark on the side of his face. No one had the right to mark him but me. Pulling back my leg, I brought it forward and straight into his ribs. He coughed, groaned, and yelled, "Stop!"

"Tell me what you're doin' here? This is Hawks MC property. Did you know that, fool? You fucked up big time comin' here. You some junkie lookin' to steal?"

"I-if I say shit, my boss will kill me."

The brothers around me chuckled. Even Beast, who would have read his lips.

"Wrong, man. They won't kill you. I will. Up to you if you want it slow or fast?"

"Please, don't—"

"Tell me."

"I, I can't."

With a shake of my head, I sighed. "Wrong answer." In seconds, his other wrist supported some gardening shears. As the man screamed, cried, and writhed, Beast stood up beside me and crossed his arms over his chest.

Fuck me.

It really wasn't the best time to be admiring.

Scrubbing a hand over my face, the guy finally quietened, and I demanded, "Answer me or it'll only get fuckin' worse."

He said nothing. His chest rose and fell rapidly, yet his mouth didn't open to fuckin' answer me. The stupid dick.

A phone chimed. Ignoring it, I picked up a knife off the bench near me. It was my tool, how I liked to work, how I got my club name, Knife.

Crouching, I touched the tip of the blade to the centre of his chest. "Talk," I ordered gruffly.

A shake of his head had me clenching my jaw in fury. Digging the blade deeper, the idiot moaned in pain but still didn't share any words.

"Knife," Dodge started.

Fuck.

Not payin' any attention to Dodge, I sliced down the guy's chest to his abdomen. He grunted, eyes squeezing tight and panting.

"Brother," Dodge tried again.

Swirling the tip of the blade against his gut, I repeated, "Talk." When no words were shared, I sank the knife deeper.

His mouth opened. "Mr Conger o-ordered me to take the child."

My body froze, my eyes widening, and I whispered, "You have got to be fuckin' me."

CHAPTER FIFTEEN

BEAST

*J*esus Christ. I saw the fuckhead's lips move and I
didn't want to believe what I read on them.
Didn't want to understand the name, but I did.

Knife's father organised for the fool to take Knife's
daughter.

Why?

I watched as Knife became unstuck and slammed the knife
into the man's gut. He screamed; only it was cut off when
Knife removed the blade quickly and sliced it across the guy's
throat. Knife stood, his shoulders moving up and down
rapidly with each breath he took.

What I would have liked was to reach out to him, to know
what was running through his head and help him fix it....
Then I could find out why in the hell he kissed me.

Bloody hell.

That kiss.

That one kiss made me feel too much, and it was dangerous.

Just when I was trying to get over him, he'd fucked it all up when his mouth touched mine.

Dodge stepped around the dead guy on the floor, to get in Knife's face.

I read his lips as he said, "Gotta talk, brother. Low just sent me something Mena found in Nevaeh's diaper bag Sana dropped off with her." Knife must have asked what, not that I could see his face, but Dodge answered with, "Wasn't easy to find, but apparently there was a note from the mother wedged between the bottom seam. Man, you need to read it. Low took a picture of it."

Knife turned enough so I saw his face and caught when he said, "Read it to me." His emotions were getting the better of him. To find out his father had ordered some dick to steal his girl was fucked up, big time.

Flicking my eyes to Dodge, he said, "Knife, I fooled you, and I'm sorry. What I told Sana was true. I have found someone to love all of me, but he doesn't want a child from another man in the house. I never wanted a baby either. Not until I was offered money to have one. Your father propositioned me, and I accepted because I needed the money. He got me to seduce you, which wasn't hard (sorry, but you need to be careful who you take to bed). I tampered with the condom because I was meant to have your child for your father. He wanted an heir. A boy for his business. I knew when I wasn't having a boy, things wouldn't be good. I stayed in a house your dad set up until it was nearing my nine months. I used him like he used me. At least I got part of the money he offered. God, Knife, your dad's a dick. Not a nice person at all, and he deals with even worse.

"He wouldn't be happy with a girl as an heir, so I faked it. Showed him a picture I stole at the ultrasound place of a baby boy. Then I ran. I hid until I had Nevaeh. I wanted to keep her safe. She's beautiful, Knife. So beautiful. But I wasn't made to have children, at least not on my own. Which was why I got Sana to drop her off to you. I know you'll fall for her and protect her. You'll have no trouble from me ever, of this I promise to you. Take care of her and make her happy. That's all I ask. Though I know you would anyway, no matter what I say. Bye, Knife."

Holy fuck.

Knife's father wanted an heir that much he'd orchestrated the whole thing and then when she ran, he would've been pissed, so pissed he got someone to try and steal the baby back. The thing was, I didn't think he knew his grandchild was a girl yet, and I honestly didn't think that was all to the story. Maybe it was the truth for the woman Stacey and how she wanted the money. But I reckoned Knife's dad had an ulterior motive to organise the whole thing in the first place.

I told Knife my thoughts. He nodded, his eyes going back down to the dead guy. "Yeah, doesn't fully fit."

Knife looked to Dive. "Will Mena have Nevaeh all night?"

"Yeah, brother. I'll take some extra shit of hers over."

Lifting my hands, Knife's gaze shifted to me. *What you thinking?*

His smile was vicious. "It's time to pay Daddy dearest a visit."

A grin lifted my lips to match his. *I'm coming.*

"We're all in," Pick added.

WE OPTED for two vehicles instead of our rides, not wanting our presence noticed until the last second. I was in a car with Dodge and Knife, while Pick and Billy stopped by to grab Dive after he'd dropped off the things I packed for Nevaeh. I was dressed in dark jeans and a black tee, with my club vest over the top, similar to what the others were wearing. We were headed to Knife's parents' house. He didn't want to wait any longer, and I couldn't blame him. Everyone was still in the car, unspeaking and barely moving. Dodge and Knife seemed lost in their own thoughts, and I couldn't help wonder what Knife was thinkin'.

It wasn't the time for it, but my mind went back to that kiss.

What in the hell did it mean?

Why in the fuck would he want to kiss me in the first place?

Or even ask if Ben and I were serious?

Confusion swamped me.

If what went down hadn't happened, I'd be demanding answers from the man sitting up front.

Knife's arm came out and pointed to a goddamn mansion of a house. I blinked slowly, once, twice, and still, I couldn't believe my eyes. Knife came from money, something he'd never told me about. It didn't change who he was to me: a brother of the club and the man who played on my mind all the time.

Dodge said something to Knife I didn't catch as we pulled into the gated drive, and Knife turned in his seat. *Can you do your thing on the gate?*

Nodding, I exited the car as the vehicle containing the rest of our brothers pulled up behind. Steppin' up to the system, I pulled out my switchblade and jimmied the box open. A few seconds later, the gates slowly opened.

As soon as my arse hit the seat, we drove down the long driveway and stopped out the front. I tapped Knife's shoulder, and he turned. *You sure your 'rents don't have guards?*

Smirking, he shook his head before answering. "Frank thinks he's untouchable with his system. Then again, he probably doesn't expect an attack from his son."

We met Pick, Billy, and Dive at the front of the car and made our way to the front door. They separated, and I got in close. I lifted my tool kit from my pocket and got to my knees. The lock was easy to pick. Fuckin' fools hadn't even clicked the deadbolt in. I swung the door open and stood, entering first. No lights were on, but with the huge-arse windows, it was lit by the moonlight. Quickly, I took care of the alarm system. Top of the line, my arse. It was easy to kill.

We spread out. I kept close to Knife's back, knowing he would have guessed where he needed to go. We climbed the million stairs and went to the right down a hall. The place was like a museum, old pricey shit all over the place.

We stopped at the door for only a second before he pushed it wide and turned on the lights. Two startled people quickly sat, blinking sleep away from their eyes.

Knife advanced. The man in his late sixties called, "What is the meaning... Jay? What are you doing?" The guy was old, looking to be on his last withered legs. Why would he decide to orchestrate an heir when he was already so old? An heir wouldn't have been of age when he took his last breath. I'd been right; it wasn't addin' up.

"Jay, what are you doing here in the middle of the night?" the woman said, her eyes going to me and then back to her son. She was worried and had every right to be.

Steppin' up beside Knife so I could catch whatever he was gonna say, I crossed my arms over my chest and sensed our brothers coming into the room. Knife's parents' eyes widened, worry gone, fear taking its place.

"You made the wrong move, *Frank*." I didn't miss the sneer when Knife all but spat Frank's name. "A very wrong move."

"What are you talking about?" Mr Conger went to climb outta the bed, only to stop and glance back at his son.

"You move, you *will* regret it."

"Jay!" I saw his mum cry.

Knife's eyes flashed to his mum. "Did you know?" he asked. He didn't wait for an answer. "Did you know the man you sleep next to, my fuckin' father, organised someone to break into the house I'm stayin' at with my child?"

Her hand fluttered to her chest. She glanced to Knife's dad, whose lowered gaze was on his son. Shaking her head, she shifted her gaze back to Knife. "You have a child?"

She didn't have a clue what her husband had done.

"Yeah, Mum. I have a kid. Just a baby, eight months old. Apparently your husband wanted an heir so much he got a slut to seduce me and get knocked up by me. Then, after she played him and ran with the baby, he sent some fuckhead to grab my kid by breaking into the house." His mum's eyes filled with tears. Knife shook his head, before whipping his gaze to his dad. "Move again and I'll have my brothers shoot you." Knife stepped closer. I was right alongside him. "You made a bad decision to fuck with me and mine. A very bad one." He looked over his shoulder. "Take her out and don't let her come back in here until I leave."

I wasn't sure who he spoke to until Dive came forward to assist Mrs Conger outta the bed. Her whole body shook as Dive led her silent, shocked form from the room, closing the door behind them.

KNIFE

I looked at my father, Frank Conger, while disgust churned my gut. He was an old fucker who thought his shit didn't stink and could do anything he wanted. Well, I was about to prove him wrong. Pick, Billy, and Dodge moved in closer. Beast was already by my side so he could catch everything that was said. If I wasn't so pissed, I would have signed for him.

"Why'd you do it?" I asked, my nose crinkling up as he tried for a gentle smile.

"Come on now, son—"

Leaning in, I roared, "Do not call me that."

"You didn't want anything to do with me. My only child wanted nothing to do with me."

Snorting, I said, "Yeah, why you think that is, Frank?"

His fist hit the bed. "They were of a legal age."

"Barely. No kid wants to find out his father dealt in the shit you did. You got them hooked on crack so you could do anything to them. Shit, not only you but your mates. Make matters worse, you kept them in a fuckin' house back in the woods so Mum didn't know and then when I found your dirty secret, you wanted me to follow in your footsteps. Not only dealin' in that shit but illegal works from the business. Fuck that, and fuck you."

Dad glared. "You know *who* I deal with in the business, yet you feel you can come here and threaten me. Foolish move, *son.*"

That caused me to throw my head back and laugh.

Still chuckling, I wiped away my tears of mirth and shook my head. "Shit, old man. Do you have any idea about my family?"

He sniffed. "You mean the men at your back? I know who they are, and I have no fear of them."

Snorting once again, I said, "Then you're pretty fuckin' dumb. You tell the men you deal with who I belong to and see what they say. They probably know us better than you do, old man. They'd know no one fucks with Hawks and gets away with it. In one way or another, they would have heard the stories, so they'd feel the fear even if you don't." Uncrossing my arms, I pulled my phone free and stalked around to the side of the bed. After tappin' a few things, I threw it to his lap. "However, I think after you see that, you'll start to realise who I am, who I belong to and then, fuckin' *then*, you'll feel the fear so bad you won't say shit to anyone. You'll want to leave me and mine alone because if you don't... I will do to you what *I* did to him." With my chin, I gestured to the phone and the photo that lay on it.

I could have laughed again when his hands shook as he picked up the phone and brought it close to see the photo. He gagged and threw it to the bed.

"Yeah, I think you understand me now." I grabbed up my phone and placed it back in my pocket. "That was the guy you sent in to get my girl." Frank's eyes widened. Shaking my head, I commented, "You didn't know I had a girl. Didn't matter to me if it was important or not to you. You still had to learn, and I was happy to bring the teachin' your way." Crouching enough so I was in his face, I shot my hand out and wrapped it around his throat. He choked as I tightened my grip. "Stay outta my life. Leave my mother, if she ain't already leavin' you, and do whatever the hell you want to, but nothing, and I fuckin' mean nothing at all will touch me, Mum, or mine. You hear me?"

"Y-yes," he croaked out.

CHAPTER SIXTEEN

KNIFE

*W*hat I wanted to do was slice him open. Instead, I would let him live feeling shit scared of his own son and allowing him to relay to others who thought to fuck with Hawks not to. I did, however, land my fist into his face. I gripped his neck and leaned in. "Tell me the real reason you wanted my girl. It wasn't some heir bullshit." Because Beast had been right; just wanting an heir wasn't enough. There had to be another reason. I reckoned the heir stuff was just some bullshit he'd spewed to Stacey to fuck me over for money. But since it brought Nevaeh into my life, I couldn't be too harsh on her, unless she came lookin' for my girl.

"W-what are you talking about?" he stuttered like a fool.

I shoved his head back so it hit the headboard hard and stood. "I'll only ask one last time before my brothers actually do start shooting. Tell me the real reason why you wanted my kid."

He glanced around the room at my brothers and then back to me. His chest rose and fell rapidly. "You wouldn't understand."

"Try me," I clipped.

"I-I promised someone something."

My head jerked back. "What in the fuck are you sayin'?"

"A client of mine wanted..." He glanced again around to my brother before landing his eyes on me. "He wanted an in with your club."

Jesus Christ.

It all clicked into place.

"So you thought you'd say you could get him an in by trapping me, stealing my kid, to what? Hand her over to him so it'd have me and my brothers do his illegal shit, and then you could sit back happy you'd done the deal with the devil and survived?" I laughed menacingly. "You fuckin' dickhead. No one would ever get control over Hawks. No one. You can tell him that after you let him know we killed his man. Hell, I'll even message you the photo to send to him." His eyes bulged. I'd guessed right. The dead guy had been one of his client's. "You also need to enlighten the fucker if he ever tries to pull this shit again, we will bring him down." Turning, I stalked from the room with my brothers following.

Only at the door, I spun back and added, "Nearly forgot, Frank." There was no fuckin' way he'd be anything other than Frank to me again, though fuckhead could work too. "You continue on with those girls, I'll come back. You don't want that to happen, do you?" It was something I should'a done a long time ago, but I didn't because they were homeless hookers and at least they had a roof over their heads for a while. Still, the thought of not doing anything, even though I was sixteen at the time I'd found out, didn't sit right inside of me. I'd got outta the house soon after and found Hawks, wanting my old life set behind me. I shouldn't have built up a wall around my dad's fucked-up deeds so high and forgotten about what he'd done.

The blame was on me for him screwin' up so many women. The knowledge fuckin' burned.

Frank shook his head in answer.

"Good. End it."

Once out the door, we walked down the hall and stairs before I looked to Dodge and asked, "Can we make sure he follows through?"

I'll set up cameras. Beast signed.

Dodge nodded. "I'll get some brothers on what fucked-up Frank did in the woods behind here. Make sure it doesn't happen again and help those women who want it. And we'll watch Frank closely to see who he communicates with. See if we can find out who this client is. I just don't understand something. Why didn't you kill him? He was gonna take your girl and hand her over to some sick fuck."

"Whoever this client is will want retaliation for taking down one of his guys. He'll realise we ain't an easy target, so our best bet for him to get what he wants was to leave Frank alive so he can take it out on that old man."

"Well, shit. You do have a brain," Billy joked, at least I fuckin' hoped it was one.

After raising my middle finger in his face, we made our way into the kitchen, where I found my mum in tears. She sat at the table with Dive standing beside her, his hand on her shoulder. She must'a heard us coming because she stood once we entered. With her hand clasped to her chest, regret shone in her eyes.

"I'm sorry—"

"Mum, don't. It ain't your fault."

"I let you leave and stay away because I wanted to protect you from his world."

"Now all you gotta do is worry about you. Want you outta his life, Ma. Can you do that for me?"

"Yes," she whispered. "I've missed out on so much from your life because of him, but I won't anymore…. That is if you'll want me in your life?"

Taking the steps I needed, I was in front of her and pullin' her in my arms. "I shouldn'ta left you either. You've always been a part of my life, but I just didn't tell you. Sorry for not reachin' out." Her arms came around my waist. "What you gonna do?"

"Leave him. Something I should have done a long time ago but didn't have the strength to do it. Not until now."

Nodding, I shifted her back to meet her sad eyes. "I'll have some brothers stay while you pack, but I gotta get outta this place."

"I understand."

Fuck me. I was the biggest dick to have left my life behind and let Mum stay with poison.

"Don't," she muttered. "Don't blame yourself. I was weak, but no longer."

"We'll talk soon, yeah?"

She offered me a shaky smile. "I would like that, and to meet my grandchild."

"Done." Leanin' in, I kissed her cheek and looked to Pick and Billy. "Can—"

"We got this, brother."

With a chin lift, I said, "Thanks. Take one of their cars. Fill it with what she needs and get her to a hotel."

"On it."

Glancing to my mum, I said, "See you soon."

"I look forward to it."

Spinning, I walked from the room with Beast, Dodge, and Dive. As soon as we got outside, I took a lungful of air, my hands clasping at the back of my head.

"You good, brother?" Dive asked.

"Thought I'd left that life behind. Realised I shouldn't have for her sake."

"She's strong, even if she said she was weak. I don't think any of Frank's shit touched her. Loved her enough to keep it hidden from her."

"She's a lot younger than him. Still got time to be happy. Truly happy," Dodge said.

"Yeah." I nodded, dropping my arms to my sides.

"You need sleep, brother. Beast will take you back. Mena will have Nevaeh for the day, rest easy."

"No—"

"Brother. Fuckin' lotta shit to absorb. Let it sink, deal, and then come get your girl." Dive knocked his fist into my arm.

The offer was great, one I wanted to take, but I needed to have my girl back. See she was safe. A tap on my arm had me turned to Beast.

Got to board up her window. Organise some more security on the house and bars to the windows. Let's get the house set before we bring her back.

Shit, he was right.

Sighing, I nodded, and after thanking my brothers, I started for Beast's car.

BEAST

He was exhausted and even after we got home, he didn't rest. He straightened Nevaeh's room and then boarded up her window while I put in cameras outside. Hell, maybe every brother should have cameras at their homes, not just the compound. Never knew what in the hell could happen, and prevention was better than anything. Somethin' I'd suggest at the next church. I already had a security system, but I hadn't activated it because I'd still been awake at the time of the attack.

Christ. What a night.

It was early hours before I stumbled in the front door, with Vin at my side, to find Knife coming outta Nevaeh's room with a bag of rubbish, probably the broken glass. His expression pinched with thoughts he shouldn't be havin'. I knew they'd be about his arse of a father, and his mum. Regret would be front and centre, and he'd also be pissed at himself for wantin' to live a life of his own without his family's shit draggin' him under.

I knew the feelin'.

My dad was the dick, and my mum the one who put up with him because she thought she loved him. When I'd left, she'd picked him over havin' anything to do with me. Exactly like Mrs Conger. Only I wasn't sure Knife saw it like that—his mum choosing the evil over her own child. He was blaming himself for leavin' her. Maybe one day he'd see it. Then again, I didn't really want him to.

He'd be better off having his mum in his life now than never having her at all.

If she came through with what she promised, leavin' her husband and gettin' back in Knife's life, then I'd leave it be, but if she didn't, I'd want Knife to see he wasn't to blame.

I reached out to his arm then signed once I had his attention. *You got to get some hours of shut-eye.*

He nodded, but then headed straight into the living room and then into the kitchen.

Damn, was I gonna have to tie him to his bed?

Hell. That thought went right to my cock and the kiss we'd shared on the couch. Lookin' to the couch, my dick jerked in my jeans.

Shakin' my head, I rubbed a hand over my face. I needed some sleep.

Kiss me.

That was what he'd said.

Kiss me.

When he touched his lips to mine, I was goddamn shocked. My body had frozen, and I hadn't realised I wasn't dreamin' until his tongue reached out to play.

Then it was on.

Kiss me.

Words I wished I could have heard instead of seen.

Reachin' down, I glided my hand over Vin's head and down his back, causin' his tail to wag. He'd been pissed earlier when I'd left him at home. I was lucky it didn't last, and he was happy to see me when I'd walked in the front door with Knife a few hours ago.

Two booted feet came into view. Knife stood in front of me. *Time to sleep, brother.* He nodded. *Just a couple of hours, then you can call the guy about bars, and then go get your girl.*

What are you gonna do?

See to some cameras at your dad's place.

Thanks, Beast.

What I'd give for him to sign my real name. Jesus, another word I wished I could have heard fall from his lips, just before he kissed me, or while we were kissing. If he'd muttered it against my lips, I would have been fine with that or when I'd slowly rocked my cock…. Christ, abort thoughts. It was time to crash.

"Gonna get a shower in first," Knife added and fucked my head up even more.

Knife stripped slowly outta his clothes in front of me. He gave me a smirk over his shoulder and slid his pants down his legs.

Blinking, I stumbled back a step, my cock hard as fuck behind my jeans.

Sleep. I needed sleep.

And to maybe tug one off.

Right, you take the bathroom—or me—and I'll grab one later. I ignored the trembling of my hands as I signed.

"Done," he responded with a smile.

Fuck me to hell.

His smile always shot right to my cock. It wasn't exactly the time for it when I was already so goddamn gone from my thoughts. I just knew I was leakin' pre-cum. Knife's eyes flashed wide.

Shit. Did I moan?

Kiss me. I urged with my mind. Only he didn't. Instead, he smirked as if he found somethin' funny and then walked past me and brushed his shoulder against mine. His scent stayed with me even though he kept walking down the hall. I was sure it was a record of mine with how fast I'd made it into my own room with the door shut, and while Vin stretched out on the floor, I tore off my clothes from my heated body and lay back on top of the sheets with my cock in my hand.

It wouldn't take me long.

I was primed and ready from only thinkin' of Knife and that kiss.

Fuck. I couldn't stop myself even if I wanted to. I *needed* to come.

I stroked up and down my length. A thrill deep inside of me had my head pushing back into my pillow and a groan falling from my lips.

Images of Knife naked in the shower flashed in my mind. I'd seen enough of him topless and with his pants down in the past to know what he looked like. His strong build, his sleek tattooed skin as he pounded into a woman, where I wished it was me, and since it was my fantasy, I replaced the fuckin' woman with myself.

He'd bend me over something, eager to get my pants down around my ankles where his hands would come down on my hips while the tip of his cock jutted out and between my arse cheeks.

Ah, fuck me. My load shot up and out the tip of my cock before I even got to the good part.

KNIFE

I'd just turned the water off when I heard Beast groan from his room next door. Bloody hell, he was jerkin' off, and I knew, goddamn knew, I would be starring in his thoughts while he touched himself. I'd seen the outline of his erection in his jeans and heard the moan fall from his lips after I'd smiled.

Shit, if I'd known my smile was gonna make him pop a stiffy, I'd have to remember to smile all the time to mess with him.

Turning the shower back on, since my dick was pointing to the moon after hearing Beast groan and thinkin' of him touching himself, something I never thought I'd get hard over, I rested my hand against the back wall and took my cock in hand. The spray of warm water slid down my body and warmed my cool skin.

An image of Beast walkin' in on me while I jerked off, and offering to help, had my balls already tightening. Christ, I was hot for the dude and liked it more than picturing a woman.

Go fuckin' figure.

What drew the cum from my body was an image of Beast stripping down, hopping in the shower and takin' my cock in his mouth.

Catchin' my breath, I opened my eyes and grinned.

Yeah, if the crap was behind me with Frank, I'd be steppin' up my moves on Beast.

All I had to do was hope he liked them.

CHAPTER SEVENTEEN

KNIFE

*G*oogle was not my friend. I thought I'd check out ways to impress the guy you wanted. I even typed in "to impress the gay guy you wanted," which I was fuckin' proud of myself for doin'. Thought it'd help me get ready to approach Beast with what I wanted.

Plain and simple. I wanted him.

At least I thought I did.

Nope, I did. It'd been a few days since the shit went down, hearing nothing from it, and it seemed life still couldn't give me a break. We'd either been too tired to talk or busy with other shit that we missed each other at times in the house.

So when I was alone one night and Nevaeh was asleep, I fired up Google and searched for a few things. Some men liked an alpha male. When I looked up to see what that was, I realised both Beast and I were alpha. Hell, to me we were. Not like I was gonna drop into Dive's and ask if he thought I was an alpha. It said some men liked a manscaped man. Again, when I searched what in the fuck that meant, I saw clean, trimmed, some shaved pubes and, fuck me, arses.

Did that mean I needed to do that?

Did Beast like a man trimmed or nothing at all down there?

I was confused as fuck and had no one to talk to.

Hell, I hadn't ever cared if women thought I was the hairiest motherfucker before, so why was I worried and caring what Beast thought?

Shit. Did Ben trim?

Then to make matters worse, I saw some even waxed down there. Waxed. Like some women did. I didn't want to look like a little boy when Beast went down there. I was certain it would be when not if Beast went down there. I'd gone to bed each night jerking off to fantasies of Beast and me, and they were gettin' hotter and hotter. Shit, I was comin' faster and faster each time, so that was another worry.

Would I blow my load before I got any action from the guy?

That'd be pitiful.

As the day went on, I kept thinking about trimming or doin' something to make my junk look presentable. I couldn't just dump it on a plate and offer him a bite to eat.

Or could I?

Nope, I had to go all out.

Besides, if women could do what I was about to, I totally could.

Shaking my head, I called the only person I knew who'd

keep their mouth shut, who was sweet, gentle, and under-standing.

"K<small>NIFE</small>," Mena whispered, stepping closer to my side with Koda in her arms. "I'm scared."

Groaning, I pushed the stroller with Nevaeh in it back and forward while I snapped at Mena, "Woman, do not do this shit to me. You'll freak *me* out."

"Maybe you should just go to Julian?" she suggested. I'd just told her why we'd met at the beauty place and she'd paled. *The woman paled.* That was not a goddamn good sign.

"No way in hell am I going to Julian. He'd probably wanna make a clay model outta my junk because it's so awesome."

Her eyes were wide with fear, and every time I caught sight of them, my gut would clench. She cleared her throat and asked, "Tell me again why you want to do this?"

Shrugging, I rubbed the back of my neck and muttered, "Just want to tidy up down there. Thought if women could do it, I don't see why I can't."

She reached out and placed her hand on my arm. "I'm sure Beast will like it down there without doing this. You need to run, Knife. Run out of this store right now."

Holy fuck. Now I was starting to sweat as panic set in.

A little wax couldn't hurt.

Could it?

"Ah, who said anything about Beast?" I snorted. "Why would I do anything for him?" I scoffed. "This is for all the lady admirers. Yeah, the ladies." I nodded.

Fuck, why would she say Beast?

It wasn't obvious, was it?

Hell, how could it be? I didn't go around drooling over the guy or carrying around his junk in my hand like a prized trophy.

"Mr Conger?"

My heart jumped, along with my body, at my name being called.

"Knife," Mena whispered, "it's not too late to back out."

Turning my head to her, I glared. "It's obvious you were the wrong person to come along for moral support."

She nodded. Christ, she agreed with me. "I've had a bad experience, Knife."

"You're coming in with me."

"What?" she yelled, then covered her mouth with her hand and shook her head. Koda laughed at her and then yelled "what?" also. "No."

"Yes," I gritted and grabbed her arm in one hand while I steered the stroller with the other over to the Chinese lady waiting for us.

"This is no sexual time. She can wait with children." The lady smiled.

Why in the fuck would she think it was "sexual" time in the first place? I was about to tear my pubes from my body. Did she think I'd want head while gettin' it done?

Fuck me.

Mena straightened. "I'm here for moral support." Hell, I was proud of her for standing up and taking charge.

The woman eyed us and pointed at Mena. "Your clothes stay on."

What in the ever lovin' fuck do people get up to while gettin' waxed?

"Mrs Chang," another woman called before stepping up to our side. "This isn't like the place you used to work in. No one comes in here for anything… um, sexual."

Mrs Chang thumped her forehead with her palm. "So sorry. I forgot not working at Blow Joe's any longer." Then she turned and went through the door.

The other lady turned to us. "I'm so flippin' sorry. I was in need of a waxer, and she came in at the right time. Do you want me to mind the munchkins while you both go in there?"

"No," I clipped.

"Yes," Mena said. "Um, Knife. It's not like she'll steal them."

"Oh, I won't. I'll take them into the break room right across from you both. I'll even leave the door open so you can see them. No other appointments are scheduled right now, so no one else will be back there."

Sighing, I nodded. We walked down the hall. The woman pointed into the right room, and I watched her take the stroller into the left room, leaving the door open like she said, and then she came back for Koda, who happily went into her arms. Guess it was good Nevaeh was asleep so she couldn't kick up a stink. She wasn't happy with strangers, seemed to only wanna take to me, Beast, Dive, and Mena.

Mrs Chang clapped her hands and then rubbed them together. "You get pants off."

Glancing to Mena, I chuckled and said, "Babe, think Dive will kill me if I let you see my awesomeness?"

She nodded, a smile playing at her lips, and then she gave me her back. I quickly took off my boots, socks, jeans, and boxers. The cool air caused me to shiver as I slid onto the bed with paper laid out over it. All the while Mrs Chang looked on. Fuck, I should'a asked her to turn around also.

I slipped the folded sheet at the end of the bed over my waist.

"You turn now and take his hand," Mrs Chang said.

"Why would she need to take my hand?" I asked, my brows dipping in worry. What made it worse was when Mrs Chang started to giggle. As Mena went to take my hand, I shook my head. "Nah, babe. I'll be fine."

She bit her bottom lip. "My hand is here when you need it."

I was about to answer, tell her I wouldn't need it, when the sheet was lifted. My eyes went there for a second, and then I flicked my gaze back up to see Mena looked everywhere but the action about to happen at the end of the table.

"Hmm," Mrs Chang hummed under her breath. I shot my gaze back down as she grabbed my legs and folded them up and out. "I need to see better. You very hairy."

"What in the fuck you doin'?" I demanded when her fingers shifted through my pubes.

"Like a jungle down here. I look for tree trunk."

Fuck me.

Clenching my jaw, I bit out, "My cock is the biggest tree trunk out there, and you'll find it right in front of you."

"Yes, yes. Very big." She patted my leg. Better not have been in fuckin' sympathy.

I grunted. "The women never complained."

"Don't worry. I clean up and he be seen better."

Would it be too much if I killed the bitch between my legs?

"You want all hair gone?"

Did I?

"Ah, I don't know."

"See how you go first," Mena suggested. Christ, she acted

like I was gonna pussy out and run around crying like a little girl.

Scoffing, I said, "I'll be fine. Just get started."

"I trim first, then wax."

Sounded like a plan. When she looked from between my legs, I nodded. She reached over for a pair of scissors. "Careful with those," I ordered.

She giggled and from what I was feeling, she picked up bits of pubes and started to hedge it like a bush, not a pussy, but a bush in a garden.

They needed background music or somethin'. All I could hear was the *snip, snip, snip* of the scissors.

Mrs Chang stood and placed her hands on my knees. She looked down, nodding at her work. "Look better already." She glanced to Mena. "You want look?"

Mena laughed nerviously and shook her head. "No, I mean, it's not for me."

Mrs Chang cocked her head to the side but said nothing else about it. "Wax warm, be prepared."

"All good." I nodded. Resting back, I closed my eyes and thought there was nothing to it when I felt the heat of the wax being spread on at the top of my pubic line. Yeah, this was gonna be as easy as… well, me.

She pressed it a couple of times. Not sure why, maybe to check if it was ready. "On three. One." She picked at the corner of the wax, and I thought it wasn't so bad, just a little sting. "Two. Three."

"Fuck me!" I screamed. "Jesus Christ, motherfucker. What did you do? Mena, look. Mena, she ripped my cock off. Fucking hell, am I dickless now? Mena, look for me, I can't."

Mena's hands gripped mine. "It's okay. It's all right."

"No, it isn't! She tore my dick right off!"

"Ready for more?" Mrs Chang asked with a smile on her face, and before I could tell her to shove it, she was already spreading on more wax.

"No, I can't do this. You women are fuckin' crazy."

"One."

"No! You bitch."

"Two."

I struggled, went to sit up, but Mena pushed me back down. "Don't move, you'll make it worse. Breathe, Knife. Breathe."

"Three."

"You cunt. You sadistic bitch!" I screamed.

"One more and then Mr Willy will—"

"Mr Willy wants *no* more. No, get the fuck away." I pushed back up, but Mena leaned over and somehow, like Mrs Chang had extra arms and was as strong as Hulk, she pushed my legs apart and slathered on the wax.

"Fuck. Fuck. Fuck, I'm gonna cry." My arms wrapped around Mena, who lay on my upper half to keep me down. "Hold me, Mena." My voice shook like the biggest pussy out there.

"One."

"I swear to Christ I will punch you in the tit if you count— Holy shit!" I roared. "You cruel, cruel woman."

CHAPTER EIGHTEEN

KNIFE

*I*n seconds, I was off that bed standing at the side
and looking down to make sure I still had a dick.
He was there, but he was as pissed as I was. I was red, swollen
and—

"There's blood," I bit out through clenched teeth. "You
made me bleed." I managed a step towards Mrs Chang before
Mena's arms came around my waist.

"Knife, you can't harm her. Calm down, please."

"If my dick had hands, it would strangle you," I warned
Mrs Chang, who only smiled back.

"Thank you," she said. "Would you like me to do your
anus?"

My head jerked back and I blinked slowly at the small
woman. Was she fuckin' serious?

"No! I don't want you anywhere near my arse. Christ, woman."

"Knife." Mena rubbed my back. "We should get going. Nevaeh will wake soon, and you'll need to shower the excess wax off."

"Let me get dressed." Bending, which hurt, I grabbed my wallet from the back of my jeans and went to pass it to Mena, whose eyes were up to the roof. I grabbed her hand, dropped my wallet in it and said, "You get the kids out front and pay, I'll be out in a second."

"Okay." She was out the door quickly.

"And you," I snarled at Mrs Chang, "leave before I do something you won't like."

"You have good day." She grinned and walked casually out of the room like she was used to being threatened.

Once I heard the door close, I looked down at my junk again.

Why in the hell did I think waxing was gonna be easy? Even though my dick looked bigger, without all the hair surrounding it, there was no way in hell I'd ever do that again.

Beast was gonna have to like what I had to offer.

Shit, maybe I could bring waxing into torturing people who fuck with Hawks.

Not that I'd suggest it. They'd ask why and there was no way I would tell them I tried it and just about cried like a baby.

Just about.

Okay, so I had tears and asked Mena to hold me.

Something she'd have to take to her grave.

MENA CAME BACK to the house and said she'd watch and feed both kids while I took a much-needed shower. I swear I was walking crooked. I wished I had a portable fan so I could pull my I-didn't-realise-they-were-so-tight jeans away from my groin and blow some cool air on it.

Hell, I was honestly considering asking Beast if he'd blow air from his mouth over my dick.

Opening the door, I came to a halt when I saw Beast, Dive, and motherfuckin' Ben sitting in the living room. Beast and Ben were on the couch while Dive had his arse on the coffee table.

It really wasn't a good day to see that dick's face.

"Yo, brother. You still got my—" Dive started, but didn't finish when I pushed Nevaeh in her stroller, further into the room and then stormed into the living room, with a slight limp and screwed up nose from the pain, to point down at Ben.

"You need to—" I started to yell.

"Knife," Mena cried, interrupting me. All eyes went to her. "Um, hi, everyone." She signed and smiled, handing Koda to Dive before coming to stand in front of me. "Nevaeh needs her lunch."

Clenching my jaw, I breathed deeply through my nose and looked over her head to glare at Ben, then Beast.

"You're right." Walking back over to my girl, who was lookin' out the side of her stroller at me, I scooped her up and kissed her cheek, causing her to giggle. Ignoring them all, I made my way back through them and into the kitchen while grumbling under my breath, "Stupid fuckin' cockhead coming here. What was he even doin' here? Christ, had Beast still been seeing him even after that kiss?"

"Is he okay?" I heard Dive ask.

"He's had a hard morning," Mena supplied, and I snorted at it.

Hard morning my arse. After going through the worst torture I'd ever been submitted to, I get home to find Beast's cocksucker sittin' close on the couch to him.

What was up with that?

And why in the hell did I sound like a jealous teen girl?

It had to be because I'd had my pubes ripped from my body by a smiling, sadistic woman.

So what if Ben was there? Obvious that kiss hadn't meant anything to Beast. Did it mean something to me? Yes, yes it goddamn did. Only then why did I tell Mena gettin' all trimmed and shit was for women?

I wasn't ready to admit to anything when nothing was really goin' on between us.

And that was *if* somethin' did. I could be all talk and end up shittin' my pants if things got hot and heavy between Beast and me in the bedroom.

It was somethin' I still wanted to find out though.

If only the fucktard in the living room would fuck on off outta his life.

As Nevaeh played with some blocks on her highchair bench, I slammed things around in the kitchen gettin' her and Koda's lunch ready. I was also flinching still with every step I took. Christ, it probably looked like I had something shoved up my arse.

There was another thing to think about.

I'd seen Beast's cock before, and it was a thick, long sucker. Would I be into havin' him enter the unknown with his monster of a dick?

Wasn't sure I could bottom.

Catching sight of a carrot, I picked it up and studied it. Needed to be thicker and longer, but could I seriously have something around that size up my arse?

Would I enjoy it or scream like a virgin?

That was somethin' I'd have to think about later. Throwin' the carrot back in the fridge, I slammed the door shut and spun around to find Beast standing there. I bit back my scream, but my body jolted.

Stupid fuckin' ninja dude.

What you up to?

Heat hit my cheeks, so I turned away from him and shrugged, then shook the bowl full of peas at him. Facing him again, once my face cooled, I yelled out to Mena, "Woman, you gonna feed your boy?"

She's gone. They're all gone.

My brow hitched up. *Why?*

He smirked. *Saw you on your rag and wanted to clear the house.*

My middle finger came up on its own accord. Beast stepped into the kitchen more with Vin following him. *Let me feed her. You go shower.*

"What makes you think I want a shower?" Did he smell the wax on me?

Mena said you wanted one. Could put you in a better mood.

Passing the bowl over to Beast, he walked around the high chair and squeezed in past me, where I felt his arse brush my sore area. I let out a hiss and for once, thanked fuck he couldn't hear me. Even though it stung like a fucker, my dick still perked up, apparently over being pissed off after what I did near it.

Still, I looked at the space between the high chair and me. There was enough for him not to be near me. Did that mean he was teasing?

Hell, if I wasn't burning below, I'd do something about it.

Beast glanced up at me. *You good?*

Clearing my throat, I nodded and stepped back, crossing my arms over my chest as I watched Nevaeh enjoy her food and babble between bites. I swung my stare to Beast again to find him watching me.

Why was Ben here? I just couldn't help but ask it.

His lips twitched. Why? He found me amusing? Did that question come across like I was jealous? I wasn't.

Who was I kidding? I was furious Ben was in the house.

He just popped in.

I considered asking if his cock accidentally popped into his mouth.

Annoyance had me fisting my hands and clenching them at my sides because Beast was being evasive. He could just tell me why he *popped* in, how long he'd *popped* in for and if any touchin' was involved while he had fuckin' *popped* in.

Instead, he went back to feeding Nevaeh.

He glanced at me because I still stood there glaring down at him like a moron.

His lips twitched again.

"How long you home for?" I asked, wanting to know how long I could take to shower.

Got the whole day.

Did that mean he didn't have the night? Was Ben there to ask him out? Was he gonna go out with Ben again?

Fuck.

I felt like throwing up.

"Be as quick as I can be."

Don't rush, I got her. Then he smiled at Nevaeh and pulled a face. Fuck me, but that was hot to see. Big, broody biker messin' playfully with my girl.

I had to get outta there and hope a shower would clear my head. Doubtful though. My head was flyin' all over the place, obsessin' over Beast and dickface.

Why wouldn't he just come out and say why Ben was there and if he had plans with the dick later?

Did he enjoy my discomfort?

Scrubbin' a hand over my face, I limped outta the room. Each step was painful, and I hoped to Christ Beast had some lotion to rub on my sore bits, 'cause I knew I didn't, and Mena had said it would help a little. Fuck, I should'a asked her how long it'd take for me to be back to normal. It'd better not take too long because I wanted to move things up with the man in the kitchen. Then, at least if things worked out, if I liked what we were gonna do, I could demand that Ben took a hike outta his life.

It took me longer than usual to get undressed and after, I stood lookin' down at myself once again. Still red and raw.

Stupid fuckin' move.

Waxing. Why in the hell did women do it? They were stronger than they looked, that was for sure. Guess if they could squeeze a baby out, waxing would be a breeze.

Next time Google could go to bloody hell.

My thoughts drifted back to Beast. He was constantly in the forefront of my mind, only that time I was thinkin' about Beast jerkin' off like I'd heard the other night, and my dick sprang to life.

If only I wasn't sore, I would have tugged one out.

Instead, I turned on the shower, got under the spray and hissed like a bitch when the water hit me.

AFTER SHOWERING and dressing in loose-fitting track pants, my phone rang. The display read Private Number. "Yo?"

"Your father is dead."

My whole body stilled. There was only one guess who the motherfucker was on the other end of the line.

"He promised me something and he didn't deliver. Since you took the life of one of mine, I've taken his." The guy talked like he was God. I was about to take him down a step and let him know exactly what I'd found out the day before from a brother who'd traced Frank's phone.

"And tell me something, dickhead. Did Frank pass on my message?"

He laughed as if what Frank had warned him about didn't faze him. "I believe he did."

"Good. Then you know not to fuck with Hawks. If you do, we'll come after you, Bryant Campbell." Silence met me on the other end of the line. I chuckled darkly. "Yeah, we know who you are. So you might actually want to listen to this warning, Bryant. We'll be watching. You even breathe in our territory, you'll never know what hit you." With that, I ended the call. Stupid fucker thought he was the up-and-coming man in the drug business and untouchable. He was wrong. Only Hawks was untouchable.

After calming my fury, I made a call to Parker, telling them to get to Frank's house to take on the case. I also rang Ma and told her the news. Her voice cracked and she cried. Only it didn't last long. She pulled herself together and we talked for a few more moments before hanging up.

I was glad Frank was dead. The world would be better off without him in it. I just hated the pain it had Ma feeling, even if it was small.

CHAPTER NINETEEN

BEAST

A few steps and a few words were what played over and over in my head. Hell, even the glare Knife used when he saw Ben in the house hit me right in the groin. What was up with the other man in the house? And why in the fuck was he limping?

I'd asked Mena and knew something was up when her cheeks had heated, and she'd mumbled, "Nothing." Dive knew it as well, which was why he got her outta the house quickly, no doubt to see if he had to kill his brother. I'd seen them havin' words just outside, both gettin' frustrated, and then after Mena had poked Dive in the chest and said something, he threw his head back and laughed. Then he doubled over, holding his stomach and laughed even more. Mena, with Koda in her arms, kicked him in the shin and with a look of fury, one I'd never seen on her face, she snapped something and then stormed off to the car.

After it, I'd turned to Ben, who'd been watchin' with a smile on his lips, and just when I was about to get rid of him, he'd stood and said he'd catch up later.

Wasn't his fault I hadn't been into our thing lately.

Not since that kiss.

The kiss that played on a loop.

Ben wasn't stupid though. He knew something was up. He just didn't know what.

Or maybe he guessed it had something to do with the man who lived with me, especially after the way Knife reacted. Which, to be clear, was a fuckin' turn-on, especially with the shit he did even in front of Dive. Like he was a jealous boyfriend.

Fuck me.

Knife jealous?

Boyfriend?

Those were three words I never in my goddamn life would have considered when it came to Knife.

The man who'd run from the hotel room in Sydney.

The man who'd ignored me for two fuckin' months after it.

Jealous and boyfriend…. Yeah, those words shouldn't be used when it came to Knife. I was being an idiot.

Then again.

He. Kissed. Me.

Clearin' my head of all thoughts Knife related, I spooned the last of Nevaeh's food into her mouth. Over the last few weeks, I hadn't seen much of her or Knife. Our schedules were different, but it was always good to have one-on-one time with the precious girl in front of me. Neither of us talked, but I could still understand what she needed, even without my hearing. Like even when her mouth moved, dribbling on about something, she had her arms wide. She wanted out of her confinement. Smiling, I fought with her over wipin' her mouth, something she got a nasty little look over. Once she was clean, I picked her up and brought her close to my chest. She was always happy to be carried around. We went into the living room with Vin following close at my side. His gaze would glance up and down all the time. He thought Nevaeh was awesome like I did. His tail went a million miles an hour when I placed her on her play rug on the floor. Vin lay down beside her while I sat on the floor and picked up some blocks to build. Nevaeh ignored my tower and instead scooted her butt along the floor towards Vin. She was gettin' fast at scootin' along. At first, she did it unsteadily, but she'd soon become a pro. She flopped herself forward, her upper body lying over Vin, who didn't seem to care at all. Any other dog I would've been worried, but not Vin.

Since I had my arse on the floor and Knife sometimes walked like a herd of elephants, I could feel through the ground his approach, so I glanced up to the doorway just as he entered, freshly showered and smellin' fuckin' fine. His face was in a scowl, probably still pissed I'd been messin' with him and not sayin' why Ben was there.

The thing was, there hadn't been a reason Ben called in. He'd been in the area and remembered my address on the forms I'd filled out. In other words, he'd stalked my arse because I hadn't been responsive to messages or at meetings for a few weeks.

Only he never got to question me since Dive showed as

Ben was at the front door.

Knife limped into the room, a look of discomfort and something else crossing his face. What in the hell did he do? Pull a muscle?

Why you limping? I queried as he sat in the chair slowly, closest to his girl.

Damn. He was blushing. Whatever it was embarrassed him and made me want to know more.

"Nothin'." He glared and then smiled down at Nevaeh as she climbed off Vin and scooted her butt over to her daddy. He leaned over, winced, but still grabbed his girl and placed her on his lap. He met my eyes and told me about the phone call he'd just received. He didn't seem cut about his father's death. Then again, I wouldn't be either. He was more worried about his mum.

You okay?

"Will be after he's buried and I know my ma will be all right."

My phone, in my back pocket, vibrated. Vin lifted his head and nudged my arm. Smiling down at him, 'cause it was his way to show me my phone made a noise, I pulled it out and looked at the name.

Ben.

Shit.

Sighing, I opened the message. **You could have just told me you were seeing your roommate. I feel like an idiot.**

Fuck, I didn't want him to feel that way. I'd been the fuckhead to lead him on, but I was also fearful of losing him if Knife was just messin' with me. Hell, that thought tightened my gut in a knot.

Glancing to Knife, I caught him pulling his eyes from me

163

back to Nevaeh, who climbed all over him chattering about whatever babies talk about.

You're not an idiot. That would be me because I don't know what in the hell is goin' on with him or me. If anything would happen. Sorry!

His reply was quick. **Always knew you weren't fully in it with me. I suspected it had to do with Knife. Now I know for sure. No man comes into a house ready to kill a person like he did before. Something WILL happen, and I know when to step back. Still, I'd like to hang?**

Something kicked my socked foot. I glanced down to see Knife pull his bare foot back, and then looked up to meet his gaze.

"Who's that?"

Before he moved in he never used to ask me who I was on the phone with.

Was Ben correct in thinkin' somethin' could happen here?

Snorting, I shook my head. I had to remember Knife was the man who'd run from the room and didn't talk to me for a fuckin' long time.

Then there was also that kiss.

Christ. What was he doin' to me?

Ben.

He narrowed his gaze on me, and I saw the tick in his jaw when he clenched.

"He only just left. What's the guy's problem?" Nevaeh took that moment to shove her fist in his mouth, so the last word was gurgled around her tiny hand. Knife chuckled and pulled it free. "I'm hungry, darlin', but not that hungry."

Grinnin', I then chuckled when I saw Nevaeh start to giggle. Damn, I wished I could actually hear them both.

Instead, there was nothing but silence for the rest of my life, and it fuckin' sucked.

Blinkin' back the emotions, I noticed Knife talkin' to me. "You didn't answer. What's he want?"

Should I mess with him more?

Nah, I wasn't in the mood suddenly. *Nothing really.*

Knife rolled his eyes. Ignoring it, I stood from the floor and stretched, watchin' as Knife's eyes raked over my body.

My dick perked up in my jeans. Damn, Knife and I needed to have words. I had to sort shit out between us. The way he'd been confused the fuck outta me and if he was just messin', I wanted to make sure so I could move on.

And I thought by movin' on, he'd have to move out or, hell, I'd go on an extended vacation and do some work in the Ballarat Charter. See if Talon could shift another member up our way to replace me since we were short on members.

Lunch?

As Knife nodded, I turned and went into the kitchen. I knew he'd have to get Nevaeh down for a nap and then, fuckin' then, I'd ask some questions.

I had some roast beef from the night before, so I made some sandwiches for the both of us. I could have used a beer or ten, but I wanted a clear head for when I spoke with Knife, even if my nerves were growin' higher and higher over the conversation to come.

Christ, I felt like my gut was eating itself. I wasn't even sure I could manage to eat.

My body jolted, and I spun around when I felt a hand on my arm. Knife was already laughin' for catchin' me off guard. The dick.

His lips moved, and I had an urge to take them; instead, I

watched him ask, "What's up? Usually you know when someone enters."

I did. No matter where I was, I had an eye on the entrance and on Vin who'd let me know if someone was coming.

I ignored his question and instead signed. *We got to talk.*

He nodded and leaned his arse into the counter. "This about me living here still? 'Cause I gotta say, it's real good how you've let us crash at your place for so long, and anytime you think we're outstaying our welcome, you let me know and I'll look for another place." He took a breath and went on. "Just haven't been lookin' lately 'cause I wanted to bond with my girl, but I know things are cool with me and Nevaeh now. She knows—"

My hand came up as my head jerked back. Where he got that from I didn't know. *Stay as long as you want. It's not about that.*

"Right. Then… is it about Ben?" His upper lip raised when he'd said Ben's name. "Is he movin' in? Are you two getting together? Shit, have you even fucked the guy? He shouldn't move in if you don't know what he's like in bed. Fuck. Not that you should—"

Jesus, stop. I chuckled. *It's not about Ben. Actually, maybe, sort of.* I shrugged.

Knife tightened his hold on the edge of the counter. "Then what's it about?"

What do you think? I raised a brow and looked to his lips, then up to his eyes.

He threw his hands up in the air and said, "I don't know. The shit I guessed was wrong, and I don't get how it's not about Ben when it sort of maybe is."

Groaning, I rubbed a hand over my face and glared at him.

Was he really that stupid?

Knife—

He interrupted, and I watched his mouth move around the words. "Call me Jay."

What the fuck?

My gut swirled.

Did he just ask me to call him Jay?

What?

He smirked. "Now who's the one not understanding?"

Smartarse.

You want me to call you Jay?

He shrugged. "Yeah, in here, the house, call me Jay."

Shock had me standing there blankly staring at him. He'd never asked me to call him by his name. Never. And we'd been around each other for a fuckin' long time.

His hand waving out in front of my face had me blinking rapidly and grabbin' my attention to see him say, "Did I break you? It's only a name, brother. You can call me whatever you want." He shrugged.

Crap, my heart thumped in my chest. Shifting on my feet, I straightened and then leaned back against the counter in the corner. *All good, I'll call you Jay. Here. At the house.*

"Cool." He smiled. "And even though you didn't fuckin' offer the same thing back, I'm still gonna call you Maddox."

Fuck me.

His lips movin' around my name was somethin' I wanted to see for the rest of my fuckin' life. I sent him a chin lift. There was nothin' else I could do because I was at a loss from losing the whole conversation in the first place.

I was also living back in the time my name left his mouth.

Shit.

If he was fuckin' messin' with me, I was gonna kick his arse.

"Right, now that's straight, I wanna eat, but before we do, what did you want to talk about?"

Screw it all. I was gonna just come out with it. *The kiss.*

CHAPTER TWENTY

KNIFE

*D*amn it. I thought I'd go in slow, lay down the rule about using each other's real name while in the house. I'd been thinkin' about it a while, and I wanted Maddox to call me Jay. And then he just blew things wide open when he wanted to talk about the kiss.

As in, *the kiss*, where I attacked his lips.

Not that he seemed to have minded at the time.

Clearin' my throat, I rubbed the back of my neck to try and cool my skin down since I knew it had heated with a blush. "Okay. What about it?"

There, throw the ball back in his court, since I wasn't ready to come out and admit I was thinking of it constantly and wanted to do it again or why I wanted it in the first place.

Still, if push came to shove, I'd tell him if he really wanted the answer.

Especially since I hated the sight of fuckface in the living room near Maddox.

A smile tugged at my lips. Just thinkin' his name felt foreign, but goddamn good. However, it was serious time. So I cleared my thoughts and face of all emotions and stared back at Maddox's glower.

What about it? He challenged.

"Yeah." I nodded. He thinned his lips into a frown and let out a hard breath through his nose. God, I loved messin' with him, but I was also panicked about talkin' about it all, about what I was feelin' because I was still unsure. At least I thought I was.

Fucked if I knew.

If anything, I'd rather just go for it instead of talkin'.

Talkin' sucked, and I knew I'd screw up whatever I was gonna say. Why couldn't I just... jump him like I had before? Then at least he'd know I'd want to.

Did I?

Want to kiss him again?

Fuck. I sighed. I did. I really, really fuckin' did, and there was no denying any of it. He'd been starrin' in my porn thoughts for a fuckin' while, and I wanted to see if reality would be better. Hell, I hadn't thought of pussy for a long time.

Jay. He signed with aggravated movements, still, I liked it, so I smiled and I didn't think it'd be possible, but his eyes narrowed even more. *Why did you—*

There was a knock, and then someone opened the door and called out, "Brothers from another mother, where you at?"

Maddox was movin' before I did, followin' Vin into the

living room. A pace behind them, I walked in to see Low, Dodge, and their girl Romania, who I called Rom, while others said Rommy.

"Sorry we're early, but once I told Rommy she was gonna hang with you guys and little Nevaeh for a while she wanted to come."

She was?

"Hey," I called.

"Yo, brother. Thanks for takin' our girl so I can take my woman out."

"Ah, no worries."

Dodge snorted. "You didn't know?"

"Well, it was Beast who I asked," Low put in. "Though I figured he would have told you."

Looking to Maddox, I raised my brow. He was still in a mood scowling at me, but he signed. *Mentioned I was busy later, just didn't say what I was doin'.*

"All good. Nevaeh would love the company. Hey, Rom." I gave her a chin lift.

"Hi, Knife. Can I pat the puppy?"

"Sure, girl."

Vin loved attention.

She came forward and rubbed her hands over Vin's face, who's tail started to thump.

"This is awesome," Low cheered. "We so appreciate it. Texas is at a mate's place and Rom would be at her girl's, but she got sick, and it's been too long for date night with my man."

"What time you grabbin' her?" I asked, though I was still watching Rom pat Vin and then I saw her get to her knees and look under Vin.

"It's a boy," she cried out. "He has a doodle."

"Rommy." Dodge groaned, his head going back, eyes to the ceiling.

"What?" she asked innocently. She stood and told Maddox and me. "I'm a girl, like Low. I have a vag—"

"Romania," Low scolded. "What did I tell you about sayin' stuff like that?"

"I should only talk to you or Uncle Trey about it."

"Preferably Low, baby girl," Dodge muttered.

Low laughed. "Yes, honey. Just us." She glanced to Maddox and me and offered, "Sorry, she walked in on her brother the other night and saw, you know. Never crossed her mind people were different."

"Ain't she like eight now?"

"Yeah, nearly nine." Dodge nodded. "And the older they get, the less chance we know what's gonna come outta her mouth."

Fun times.

IT ENDED UP WE WERE HAVIN' Rom until nine that night. Dodge was takin' Low to dinner and a movie, but first they had some things to do at the compound. Though, I was sure work wouldn't just get done at the compound.

After Nevaeh woke, Rom and she played together, and it was an awesome sight. Even though the girl didn't shut her trap once, even nearly choking on a cookie tryin' to talk, I was lookin' forward to Nevaeh growin' because I wanted to hear what she'd come out with. Wasn't sure if it'd be the same as Rom, and at times, I prayed it wasn't since she spoke about when her poop was hard to come out, and the time she ate her snot, until Low told her it was bits of dirt up her nose mushed together. She didn't like dirt apparently; after all, she'd tried it when she was younger.

The girl needed to learn TMI moments, but still, I found myself not giving too much of a fuck. She amused both Maddox and myself. Lost count of the times she'd made us laugh.

I'd been grateful for her arrival since it put off the talk with Maddox. I was even more so when I watched him with the girls. He fuckin' loved it. Never would have thought a big, rough man like him was such a softy.

He'd just thrown his head back and laughed after he'd read Rom say, "Texas was so angry with me, but I just wanted to look at his magazine I found under his bed."

Snorting, I shook my head. The little monster shouldn't have been under her brother's bed. I could guess what kinda magazine she'd found.

We were sitting in a burger joint eating dinner. Neither Maddox nor I wanted to cook, so we brought the girls out. I'd already had a booster seat for Rom, that Nevaeh was to grow into. Rom was still on the small side, so she needed it.

Nevaeh was in a high chair munching on some fries. Actually, she was squeezing the hell out of them in her tiny fist before it even made it to her mouth.

It was there and then that it hit me.

I was sitting across from Maddox, he was next to Rom, and I had Nevaeh at my side, and I liked the scene.

I liked it a fuckin' lot.

It was free and easy.

Yeah, I could say I'd have the same with a woman, but I didn't want that.

My heart thumped rapidly in my chest at the realisation I wanted what was right in front of me. The man who was trying to teach Rom how to sign some words. Who was smiling down at her.

Fuck.

Who'd have thought?

Not me in a million fuckin' years.

But I did. I wanted Maddox.

So fuck hiding it. Fuck putting shit off because I was scared.

It was time to sort it.

BEAST

Somethin' in Jay—Christ, I couldn't get over how good it felt callin' him Jay—had changed. The change in him seemed like a weight had been lifted off him, and it happened at dinner.

When we'd got back to the house, Jay got Nevaeh ready for bed with Rommy following him around asking questions, so I went to the fridge and grabbed a beer. Maybe I needed sleep, but I was sure Jay was messin' with me more. He was always close. His hand seemed to touch my arm more times than I could count that night than over the span of time we'd been around each other.

My body was hyperalert when he was close. My dick acted like it had a string tied around it and jerked when Jay was near.

Earlier, he hadn't seemed willing to talk about anything, and yet there he was playin' with me, with his little touches when he could.

Yeah, somethin' had changed, but since I was dog tired, I wasn't ready to talk to him about it. I'd been doin' overtime due to a shortage of workers at the garage since more brothers were covering the strip clubs.

I'd just drained the rest of my beer when Vin nudged my leg; someone was at the door. As I made my way into the living room, Jay, with Nevaeh in his arms, and Rommy came from the other room. I stopped in the living room since they were closer to the front door. Jay opened it, smiled, and stepped back sayin' something. Rommy dove forward as Dodge stepped in and swooped her up into his arms.

Made me wonder if.... Fuck, I couldn't go there. Jay wouldn't live in my house forever with Nevaeh.

"Was she good?"

Since his eyes were on me, I nodded with a smile. *She only ate about a billion cookies.*

Dodge relayed what I'd signed, and Rommy's mouth opened wide. Her eyes bulged and she said, "I did not, and Beasty kept feeding them to me."

Beasty.

Shit, that was cute. Had anyone else tried that shit, I'd kill them.

Dodge smirked. Glaring at him, I shook my head. *You're early.*

"Low hated the movie, thank fuck. It was girly shit."

Snorting, I smiled. *You got off easy then.*

"Hell yes."

I gotta hit the bed, I'm buggered. I yawned.

175

"Yeah, thanks for the extra time at the garage and mindin' this monster."

"Can I come back tomorrow?" Rommy asked, pulling Dodge's face towards hers to meet his stare.

"Not tomorrow."

"Monday?"

Dodge shook his head, laughing like Jay and I were. "School."

"School sucks."

"I know, kid, but how else you gonna get a good job to take care of me and Low when we're old?"

She thought about it for a second. "Do you think I'll have enough money for all of us if I become a gyno?"

Dodge coughed. Jay threw his head back and laughed, and I shook my head chucklin'.

"Darlin', where'd you hear gyno from?"

"From Texas's friend. He wants to be one."

Dodge's face darkened. "How 'bout we talk about it later and you say goodbye to Beast and Knife?"

She smiled. "Okay." Dodge placed her down, and she ran towards me first, wrapping her arms around my upper thighs. Goddamn, she was cute. Dodge had said her learnin' and growth was behind due to her shit mum. If it were me, I wouldn't want her to grow up.

After they'd left, with the door closing behind them and Jay lockin' it, he turned, and I signed. *Headin' to bed.*

All he did was dip his chin at me with a smirk on his face, a smirk I read where he was up to something. Before I could question it, he was already on the move with Nevaeh back down the hall and into her room.

Vin followed me down the hall. I made him stay in my

bedroom while I went and did the stuff I had to in the bathroom. I'd just closed my bedroom door and stood beside my bed pulling my tee over my head when I noticed Vin raise his head.

Glancin' over my shoulder, I paused with my tee still in my hands when I spotted Jay standing in the doorway. He didn't stay in one spot for long. He kept walking and, with each step he took closer to me, my blood heated, my heart pumped harder, and my body shivered from the teasing smile playin' on his lips.

What in the fuck was he doin' in my room?

CHAPTER TWENTY-ONE

BEAST

*J*urning wasn't an option. My body was frozen, so when Jay got close, right behind me, and then slowly—so fuckin' slowly—he shifted forward and touched his warm lips to my shoulder, I didn't move a muscle. I was the taller out of us, and usually I didn't notice it. But I did then.

My breath stalled in my lungs as he looked up into my eyes. He pulled back, smiled, and then walked around the bed, my gaze following him the whole way.

Holy fuck.

Was I imagining this shit?

I blinked slowly, and yet he was still there, only he'd come to a stop on the other side of the bed.

Motherfuck.

He placed the baby monitor down, one I hadn't even

noticed he'd carried in, and tugged his tee from his body, throwing it to the floor, all while watching me and smiling. Next, I gulped hard as his hands went to his jeans and he undid the button.

I wasn't dreaming. It was in fact happenin'; Jay was gettin' undressed like he was gonna slip inside my bed.

Fuck, like we did it all the time.

My lungs filled with much-needed oxygen and I faced him on the other side of the bed as he slid his zipper down and hooked in his thumbs to drag his jeans down his legs.

What are you doing? I demanded.

He ignored my question, kicked off his jeans, pulled off his socks and then, fuckin' *then*, he pulled back *my* blankets on *my* bed and slipped right on in to lie on his back with his arms up, so his hands went behind his head. He stared up at me, still goddamn smiling.

What. Are. You. Doing? I signed slowly.

"Thought we could make out for a while."

My eyes grew wide. I coughed, rubbed a palm across my chest because my heart was going crazy and I willed my dick to stay down.

"Or we could snuggle. I'm pretty good at it." He winked.

Fuckin' winked.

Where had this man come from?

He wasn't like the one who ran from the hotel room.

Shakin' my head, I pulled a brow up and asked. *Are you high?*

I watched as he closed his eyes and laughed. His whole body shook with it, and Jesus Christ, seeing his body in my bed near naked... what a sight.

179

After his laughter had faded, I told him with my hands. *We can't do this. I'm tired and—*

His hand came up. "Hold up. Why can't we do this? And I did mention snugglin.'"

Jay. I groaned and scratched at my chin. *You don't know what you want. I don't understand what's changed, but this shit messin' with me won't cut it.*

He sat up, leanin' his back against the headboard and his expression changed from teasin' to annoyed. "I ain't messin' with you. Fuck, do you know the strength I used to even walk in this room? I wouldn't be in here if I was foolin' around." He ran a frustrated hand over his head. I dropped my tee to the floor and fisted my hands at my sides. He was right on one point; he wouldn't have come in here if he wasn't serious.

Only what did he want?

A kiss?

A thrill for the night?

Tell me straight out what you want, and I'll see if I can give it.

Hell, I wanted to grin when I caught him swallow hard in his throat. His eyes flicked all around the room as he fought with what he wanted to say.

His mouth moved around some curse words. Then he threw the covers off him, and I knew he was gonna walk outta that room. My gut sank. Shit, I should be used to watchin' him walk away.

Only he didn't.

Turning, I faced him as he stopped just in front of me. He shrugged, his head tilted to the side, and he gave me a timid smile. "A kiss."

You want a kiss?

"Yes."

Why?

He rolled his head back to look at the ceiling and then straightened to glare at me. "Fuck's sake. Just goddamn kiss me, you prick."

Pissed Knife was comin' out to play.

I just don't—

He threw his hand out to point down low. I glanced there to see the outline of my erection behind my jeans and then quickly looked up to Jay. "At least a part of you ain't fuckin' questioning everything."

You don't get—

"Fuck it," he bit out and glared.

His hands came to my shoulders and he roughly pulled me in. Our chests collided. I didn't get time to take anything in because Jay's lips landed on mine. They stayed there still. I opened my eyes to see what in the hell he was doing, and I saw his expression was screwed up in confusion, only it quickly changed and relaxed. He shifted, his mouth moulding more to mine.

Screw this.

My heart raced, my blood pumped, and I fuckin' wanted to see how he would react when I let go.

I wound my arms around him, one at his waist the other at the back of his head. I saw and felt his smile against my lips before I closed my eyes and invaded his mouth with my tongue.

His was eager and swirled quickly around mine only to pull back, so I gave chase. I wanted to taste him more and was rewarded with another swirl and swipe of his tongue.

Fuck.

Christ.

This was Jay.

Knife.

I had him in my arms, and I was goddamn kissin' him.

If it wouldn't have seemed like I was the biggest pussy out there, I would have cried. I'd been in love with the man forfuckin'-ever and finally, and bloody finally, I had him where I wanted him, and he'd been the one to choose to come to me.

He came to me. I had the proof in my arms.

Pullin' away, only because I needed to catch my breath, I couldn't look at him. Without lettin' go, because I wasn't ready to, I rested my forehead down on his shoulder.

Fuck me.

This was Jay.

Knife. The obsession of my life.

His hands slid down my shoulders, and then he moved back a little to get his hands between us. Since my eyes were open, gazin' at a fuckin' smokin' body in boxers which, I was surprised to find, tented, I saw his hands move.

That was pretty good.

A snort left me. Then I started chuckling. I didn't know what to say or do. Jesus, I even reverted to my teen years and playfully shoved Jay back a step.

"Well, it was." Again, he pointed to my junk and then his. "It's obvious." He nodded.

I need to get some sleep.

"That's it? One kiss and you're done with me? Actually, maybe it's best since... never mind."

Since what?

"Nothing." He shook his head and went back around to the other side of the bed.

I clicked my fingers. *Since what, Jay? And what are you doing?*

He looked to the bed, to me, and back to the bed before meeting my gaze and stated, "Goin' to bed." He winked and once again, slid between my sheets, pulling the top one up over him.

He was the worst, most stubborn bastard I knew, and I was too tired, even if my body was raging to go. My head was too drained to argue with him. So, I dragged my jeans off, pulled my side of the blanket back, and got into bed.

I lay on my back staring up at the ceiling. The light was still on. I fuckin' forgot to turn it off because *Jay* was in my bed. Beside me, who, I felt and glanced out the corner of my eyes, had rolled to his side to face me.

He got to his elbow and looked down at me. "The light's still on."

I know.

"You gonna turn it off?"

In a second. I wasn't ready. I needed to remember this moment for the rest of my fuckin' life. Jay looking down at me smiling, his eyes soft, his expression relaxed, and... he was in bed with me.

"Thought you were tired."

I am.

"Okay." He nodded and then, fuck me, he leaned down and touched his mouth to mine, once, twice. When his hand landed on my gut, I jumped and felt his grin against my mouth. Only when he glided his hand up to take hold of my chin and deepen the kiss, I wrapped my arms around him and dragged his body close. He groaned, his chest rumbling against mine. I couldn't help it; I couldn't stop. I slid my hand down his back and grabbed hold of his arse forcing him against me more where I felt his hard cock at my side.

He abruptly pulled back. He moved his whole body off mine and was back to on his elbow running a hand over his face, breathing as hard as I was.

When I had his eyes, I asked. *What happened?*

He shook his head. "Nothin'."

Jay, what the fuck happened?

His chest rose and fell with a deep sigh. "I'm, ah, fuck, just sensitive."

My head jerked back in the pillow. *How? Where?*

"Don't worry about it. I'm tired, let's sleep." He went to get out of bed, maybe to turn off the light, but I grabbed his wrist and pulled him back down. He lay flat on his back, and I moved quick enough to be looming over him.

Where?

"It's nothin', Maddox." And then his whole face and neck blushed, so I knew it was gonna be embarrassing for him. He didn't get shy over a lot of shit, but he was then.

Tryin' to fight my smile, I asked. *What did you do?*

"Get the fuck off me." He glared.

He knew better than that. I was bigger and a little stronger, so when he tried to struggle, I lay an arm over his upper body, plus a leg over his thighs and then flung the blankets back to search his body. Keepin' an eye on his fuming face while he cursed me, I ran my free hand over his chest, ribs, and sides. There was no reaction, other than being pissed, until I started lower. With my palm flat, I ran it over his stomach, and his jaw clenched. Lower, his nostrils flared. If it wasn't for the glare, I would have thought he was turned on. Shit, okay he kind of was, another shock for me, since it was all new and it was Jay. His cock was half-mast.... Hang the fuck on, he only shifted away when I'd pressed his lower half into me.

My hand paused just above the waistband of his boxers. I glanced up to meet his furious gaze. *What did you do?* I asked with a smirk.

He shoved at my chest, but it was only half-heartedly like all his struggles had been. If he wasn't embarrassed, I reckoned he liked me touchin' him, looming over him.

"Get off me," he demanded, his upper lip raised.

Show me.

"What? No!"

Jay. I smiled. *Just show me.*

"You were tired. Let's fuckin' go to sleep."

Fine. I nodded. Except I lied. I pretended to slowly move up to my arm and then swiftly, I grabbed the front of his boxers and pulled them down.

Damn.

I winced.

Jay managed to shove me off. I knew he was yellin' at me as he climbed outta bed. Standing, I grabbed his wrist and turned him to face me. *Deaf remember. Can't hear your threats.*

"Yeah, well, fuck you."

He went to walk past, but I stepped in front of him. *What happened?*

"Google happened. I fuckin' tried to search what... shit!" He blushed again. "Thought gay men liked it clear around the junk, so I got waxed."

Be still my goddamn motherfuckin' beatin' heart.

He'd done it for me.

He did want this.

Wanted something to happen between us.

Crap, if that hadn't shocked the hell outta me, I would'a been on the floor laughing my arse off, so I guessed it was good the shock won out.

CHAPTER TWENTY-TWO

KNIFE

J wanted to crawl in a bloody hole and die. Hell, I'd even take a sharp shooter on the next-door neighbour's roof aiming to take my head off through the window. Anything, and I meant *anything,* would have been good to distract Maddox from what he'd just found out.

Maybe I should have left my approach for another day. If that kiss hadn't got hot, and it was damn hot, he wouldn't have found out, and I wouldn't have blushed like a goddamn virgin on her wedding night.

Shit.

All I wanted to do was run from the room.

Until I felt his fingers under my chin, where he gripped and turned my face so my eyes could meet his. If he'd been on the verge of laughing, I would have punched him. Instead, he looked serious, with only a little lip twitch.

His hand left my face to sign. *Looks sore.*

"It is. Can we just go to sleep now?"

Sure. But go get some cream and I'll rub it in.

Did I read his hands right? "You want to rub cream into it?" Shit, I could think of something else he could rub. Just thinkin' of his hand around my cock had it stiffening.

Maddox happened to glance down. He looked back up smiling. *Fuck, Jay. Never thought you'd get hard for me.*

With a snort, I shrugged. "Seems that way all the time now."

His smile went wider. *Yeah?*

I nodded. I couldn't respond since his eyes just heated.

Go get the cream. Let me take care of you, babe.

Jesus, had someone snuck in and shot me full of adrenaline because my heart raced behind my ribs.

Babe. Christ.

He'd said babe to me.

A dude, a *male* called me babe.

And I fuckin' liked it.

Maddox must have guessed, because his smile softened. He leaned in and touched his mouth to mine before ordering. *Go get the cream.*

I was back in the room within seconds. Maddox hadn't moved except for turning towards the door to see me enter. I walked over to him and held out the cream, then swallowed thickly.

Maddox, as in Beast, was gonna touch right near my cock, and I wanted him to.

Fuckin' hell.

Usually I wasn't shy. Hell, I'd fucked in public before and hadn't given a shit who saw, but suddenly I felt nervous about

Maddox lookin' at me there. What happened if he thought I wasn't what he liked? What type of dick was he used to?

Bloody hell, it wasn't the time to think of other guys Maddox had been with.

I watched as he undid the cap, squirted the cream onto two fingers and then flung the tube and lid onto the bed. Maddox stepped closer, and I had to admit, I'd started breathing heavily when his free hand hooked fingers into my boxers and slowly, painfully slowly, pulled my boxers down. They slipped all the way to the floor.

Maddox got to his knees in front of me. His face, his mouth, inches away from my dick, who perked up to say hello.

The man on his knees looked up and raised a brow at me. Snorting, I said, "Can't help it when you're that close."

He hummed under his breath and smirked. I jumped when the cold cream touched the top of my warm skin. With my arms at my sides, I fisted my hands as I watched Maddox's eyes travel all around me in that area.

What was he thinkin'?

Did he like it?

Shit, did I look too young since most of my pubes were gone?

He was gentle with each touch, so fuckin' sweet. The cream took away the slight sting and cooled my skin nicely. So nice, I closed my eyes and enjoyed the sensation while trying to calm my dick by letting it down gently and telling it there'd be no action.

But then my eyes sprang wide, and my head tipped down when I felt a new heat, a warmth spreading over the tip of my erection.

"Fuck," I gritted.

Maddox's eyes were up, and his mouth surrounded the end of my cock.

"Shit," I hissed when his tongue swirled around the end. Then, when his wet, hot mouth slid along my shaft, I grunted through a moan. I wanted to close my eyes and enjoy the feelin', relish in it, but there was no fuckin' way I was missing out on seeing Maddox on his knees with my cock in his mouth.

Christ. I clenched my jaw when he tightened his lips down around the base and sucked all the way back up.

"Feels so fuckin' good," I told him, unable to hold those words back.

His hands landed on the backs of my thighs, where he held me steady as he sank his mouth up and down on my cock faster than before. Hell, my balls were already drawing up, until Maddox coaxed them back down with his hand.

All pain, all sting was gone and was replaced with plea-sure. His mouth... holy fuck, I couldn't believe it was his mouth on me. I had a guy, not just any guy, but Maddox, a friend, a brother, suckin' me off.

Actually, he was givin' me the best blow job I'd ever had. I wanted to marry his mouth.

"Fuck," I grunted. I had to touch him. I placed my hands on the back of his head, gently rubbin' his short hair, so close to blowin'. "Christ, I'm—you gotta back off," I warned. He didn't move. His eyes stayed on mine as his head bobbed up and down. His mouth slicker than before from all the saliva, making it impossible to hold off. "I'm, fuck, yes," I hissed low as the first shot of cum erupted into his mouth. "Goddamn, take it all," I ordered. He hummed, and more cum squirted into his mouth. The suction of Maddox swallowing as I came had me juicin' even more.

I loosened my fierce grip of his head; I'd been holding him tighter as I'd pumped my hips forward until the last drop. "Jesus." I sighed, then laughed. He drew out the dregs and then licked the tip one last time.

He bounded up to his feet. I only wished I could move, but it was as if he'd sucked all my energy out with my cum. If I could have, I would have then gone to bed, hopped in it and hugged him before I crashed.

That was until I saw how fuckin' hard he was under his boxers.

It was my duty to fix it, even if I was dead on my feet. Drained, only for the better.

He grinned and flicked my nose. *You're good now.*

Was he tryin' to play it off as casual? Too bad I wouldn't let him. "I fuckin' am." I placed my hands on his waist. "That was the best head I've ever fuckin' had, and I look forward to seeing what else we can do together."

His eyes widened a fraction more. He nodded, stepped away from my touch and went to his side of the bed. Only turning to sign. *Grab the light, will you?*

Grab the light? Like I didn't see his hard-on tenting his boxers, like he thought I wouldn't want anything to do with it...? Well, the bastard didn't give the best fuckin' head I'd ever had and not expect anything in return.

He lay on his back on the bed and pulled the sheet over him, closin' his eyes. I tugged my boxers back up, flinchin' as my waxed area pulled, and stomped my way to his side of the bed. Ignoring Vin's glare for wakin' him, I snagged the sheet in my fist. He must have felt the grip because his eyes opened when I shifted the sheet off him and roughly dragged his boxers down his legs.

What are you—

My hand came up and out to stop him. I barked, "Shut it."

His lips twitched. His hands rested behind his head, and with his chin and eyes, he gestured down to his junk, as if to say, "Have at it."

"Be ready for me to blow your mind," I warned, glaring down at him. The prick shrugged. Reaching down, I squeezed his cheeks together so his lips puckered where I kissed him hard and pulled away to state, "Don't be a cocky dick."

He chuckled.

Blow my mind then.

"Fuckin' fine."

Right. I could do it. Just like suckin' that banana one time, when I got caught and bit it off. Shit, I'd better not take a chunk out of Maddox's dick.

Damn. I'd forgotten how fuckin' sexy it was. Longer than mine, only slightly thinner, but he was trimmed nicely. I nodded. Enough admiring, it was time to get down to business.

Climbin' on the bed, I got between his legs. It was a tight fit, with my width, but we made it work. Smiling, I glanced up at him. His jaw clenched, maybe from nerves or excitement, I didn't know. Though, what I did know was there was no way I was runnin' now.

Fuck what anyone else thought.

The man before me drove me crazy, and I wanted to know all there was about him in bed, what drove him crazy, what set him off, and what he enjoyed the most.

I scooted down a little and lay. I glided a hand up his thigh, and his body shivered. Wrappin' my hand around his shaft, I tugged up and down. It was like jerkin' myself off, only different. I knew what I liked. Would he like it also?

Never thought I'd find myself between Maddox's legs with my hand surrounding his cock, but there I was, and hell, it was a moment in life I'd do again. I already knew that.

Lickin' my lips, I moved up so my head was over his dick and then pulled his cock back so I could taste the end that was already leaking pre-cum. Holy shit, my gut dipped when I heard him suck in a sharp breath. I was nervous as fuck that I wouldn't do any good, but I was aroused by havin' his hard cock under me and about to be in my mouth.

I lapped at his tip a little more before securing my lips around the tip, and then slowly, I slid my mouth down along his cock while rubbin' my tongue around it.

Maddox groaned from deep within his belly.

Fuck yes.

He liked that.

Glancing up as I dragged my mouth from him, I caught his hooded eyes on me. *Feels so fuckin' good. Seeing you there, havin' you between my legs, I ain't gonna last.*

Takin' my mouth from him, I said, "Then let me take you to the edge."

Do it.

On one elbow, I went up higher and sucked him back into my mouth. I slid up and down faster on his cock and made sure to tease and taste more with my tongue. I cupped his balls and then jerked him off when my mouth was at the tip.

His back arched, the muscles in his neck tensing, and he gripped the sheet between two fists.

Down once again, with my hand drawin' down his balls, I

knew he was close. His hand let go of the sheet and came to the side of my face. Gently he touched there, only to then run his finger on the top of my lip.

Yeah, he liked what he saw. His cock in my mouth pleased him.

When he threw his head back into the pillow, I knew that was it. I got the first taste of his cum in my mouth. I drank it down. It was salty and thick, and somethin' I didn't mind at all. So when Maddox groaned deep and more burst into my mouth, I swallowed it all down, right until the end.

When I pulled away, I couldn't help but chuckle. Maddox was breathin' heavily, an arm flung over his eyes. So I tugged his boxers back up over him. As I did, he removed his arm and looked down at me. Gettin' to my knees... fuck me, but I blushed again.

"Was it, Christ, okay?"

His jaw clenched before he sat, grabbed my wrist and forced me down to lay on top of him where his mouth took mine in a deep, heated kiss.

I was gonna take that as a yes.

Damn, I was good.

CHAPTER TWENTY-THREE

BEAST

I woke on my side, warmth at my back and a hand in my boxers cuppin' the base of my dick and balls. A grin spread over my face when the night before came back to me, and I knew the man at my back was the man I fuckin' loved. How he was spoonin' me with his hand in my boxers I didn't know; we'd fallen asleep with me on my back and him on his, close to my side after another sinful make-out session.

Blinking my eyes open, I looked at the digital alarm clock on my bedside table and knew we wouldn't have long before Nevaeh was awake.

Shit. A thought had the grin disappearing from my mouth.

What happened if when Jay woke, he freaked?

Honestly, I wasn't sure my heart could take it, not after what I'd experienced the previous night.

He wouldn't freak, would he?

Just thinking it had me near panicking.

Maybe I needed to make a break for it before Jay woke, then at least it'd be me leaving the room first. Only before I got the chance to peel myself away from the warm body at my back, he stretched, and his grip tightened around my dick and balls, ripping a groan from me.

Fuck. I needed to get up before he fully woke. Slippin' my hand under my boxers, I grabbed his hand to remove it when he squeezed. My eyes closed from the shot of pleasure that ran through my body.

Jay moved again, his body a little away from mine. With the hand securing my junk, he gently forced me back to lay flat, and on opening my eyes, I found him smiling down at me.

"Seems even in my sleep I know what I want." He winked.

My heart jumped double time, so fast it hurt in my chest; it hurt because of those words, that smile, his warm eyes and Jay still in my bed, not freakin' for a second, meant so goddamn much to me.

You good? I couldn't help but ask.

His mouth tipped up even more. "Oh yeah." His hand left my balls, only to wind around my dick and tug up and down. I clenched my jaw but kept my eyes on Jay. "And I'll be even better soon."

Nevaeh.

He glanced at the clock and nodded. "We'll have to make it quick then, meaning both of us need to get off at the same time."

How do you plan to do that?

He licked his lips and then bit his bottom one. "I've only just woke, so I'm leaving the planning up to you."

Right then. I smirked and then lifted up, flipped him to his back and tugged the front of his boxers down as I straddled his thighs. His breathing had already picked up as his eyes hooded and lust rose between us. He watched me as I pulled the front of my boxers down before I took hold of him, guiding it up with one hand as I grabbed mine with the other and took it down to meet his. Then with one hand, I wrapped my fingers around both dicks and tugged once.

"Fuck," I read on those fuckin' sexy lips and watched him focus on our cocks in my hand.

Leaning down a fraction, I rested one hand at the side of his head. He looked up and grinned. "Now this is a good plan."

Laughter escaped me, another shock to my system. Usually my bed partners knew I only wanted them for one thing and that was to fuck 'em. They hardly talked, never made me laugh or smile, and I knew why.

They weren't Jay.

Even if I had've given them permission to talk freely or some shit, I never would've achieved a reaction like one Jay could bring from me.

Closing my eyes, I just wanted to feel, to remember in case it never lasted. I could be just an experiment for the man under me, and even if it killed me, I still wanted to get my fill of him, in case I never got a chance for it ever again.

His hands were on my thighs, his body wiggling under mine, which meant he was into it as much as I was. I slipped my hand up and felt both of us leaking, so I used the pre-cum for extra lube and ran it down over both our cocks.

Startled for a second when I felt his hand on my neck, I opened my eyes and looked down, meeting his gaze.

Fuck me.

Fuck yes.

He was into it. He was really fuckin' into it. I'd dreamed of it, but never thought I'd see it.

With his eyes on me, all over me, us, his mouth parted just a little, and it showed all over him, every fuckin' inch of him how much he liked it.

He looked back up, met my gaze, and I read there on his lips. "Fuckin' love this."

Jesus Christ.

His hand at the side of my neck squeezed and then tugged me down towards him. Our lips met, our heads turned and then our tongues tangled. We ate each other's groan as I pumped my hand faster over the both of us. However, with both of us close, it became more awkward to pull, so I swiped my tongue over his one last time, before planting a kiss on his sealed lips and moved back. I wanted to see him come. I wanted to see our cum mixed together on his body.

Fuck, just thinkin' it had my balls drawing up into my body.

"Shit, fuck. Gonna—" His hands landed on my thighs, his grip hard. He opened his mouth, what I could guess a groan or a grunt fallin' from his lips as a shot of cum first coated his stomach. Seeing it, watchin' him get pleasure from what I was doin' had my own release firing up and out. I pumped my hand fast, right until the last drop came out. Jay's stomach was covered in our combined cum, and I fuckin' loved seein' it.

It was then Vin stood, shook, and headed for the door. Nevaeh was awake.

Jay's hand tapped my thigh. I glance back down to see a

smiling man. "See, we had time. But you're grabbing Nevaeh while I shower since it was my gut we came on."

I was goddamn floored by how direct and easy he was bein'.

God, it made me love the fucker even more.

There was no way I could contain my smile of pure fuckin' happiness. Bloody hell, even my stomach was stumbling over itself in glee. I climbed to the side, only to lean back over the bed and touch my mouth to Jay's before pulling a bottom drawer open and draggin' on some track pants.

You shower. I'll quickly wash up, get Nevaeh, and put the coffee on. Know how much you're a bitch without it. Seeing Jay laugh warmed me. If I had the time, I would have stayed in that spot and watched him. Instead, I grabbed some tissues on the bedside table and threw them at him before leavin' the room.

After washing my hands and face, I went into Nevaeh's room to see her gabbin' with Vin, who was at the side of her crib. If I wasn't already grinnin', I would have from that sight.

She came straight up into my arms with her own smile. Vin followed us out of her room, through the living room and into the kitchen, goin' right out the dog door off the back door via the kitchen.

I'd managed to get the coffee on, Nevaeh in her seat and her oatmeal warmin' in the microwave before Jay made an appearance in the kitchen. My heart thumped in my chest when, without a care, he walked right in, kissed Nevaeh on the head, cooed at her about something and then came my way to kiss me on the lips before heading to the microwave after it beeped.

Motherfuckin' hell.

How much more was the man going to shock me? I'd been

thinkin' he'd play it cool in the house, no PDA in front of Nevaeh or any for that matter unless in the bedroom.

I'd been so wrong.

He stopped right in front of me. "You good?" he asked, his brows dipping in confusion. Maybe because I was frozen in one spot and had been watchin' him in... I didn't know, probably, awe.

Nodding, I landed a hand on his waist and leaned in to kiss those lips I'd dreamed of many times. *Yeah, all good. I'll finish the coffee, feed your girl.* I responded when he pulled back.

He winked. "Done. By the way, forgot to tell you. My ma is droppin' in this morning. She called a friend in at the hotel so she had someone with her when Parker and Lan arrived to announce his death. But today she wants my help to organise a funeral." I gave him a raised brow. "Yeah, I'll do it. Help her, but she knows I won't be there to attend it."

Nodding, I asked, *You want me to clear out?*

He shook his head, his lips thinning. "No. You should be here when I tell her about us."

I choked on the air I drew back too quickly into my lungs. My hands landed on the counter behind me while I coughed like a ninety-year-old smoker.

Jay patted my back a few times before he walked over and sat in front of Nevaeh, carefree, as fuckin' if he hadn't just blown my head off by tellin' me he wanted to share with his mother, his bloody *mother*, about us.

What were we?

We were an us?

Since when?

I'd thought he was just experimenting.

Rubbin' my chest, I made my way over to their side so he could see me. *Are you shitting me?*

His head cocked to the side before he smirked and spooned a mouthful of food into Nevaeh's mouth. Then he finally looked back up and said, "Nope."

Wait. Hold up. What the—I shrugged—*Hang on. Let me get this straight. You want to tell your mum what about us?*

He chuckled. "I don't just bang anyone and move on."

I snorted.

He rolled his eyes. "Okay. I *used* to bang anyone and move on. Not with you."

There went my heart again.

Fuckin. Boom.

What do you mean?

"Wow, and there I thought I was the slow one." He chuckled, then said something to Nevaeh about how I was an idiot sometimes.

Rolling my eyes, I tapped the top of Nevaeh's high chair with the back of my knuckle to grab his attention. Nevaeh thought it looked fun and decided to try it out herself, causing me to smile even when my insides were active with too many emotions.

Jay. I signed.

Scooping the last of the oatmeal into Nevaeh's mouth, he stood with the bowl, leaned in and kissed his girl's cheek and then straightened to face me. "We're dating."

My eyes widened as my head jerked back from the shock while a thrill shot through my body. *We're dating?*

He smirked. "Yes."

Dating. I repeated.

He laughed and nodded. "Fuck yeah."

CHAPTER TWENTY-FOUR

KNIFE

*G*oddamn, he was cute when he was surprised. Bet he never thought I'd want to date. Actually, I hadn't. It wasn't until the previous night as we lay in bed driftin' off to sleep that I realised I didn't want what we were gettin' into to be casual.

Fuck that.

The thought of walkin' away, or having Maddox walk away, didn't sit well deep inside of me. So much so it took me a while to find sleep, even after coming hard. I liked the way I woke in bed with him, with his junk in my hand, and then the way he dealt with both our morning woods... Christ, perfection.

I couldn't deny the attraction between us. There was a fuckin' heap of it.

But attraction wasn't the only thing we had goin'. Since I'd opened my eyes to the possibilities, I'd had an inkling Maddox liked me a hella'va lot, maybe even loved me and had for a while. I should'a paid more attention to the little looks, but I hadn't, too wrapped up in the club, drinkin', and pussy.

Though, since I'd thought about it, I liked knowing how Maddox felt. I could only hope I wasn't puttin' tickets on myself and dreamin' it all up. But I was sure what Maddox felt for me ran strong. Then there was also what I was feelin' for him. Hell, I couldn't wait to see him when we were apart. I wanted his time, his eyes, his words, his thoughts. And I wanted his body. I wanted everything from the man and the thought of not havin' it fuckin' lit a fire deep, and it wouldn't simmer until I had the man all to myself.

Fuck it. I was claimin' him.

He was mine. I was his.

We needed to see where it went and just from the glimpse of what we could be, I knew it'd be fuckin' awesome.

Shit, I couldn't keep my lips off him. Right then I stared at said lips as he fought through his shock.

Shruggin', I picked up the toy Nevaeh threw on the floor and passed it back before shockin' the man before me some more.

Steppin' closer, where I could place my hands on his waist, to which he looked down at and then up at me, his brows pulled low. He was probably thinkin' I didn't mean what I said. After all, I'd been the one who ran after our first experience together. He'd soon figure out I wasn't running, and I wouldn't let him either.

"I don't give a fuck what anyone thinks as long as you and me are happy. But I want this. You and me. Together. Yeah, I'm new to it all, but fuck, Maddox, I want to learn, and I want you to teach me. I ain't goin' nowhere, and neither are you. We got something between us that could be so damn good. Nothing and no one will step in the fuckin' way. Which also means Ben has gotta fuck the hell off. I won't share. And I know you won't either. Thing is, I wouldn't look for anything, not when I got you to come home to."

Shut up. He signed.

Yeah. He fuckin' loved me. I could see it in his misty eyes. He also loved each and every word I'd just said.

I knew it when he grabbed me roughly and melded his mouth against mine.

The kiss was hot, the man in front of me even hotter, and I knew I'd said the right thing because I wasn't messin' around. I wasn't scared. I knew what I wanted, and Maddox was it.

We broke apart, and he flicked his eyes to Nevaeh, so I looked there also to see her watchin' us. My girl would have to get used to PDA quickly because there wasn't a chance I'd hide what I was feelin'.

Looking back to Maddox, he met my gaze. "You over bein' shocked?" I asked.

He threw his head back and laughed. I loved seein' it and the smile after it. Leaning in, I kissed his jaw. His hands ran up and down my arms while I tasted his skin.

With a final kiss to his lips, I said, "You'd better get a shower in before my ma gets here."

You sure about this?

"Hell yes."

Not sure you realise what you got yourself into. Some people still hate. He gestured between us, meaning two guys together. *Sure you don't want to think on it longer? Only been a night.* He smirked.

Chuckling, I shook my head and said, "Nope. I'll deal. And shit, it's been... you've been on my mind for a fuckin' long time. Want this with you."

Jay. It's a lot.... Maybe think a bit longer. I'm a possessive fucker, and once you say you're all in, then I won't let you back out.

"Good. I'm all in. Now, I have a question on my mind."

Grinning, he shook his head as if he still couldn't believe I wanted this between us. *What?*

"Do you top or bottom?"

He froze, and then another laugh rumbled up out of him. He brought me against him in an embrace.

He then pulled away and signed. *Christ, you ever not gonna surprise me?* I shook my head, smiling. *Usually, I top.* His eyes heated. *But for you, I'll bottom.*

My dick jerked behind my jeans, and my smile grew wider. Maddox saw it, which caused him to laugh again.

"Wanna get tested."

Maddox nodded, all serious. *Me too.*

"Know I'll be clean, but still wanna do it. 'Cause when I have the chance to be inside you, wanna feel all of you.... Christ, I'm hard just thinkin' it. You?" His gulp and thrust of his hips into mine told me he was. "Right. Shower, or Nevaeh'll get a show her eyes shouldn't see."

BEAST

Holy motherfuckin' Christ.

I trembled with need. My heart pounded fast in my chest with too many emotions runnin' through me. Even as I stumbled outta the kitchen with shaky hands, I still couldn't fully comprehend what just happened.

Jay Conger wanted to date.

Me.

No, the way he'd spoken, it was more he was claimin' me.

Could this actually be real?

I ran a hand over my face as I climbed into the shower. Vin, who'd come back into the house when I was kissing Jay, sat on the floor outside the shower.

I still wasn't sure if Jay was rushing into something he didn't fully understand. Would he actually want people to know? Yeah, he'd said he was gonna tell his mum, but she wasn't the only person in our lives.

The brothers.

How would he be if they found out?

Fuck. Would he go out to dinner or the movies or some mundane thing with just me? I wasn't a hand holding type, but if the urge came over me to kiss someone, I'd do it. So, if I did it while we were out, how would Jay react?

What in the fuck was I thinkin'?

Ben had been the only guy I'd been out to dinner with and those times weren't really a date. No urge to kiss him had come over me, yet I was already thinkin' about dates and everything else with Jay.

Because he was different.

He had always been it for me. Only, I'd never thought I'd have what I'd always wanted.

Never.

Until now.

Christ, I'd never been a smiling guy, but I couldn't seem to stop. The warm and fuzzy feelings really did a number on a person.

All I had to do was pray no one and nothing would fuck this up between Jay and me. Not when Jay was takin' a huge fuckin' leap for us.

Still, I reckoned I should suggest that we take things slowly. What worried me was if we went full blown into a relationship, it'd be good for a while and then fizzle out to nothin'. I didn't want that to happen.

Fuck me.

Honestly, I didn't have a clue what to do or what way would be best. I was just as green as Jay when it came to a relationship. He'd be the first guy I'd ever been in one with. Yeah, I'd dated a few women in my younger years, but I knew it wasn't ever serious. The men before Jay had been some random I'd picked up for the night from a place no one knew me. A gay club where I knew it'd be easy pickin' in finding a bottom. I hadn't lied to Jay. I was usually a top. On rare occasions I'd bottomed for guys who were bigger in body size than me, and I'd enjoyed it enough. Still, I knew I'd love it with Jay.

Damn. Just thinkin' of havin' his cock slide in my arse gave me an erection.

Even better, he wanted it bare.

Another thought shot to my cock, of Jay comin' inside of me. Fuck, it was somethin' I'd want to do to him as well.

Suddenly, the shower curtain was pulled aside. I jumped and tried to cover my dick, only to find Jay standing there with his gaze dipped.

He pulled it up to glare at me. "You don't fuckin' jerk off when I'm not around. That"—he pointed to my dick—"is now mine. Means you don't touch it unless it's for a piss. Get me?" His face was scrunched up since he was fuming.

What I felt like doin' was laughing my arse off, but not only was I turned the hell on from him thinkin' he could order me around—something I'd let him have at that moment —but I was also pleased he was pissed and wanted to handle my cock himself.

You gonna deal with it then? I asked while jutting my hips out and placing my hands on the top of the shower rail.

His eyes hooded, until he shook his head and glared at me. "Ma's just arrived. Save it for later. You get me?"

Smirking, I pulled an arm down and wound my hand around my dick to jerk once, twice. *Not sure I do.*

His jaw clenched right before he leaned into the shower and turned off the hot water. Frigid cold water sprayed out and down over my body. I gasped, cursed under my breath and turned off the water.

Scowling at Jay, I found him chuckling. "Looks like you got nothing to deal with now." He was right. My dick had got scared from the frozen water and deflated a little. "Now get the fuck out," he ordered, and stormed to the door, opening it roughly, to stomp on out, and closing it behind him.

Well, fuck me.

Control was something I relished.

However, I thought I could give some control over to Jay because, fuck, I liked it.

Lookin' down to Vin, I rolled my eyes at him. His head lifted up as if he were grinnin' at me.

Thanks for the warning. I signed. He barked.

CHAPTER TWENTY-FIVE

KNIFE

*D*amn, if my ma wasn't in the house and if Nevaeh was asleep, I would have gladly taken Maddox's dick in my hand or mouth. Just seein' him hard in the shower, his skin all wet and warm was a fuckin' turn-on. In fact, I had to adjust my dick in my jeans as I walked back down the hall. No wonder it was takin' him so long in the shower. At first I'd thought something had happened. It had, only it wasn't life-threatening. Unless he decided to deal with it himself.

Obviously he understood that when I claimed him, I meant all of him.

Any sexual desires were mine to dish out. His body was no longer his, like mine wasn't mine. I knew I'd leave all orgasms to the man I'd just walked outta the bathroom from. Hell, if I could still walk and have him suckin' me off 24/7, I'd do it. Then again, I wouldn't want him to get a sore jaw or anything, so maybe 24/7 wasn't the best option. I was caring like that.

"All good. Vin was in there with him," I said as I entered the living room to see Ma, who was in designer gear, sitting on the floor next to Nevaeh. I'd told her about how Maddox was deaf and didn't talk, so I used the excuse of how I wasn't sure he had Vin with him to go and see what was takin' him so long. It was also because I'd fuckin' found myself distracted talkin' with Ma because I was thinkin' of him.

Never thought about a person so much in my life. Usually I was self-absorbed. Well, that was until Nevaeh came along… and since that night in the hotel room.

"I'm glad." Ma smiled.

"It's good to see you here," I told her as I sat on the couch opposite to where she and Nevaeh were. We'd talked a few times over the phone, even before I shared with her the news of Frank. She was situated in a hotel for a while until she found her own place. I had asked why she hadn't wanted the house. She wanted a clean slate. I was glad she went for that option since Frank was offed in the house. What worried me was how I could see the sadness in her eyes. She had a lot of guilt; so did I. But it was time to move on and gain back a relationship without that fucktard in our lives.

"It's great to be here. I can't tell you enough how beautiful she is, Jay." When she'd entered earlier, she'd burst into tears on seeing Nevaeh for the first time. I was sure that wasn't the only reason; her emotions would be running high. "The mother, she won't—"

My hand came up. "Not in our lives and for the better. If she ever tried to come back, she'd regret it. Somethin' she'd know."

Ma nodded. She knew exactly what I was sayin' and didn't care. She'd always wanted me happy, and at the start, when she knew I was leavin' for Hawks MC, she was sad but pleased I was finally content with life.

"How you doin', Ma?"

She nodded, only to look up and see the scepticism on my face. She smiled softly. "I'll get there, Jay. I regret so much, most of all losing time with you. He was my husband for so long, though. It will take time to adjust, but I will." Even quieter, she said, "He wasn't a good man. I knew this. Another reason I regret my time with him. In a way, he deserved what he got for his dealings. But... it's still hard to take."

"Shit, Ma. I can understand that. You're strong, always have been, so with time, I know you'll be fine. And we can make that time back, and now you got a grandbaby to look forward to getting to know. Nevaeh's life is only startin' out. You can be there for both of us from now on."

More tears shone in her eyes. Her bottom lip wobbled. "I would so love that."

Even with time, I knew we'd never have a deep mother-and-son relationship, but respect had me callin' her Ma, and still I knew I wanted her in my life because she'd been a good mum when I was a young boy. She'd been weak against her husband; that was all I could put it down to.

Nevaeh would need a woman in her life, and with help from both of us, we'd get her grandmother standing on her own two feet without a fear in the world.

"I was very nervous about coming here, Jay."

"Can understand that, Ma. Again, in time those nerves will go. You just gotta remember you can be whoever you want to be here, around us, and we'll be the same."

"I will."

Shifting forward, I rested my elbows on my knees and clasped my hands together. "Something I gotta tell you."

"Yes?" she asked as Nevaeh climbed onto her lap.

Only it was then I heard Vin's nails clip cloppin' on the floor, so I knew Maddox would be behind him. Jesus, my heart was bursting with knowing Maddox was comin' down the hall. I could feel Ma's eyes on me, but I was already looking towards the hall. First came Vin around the corner. He went straight towards the people on the floor and then in stepped Maddox dressed in jeans and a black tee.

Fuckin' perfect.

His eyes landed on me right away, and he grinned. I was already smilin', so I signed. *Hey.*

He shook his head, chuckled too low for me to hear, but I could see, and I liked seeing it.

His eyes went to the floor, so I looked there to see Ma already watchin' me. A soft smile was on her lips. Clearin' my throat, I said and signed, "Ma, this is…" Fuck, did I call him Beast or Maddox? I didn't really want her to call him Beast, but Maddox was also something I wanted just for me to call him. Still, it didn't feel right. If she was in our life like I wanted, then… "Maddox." I finished and looked to Maddox. He was glancing at both of us. "Maddox, officially meet my ma, Lisa Conger." He started to walk towards the couch with a wave to Ma when I added, "Also, he's my man."

I snorted when Maddox stumbled the rest of the way over before planting his arse next to me on the couch with a blush to his cheeks.

"Um, Jay. How do I sign?"

Tearing my gaze away from a glaring Maddox beside me,

who I was grinning at, I told Ma, "You can just talk, but make sure you have his eyes. He can read your lips and I can translate what he wants to say."

Maddox looked to Ma. "It's nice to meet you, Maddox. You have a nice home here."

As I watched Maddox's fingers fly, I repeated the words, "Nice to meet you too, and thanks. Sorry about your son layin' that on you like that. He's an idiot sometimes." I laughed.

Ma giggled. "He's always been straightforward. Something I appreciate. Though he didn't need to say anything. His look at you was enough for me to know."

Holy shit. It was?

"A mother always notices these things. If you're worried others will—"

Quickly I shook my head. "I don't care if people do." Turning to Maddox, who was already lookin' at me, I asked, "Do you?"

No.

"All good then." Placing a hand on Maddox's thigh, I leaned back on the couch, relaxed, and just talked. It took some time for Maddox to get settled into it, but he'd have to get used to me wantin' to touch him all the time. And everyone else we were around would have to do the same as well.

Later Ma mentioned she was lookin' at places near us to buy. That was if we didn't mind, which we didn't. As the time went on, I realised I had missed her. Havin' her in front of me brought back memories of how she used to be with me. Even though we had money back then, I didn't have a nanny. She did everything herself. Cooked, cleaned, helped me with homework, and even played Lego and shit with me. I wasn't sure where or how she'd lost her way, but she had to have felt stuck with Frank to have not left sooner.

She was a lot younger than him, only looking about forty-five, a few years older than Maddox, but she was actually fifty-two, where I was thirty-five. She still had a lot to give, a lot to look forward to in life, and a chance to find happiness.

Ma had stayed all day. Maddox made us some lunch while Ma and I took Nevaeh on a walk in her stroller, something my girl loved to do. It also helped her sleep after lunch. There was never any awkwardness between any of us and each time she saw me touch Maddox in any way, her smile would turn soft. It told me she was happy because I was.

As she was leavin' after dinner and after we'd gone through some things for the funeral, she asked if once she was situated, she could have Nevaeh for the night. Worry bombarded me; still, I found myself agreeing. It didn't mean it'd be soon. I wanted them around each other more before I gave Ma a chance at taking her for the night. I'd also asked Maddox once she'd left, for him to install security at her new place. I'd never take a chance and not have something top of the range when my daughter was gonna be in that house. He quickly agreed, with a look that told me he'd already thought of it.

I'd enjoyed the day with my ma there, but I'd also felt guilty for wanting her gone. Each time I found Maddox lookin' at me with warmth in his eyes, I wanted to crawl into his lap and kiss the fuck outta him. I probably could have done it in front of Ma, but then again, I knew once I got my mouth on him, I'd want to take it further.

Which was why, when after I'd asked him about security, I

plastered myself to him near the front door and took his mouth. He was just as eager. His hands gripped me just as quickly and roamed my body.

As I ground my denim-clad cock across his, a phone rang. I ignored it until Maddox pulled away and glanced down at Vin at his side. Maddox breathed heavily, like I was, as he stepped back and pulled his phone free of his pocket.

He read a text, and when he looked up, I said, "I swear to fuckin' Christ, if that's fuckface Ben askin' what you're doin', tell him me or I will."

He snorted and shook his head. Replacing the phone, he signed. *Dodge. Gotta work security at a strip club tonight. Some brothers are out sick and others are workin' at Pick and Billy's bar.*

"Fuck." I groaned and ran a hand across the back of my neck. I didn't want him to leave. Strange since I'd never felt that way before about anyone. But I knew he had to. "Dodge and Talon have got to talk. Since Pick and Billy got the bar and shits goin' down at other strip clubs, everyone is runnin' down."

Think Talon's gonna shut down a club or two now the bar's making a shitload.

"Good. But you have to leave."

He smirked, knowing I didn't want him to. *Yeah.*

"Fuckin' sucks."

True. But maybe it's for the best. We should slow things until we get results.

I called bullshit. Okay, so that may be a small reason to want to slow things down, but I was sure he was still worried I was gonna bail on what we had goin' on. "Ah, hell to the fuck no. Tomorrow morning before you head off to work, I'm takin' your cock in my mouth whether you like it or not."

He laughed. *Pretty sure I'll like it.*

"We don't need to go slow, just be careful. Not that I think either of us has shit." Stepping close to him again, I added, "You gotta get it through that thick head, I ain't goin' anywhere."

He nodded, kissed me in a way that I got hard, then ordered me not to touch myself before he walked outta the door with his club vest over his shoulder and Vin followin' him to his car.

God. To think I'd been so scared about my feelin's for him. That was just plain stupid.

We hadn't talked about it, but when I eventually went to bed, I did it in his room and his bed.

After all, I did promise to suck him off in the morning. I was only makin' it easier on myself. Instead of stumbling in from another room, I was already there, and I'd be ready and raring to go.

CHAPTER TWENTY-SIX

BEAST

*N*ever really waited for something in my life like it was so goddamn important, not until it took three fuckin' weeks for our results to come back in. Over those three weeks, Jay and I took every chance we could to fool around. That was if I wasn't working, which I seemed to be doin' more of those days. Work was also something Jay felt he needed to get back into. He was worried he'd have no money for Nevaeh's college fund in the future. I'd told him not to worry about it, and to quit paying for shit around the house. But he told me to get fucked, that he wasn't some kept boyfriend just sitting around waiting for me to get home so he could suck my cock. Something he loved to do, even with the condoms we were using until we got the results. We'd let the first couple of times slip by without protection and marked it down to we'd been too hot for each other and hadn't thought.

Even though we fought about Jay workin', I knew where he was comin' from. So I told him to pay Mena to babysit Nevaeh since he didn't want to put her in day care. Last week he approached her, and she was more than happy to do it. So Jay was startin' back in the garage. He was only doin' small hours to start with so Nevaeh could get used to the change.

He treated his girl like she was a princess, and she deserved all the attention. If she wasn't sleepin' or eatin', Jay was doin' things with her, and if I happened to be around, Jay involved me in every way he could.

Hell, it felt fuckin' unreal, like we were our own little family.

Happiness had been hard to come by, but in the past few weeks, I'd never been happier than any other moment in my life.

The man who was working repairs on a bike not far from me, had me smiling more, lightened my world, and had me looking forward to each and every day. What was also fuckin' brilliant was the way he went off in the bedroom. His questions of, "Am I doin' it right?" or "Do you like that?" proved how much he wanted everything to be smooth sailing. What he didn't get was that no matter how he did anything, I would fuckin' love it, because I loved him. Not that I'd told him. We were still new, and I wasn't sure if those words would scare the hell outta him.

Still, just the other night I'd come close to saying them.

Relaxing with Jay was something I enjoyed a lot. Even though I loved having Nevaeh with us, night-time was our time together. Jay walked from Nevaeh's room with a smirk on his face, his gaze roamin' my body, sending a thrill to my cock. He made his way over and instead of sittin' beside me, he straddled my lap. I grunted at first, not expectin' his weight and then grinned up at him as he scooted forward. Leaning down, he kissed me. At first it was only a peck, but like most times, what started out gentle soon led towards something harder and hotter.

I groaned as Jay shifted forward enough to grind down on my erection. My hands, placed on each side of his neck, trailed down his body to his hips where I pressed his weight down and my crotch up while shiftin' him back and forward.

Shit. I could easily come like that.

But I wanted more, only not for me, but for Jay.

Thank fuck he was only in loose track pants. I lifted my hips so he was up and then slid them down enough so his dick sprang free and I could palm his arse. His moan travelled out of his mouth and down into mine.

While he shifted leisurely over my cock, I pulled back enough to sign. **You trust me?**

"Hell yes," he replied instantly, causing my heart to fuckin' flutter and a smile to light my face before I could claim his mouth again. With one hand, I stroked his dick, makin' him pick up his pace as he slid down over my own dick. I brought my other hand up and slipped a finger inside our mouths. He leaned back and sucked more on my finger, licking all the way around it up and down.

"Fuck," I mouthed. I gripped the back of his head and tugged him down, wantin' his mouth again. As soon as I had his lips, I removed my hand from his hair and jacked him off while using my slick finger to gently run it up and down Jay's arsehole. At first he stiffened, then relaxed when he realised, for now, I wasn't going further. I rubbed his ring and palmed his cock while our mouths and tongues caressed each other. Too soon the salvia dried, so I brought my hand up, moved my *lips from his for only a second and spat onto two fingers. Catchin' his eyes, I took my hand back around to his arse while rubbing my spit over my fingers with my thumb. Lube would have been better, but there was no way I would stop what we already started.*

He watched my face intently when I placed my fingers against his hole again and moistened the area. Runnin' my fingers up and down and as he licked his lips, I eased a finger just inside his rim.

Fuck, he was tight.

His mouth opened as a heavy breath escaped and brushed over my face. I eased my finger out and ran it around the edge again as my hand on his dick picked up speed. He grunted and again ground against me. I slide my finger back in, waiting for him to pause again, but he didn't. He leant into me and kissed, bit, and licked my neck.

Fuck. So good.

I pressed in more, past the tightness, thinkin' he was relaxed enough from me jackin' him. He didn't tense as I kept pushin' until I hit his prostate.

He reared down on my finger and up off my body. "Fucking hell." I read on his lips before he groaned again as I rubbed inside of him. He attacked my mouth with his, leaving enough room between us so I could still pull him off. His rockin' over me became urgent. My mouth ate his moans I felt from his chest against mine.

Christ, he was fuckin' lovin' it.

He arched back, his desire-filled eyes on mine. "I'm gonna come. Fuck. More. Faster." I did and in the next second, his cum squirted up between us all over my tee. Removing my finger, he trembled and rested his head on my shoulder, breathing heavily. Finally he looked at me, a blush coating his cheeks. "That was... fuck, so much."

I nodded and then gestured towards the hall with a chin lift, meaning the bathroom. Some guys got awkward seeing a guy's hand after they'd played with their arse. I didn't want Jay to feel that way, so I didn't sign what I was getting at.

Jay shook his head. "Soon. I wanna test if I can have you losing control in seconds like you did me."

My eyes widened for a moment and then went low with arousal as Jay climbed off my lap, helped me remove my tee before throwin' it to the floor, and then ordered me to shift my arse to the edge of the couch so he could play. It was then a need to tell him I loved him came over me, because honestly, I wasn't sure how I got so lucky, but I was so fuckin' glad Jay woke that night in Sydney rubbin' his dick into my arse so many months ago.

I caught Vin lifting his head from the floor which brought my attention back into the garage. There was only one problem with Jay working in the same area as I was. Thoughts of him and what we'd get up to at home always bombarded my mind every chance they could. Just from a quick look, as he walked around the garage, I visualised just about everything we did in private.

I was fuckin' obsessed with Jay Conger.

Lookin' out the opened garage doors to see who held Vin's attention, I saw Mitch, the dog trainer, walkin' my way with a smile on his face. I flicked my gaze to Jay to see he hadn't noticed Mitch yet.

"Hi, Maddox," Mitch called with a wave.

Fuck me.

I sent a chin lift to Mitch as he still made his way over and then looked to Jay, who was standing beside the bike with a furious look on his sexy face and his hands at his sides clenched.

Vin stood beside me as Mitch stopped just in front of me. "Hi, Kevin."

Just Vin. I told him.

"That's so cool. How's everything been going? I tried at your place first to come and check on things, but when no one was there I assumed you'd be at work and look, I was right. So, how have things been with Ke—sorry Vin? Did you want to grab a coffee so we can talk? Or have you had lunch? I saw a nice diner around the corner if you're having lunch soon."

Movement caught my eyes over Mitch's shoulder, and I glanced there to see…. Holy shit. Ben was heading towards me. Again, I flicked my gaze over to Jay. He was stalkin' Ben with his narrowed eyes.

We hadn't said anything to the brothers about us. Really, it wasn't their business what we did behind closed doors. And honestly, I wasn't sure Jay was ready to come out. The brothers knew he was a pussy lover, until he'd got a taste of my dick, so we both knew the brothers would give him hell. I wasn't sure if he understood just how much crap they'd give him.

Jay wasn't a rational person when pissed, and the way he looked at Mitch and Ben could cause a problem he didn't need. Knowing Jay, he'd want to stake his claim over me in front of them. He was as possessive as I was. Once, we'd been out with Nevaeh at the park, and a guy kept lookin' over at me. That was until Jay gripped my tee in his fist and pulled me close to kiss me.

Hi. Ben mouthed as he stopped beside Mitch, who eyed Ben up and down before licking his lips.

Ben, Mitch. Mitch, Ben.

They greeted and then looked back to me.

Ben helped me with sign language. I told Mitch and then to Ben I signed. *Mitch is the one who trained Vin.*

They said a few things to each other, but I wasn't paying attention. Instead, I looked for Jay. He was no longer standing next to the bike and glaring our way. He was nowhere I could see. Didn't think he'd up and disappear like that.

A tap to my arm had me turning back to look at Mitch. *Ben said he would come to lunch if you have time.*

Glancing to Ben, he smiled. *Was around this area. Thought I'd call in to see if you had time for lunch myself.* He gave me wide eyes. He knew, like I did, Mitch wanted a piece of me. Only in the last few weeks, I'd let Ben know there wasn't gonna be anything happening between the two of us. He'd asked if Knife had stepped up. Smiling, I'd nodded and then told him I wasn't gonna be attending class again. It wasn't for Jay's sake, but I no longer needed to go. Still, I had warned Jay after that I was still gonna talk to Ben since he wasn't a bad guy. Jay's nostrils had flared, and then he'd clipped out, "Fine. But I swear, if he touches you, I'll cut off his hand." A threat I took seriously, and admittedly turned me the hell on. He'd never shown his desire to claim someone in the years I'd known him.

Until then.

For me.

It was no wonder the guy had turned me into a happy fool. Shit, even the brothers had been asking whose magic pussy I was dippin' into for me to smile as I had been.

Jay thought it'd been hilarious when I'd told him.

His cockiness didn't need the boost, but since I'd shared

that just the other night, his confidence had grown, and he no longer questioned if I liked what he was doing.

So lunch? Mitch asked again. I really needed to pay attention more instead of thinkin' of Jay.

Motherfuck.

The man himself suddenly burst outta the office and started our way. His scrunched up face was enough to tell me he was about to do something.

I just wasn't sure if I should stop him or not.

CHAPTER TWENTY-SEVEN

KNIFE

*W*hat in the Christ did I have to do? Put a note on Maddox stating he was my property? Seeing him standin' there talkin' to two guys I knew, I motherfuckin' *knew* wanted a piece of him, pissed me the hell off.

"Yo, Knife," Billy called with a smirk on his face. "Who're those guys?"

Who were they?

Arseholes, that was who they were.

After sending Billy the finger, to which he laughed, I thought my idea of a note could be a good way to go. I stalked into the office to find Low sitting behind the desk and Dodge leaning his butt against it lookin' down at his woman, until I entered.

"Yo, brother. What's up?"

All I managed was a grunt in reply as I grabbed a piece of

paper outta the printer and wrote on it. My handwriting was hard and quick as anger burned low in my gut.

Low leaned over to see what I was writing, then giggled. "Knife, not sure that's a good idea. Why don't you just kiss him in front of them?"

My hand stilled. I turned my head towards her to meet her amused gaze. Then flicked my eyes up to Dodge's to see him smirking.

"Brother, you honestly didn't think we wouldn't notice you two have got something goin' on? You started back just the other day, and I reckon' just about everyone's noticed the smiles and looks you two send each other. Fuck, it's like back in school days and first crushes. The amount of heat you two send off could even get me hard."

"Just grab the fucker and kiss him," Low added again with a nod.

I clenched my jaw. Was I ready for everyone to know? From what Dodge was sayin', they already did, so could I walk out there and kiss Maddox?

Low stood, only I didn't watch where she went. My eyes went back to the paper as my mind rolled around the thought of staking my claim for the man I loved in front of everyone.

Dodge scooted closer. "You worried what the brothers will think?"

I wasn't really. I was goddamn happy, and if they had a problem with it, fuck 'em.

What was holding me back?

Maybe the fact that Maddox had kept his preference for men to himself for so fuckin' long. What would happen if I did walk out there, kiss him, only to have him shove me away if he didn't want anyone to know?

When I didn't say anything, Dodge continued in a quieter voice, "Who cares what the others think? Fuck, brother, we're all searching for what's ours. I found mine in my little bird. Dive found his in Mena and so on. Have you found yours? If so, don't let anything stop you from keepin' it."

Hell, he was right.

I'd found mine, and it was Maddox.

"Hoo-boy, they're getting pretty chummy out there," Low said. I glanced to see her lookin' out the office window. "From what I can read, they're asking him to lunch."

That was fuckin' it.

I threw the pen down and stalked to the door. Low jumped outta the way as I threw it open. Each step I took ate up the concrete in seconds. I caught Maddox looking at me, his brows dipped in confusion, but I also caught his lips twitching.

As I reached them, I shouldered fuckface Ben outta the way, tagged the back of Maddox's neck and pulled him into me, finally slanting my mouth over his.

I waited for the shove.

For Maddox to push me away.

Only he didn't. He smiled against my lips before he opened his mouth and took my kiss, turning it into a hard, possessive one.

Cat calls and cheering broke out around us. I pulled back, turned, and signed while saying. "Got it?"

Ben was already smiling and then gave me a chin lift. Mitch looked a bit put out but nodded.

Yeah, they fuckin' got it.

Maddox was mine.

I shifted to where Maddox could see me. "Right, I'm

goin' back to work. Have fun at lunch, but lay one hand on him, I'll slit your throats. They don't call me Knife for no reason."

Maddox threw his head back and laughed. I glared at the two dicks and then walked back over to the bike I was workin' on.

Maddox left soon after. At first I didn't think he would. But then I remembered it was Mitch's job to check up on everything, and Maddox still wanted to be friends with fuck-face. Didn't mean I had to be happy about it.

I was bent over tightening the last bolt when I heard behind me, "Sick fuck."

Straightening, I spun around to glare at the little fucker in front of me. "What'd you say?"

He rolled his eyes and started to walk off. I grabbed his arm and yanked him back to face me. "What. Did. You. Say?"

"He called you a sick fuck, Knife," Muff offered from not far away.

"Who the fuck are you, boy?" I asked, crossin' my arms over my chest.

"Prospect."

With a menacing chuckle, I shook my head and said, "Didn't ask what you are, but who."

"I'm only called prospect, like the others." He glared. Yeah, he was right there. New recruits didn't have a name until they were through their trial run. They didn't matter until they'd proved themselves.

Steppin' closer so I was in his face, I clipped, "I've been away, so you don't know me, but you think you can come near me and say shit like that... boy?"

"Guys like you shouldn't be allowed in the club." Wasn't

sure where he got his balls from, but he was about to eat them.

"Oh fuck," someone muttered near us.

Yeah, the boy heard it and I saw his eyes flash with fear.

Glancing over his shoulder, I caught Dodge standin' there with his arms crossed. "Prez?"

"Back room."

The grin that lit my face had the boy gulpin'. With a quick move, my hand was around his throat, and I was draggin' him backwards. He struggled, gurgled, and tried to pry my hand away. Nothin' worked to stop me.

Muff, already ahead of me, had thrown the door open. Entering, I threw the boy to the floor. "Get up," I ordered.

Some brothers filed into the room behind me. I didn't look, only scowled down at the teen on the floor. Pullin' back my leg, I kicked him in his arse. "Get the fuck up."

He stumbled to his feet, his chest rising and fallin' rapidly.

"Get the other prospects in here," Dodge called. "Wait a sec, brother."

The boy sneered at Dodge. "How can you call him brother when he's—"

"What?" I asked. "Gay, bi?"

His hands balled at his sides. "A sick fuck."

"Who you belong to?" Dodge demanded on a growl.

"No one."

"Who brought you in?"

"Fang." Jeremiah, also known as Fang, was only a year outta bein' a prospect himself. He shouldn'ta been able to bring anyone into the club. He'd also come from the Venom MC, not that it mattered. He'd had Hawks blood running through his veins when he went behind Venom's back to keep tabs for us. Still, what was he thinkin' bringin' in a bigot like the little shit in front of me?

Dodge called to another brother, "Get him here as well."

"What you gonna do? You can't do shit for sayin' something."

Brothers around the room chuckled.

"You all for that shit to happen in front of you? Two guys goin' at it?" the idiot asked.

"'Fars I could see they had their dicks in their pants, so they weren't goin' at it," Billy said.

"They were kissin'," he yelled it in a way as if it was a sin. "You all are fuckin' sick for lettin' that shit happen. Heard the Hawks was weak. Didn't know how much until I saw that goin' on." He shrugged outta his prospect cut. "Don't want no part of Hawks. Just let me leave."

Brothers chuckled. Vicious stepped forward. "You're leavin', after we teach you a lesson."

"You can't do shit. I'll go to the cops."

"Detective here." I glanced at the left wall to see Parker leanin' there with his hand up in the air. Snortin', I fought the smile wanting to rise. Christ, it was good to see who had my back.

"What's goin' on?" Fang asked as he entered the room.

"This boy here said some shit to Knife," Vicious explained.

"He was kissin' another dude, in front of everyone. Faggots, the lot—"

"Shut the fuck up," Fang snarled.

"You still vouchin' for him?" Dodge asked.

"Nope," Fang answered.

Glancin' over my shoulder, I asked, "You think he'll piss himself?"

Fang snorted. "Could. Not that I care. I only brought him in as a favour to his father."

"You let them touch me, you won't see my sister again."

Fang rushed him, gripped his tee, and pulled him up to his face. "You touch Poppy, I'll fuckin' kill you."

The idiot snorted. "I don't have to touch her. Haven't you noticed she ain't been around? It's 'cause dearest daddy has already had a taste, and he's willin' to share when I'm older."

The room went silent.

That news was fucked up, and Fang didn't take it lightly. Like none of us would.

The boy knew he was in trouble. He paled before Fang roared in his face and then threw him into the wall. Fang's fist smashed into his cheek first, then nose, gut, and face again. The boy fell to the floor. Fang glanced over his shoulder, his eyes cold. "He's all yours," he stated before making his way to the door.

"Fang, don't go in it alone."

Fang paused at Dodge's words. His hand tightened around the handle. "Don't know what you're talkin' about," he said before he threw the door open and stalked out.

"Fuck. Vicious, Muff, Pick, after him. Take his back."

The brothers quickly left the room.

Shit was about to go down, and it wasn't gonna be pretty.

"What you want done with him, Knife?" Billy asked.

Shit. I had better things to do than deal with the piece of crap lyin' on the floor bleedin' from his mouth and nose while groanin'.

"Think he's already got the message. Still…" I tapped my chin in thought. "No one calls me or anyone in Hawks faggots. He needs to bleed some more."

"No. Stop, fuck, it's the drugs. They mess with me," he said as he scooted to his arse, wincing while he rested his back against the wall.

"Boy, Hawks don't take kindly to words like that. We ain't weak. We take care of our own, and you'd best remember it and spread the word. After I'm done with you that is."

The door burst open and in it stood Maddox. "Now, I would have gone gentle to some extent, but now Beast is back, you're fucked." I grinned down at the boy and saw a wet patch soak through his jeans as he took in Maddox's huge-arse form and the deadly look in his eyes.

"Close the door, babe. We got work to do."

Maddox grinned, and it wasn't a nice one.

CHAPTER TWENTY-EIGHT

BEAST

$\mathcal{B}$y the time we'd picked up Nevaeh and got home, I was exhausted. I was also pissed I'd left for lunch and Jay had to deal with the little fucker who'd called him a sick fuck. No bastard had the right to say shit to Jay and get away with it. Sucked Fang had already had a go at him. Still, I understood why when Jay explained everything when we'd walked into the bathroom in the compound to clean the blood away. The kid still lived, barely. Parker ended up taking him to the hospital sayin' he got involved in a hit and run. What helped was when Parker rang later and the doctors had found traces of a heap of drugs in the kid's blood. So even when we scared him enough to not breathe a word, if he slipped up one day, no one would believe a drugged-out idiot.

But I wasn't sure how long of a life he had if Fang got his hands on him again.

Just before Jay and I left for the day, we went searching for Dodge to see if he'd heard anything about Fang's situation. He had. Apparently, things with Fang were about to change, but he let us know Fang and the others had a handle on it and then sent us home.

"If the brothers are still dealin' with it, you need us to take a spot at the clubs or bar?" Jay had asked Dodge on the way out.

"Nah, brother. All good. Talon sent a few up. They're taking care of things with closing down a club, and since the other clubs got renovated from the fires and are bringin' in more clients, he's having them stay for a bit until this shit with girls gettin' beat and shit settles. And besides, Handle's back."

All that was good news.

It meant things could start to calm down. All that had to be done was for someone to find the cunt harmin' the strippers so we could pull back on security.

I stretched as I stood in the kitchen, watching Jay feed Nevaeh her dinner. I wasn't hungry from lunch. Something I could have done without since both men bored me and all I'd wanted to do was get back to see Jay. Never expected to be told by a brother what went down when I'd got back. Shit, rage had all but consumed me.

Fuck. I just had to remember it was dealt with and no other, even the other new prospects, would do or say shit to us again after what they'd seen us do.

Running a hand over the top of my head, I turned to the fridge and grabbed out the leftover Chinese takeaway then dished it onto a plate. After heating it, I pulled it free and sat it in front of Jay. *Eat while she is. I'm gonna get a shower in.*

He glanced from me to the plate and then back up to me and grinned. "Thanks, babe."

Fuck.

I didn't think he realised he'd called me babe back in the compound when I'd entered the room, but he had, and if I hadn't been in a foul mood, I would have kissed him for it. But that babe he'd just used shot straight to my cock.

Christ. We were a couple of badarse motherfuckers, yet we turned to mush when we each used the word babe. Yeah, I'd seen the way it affected Jay when I'd called him that, and I could understand why he'd liked it so much.

I'd have to save my appreciation for later though. I wanted to take my time when I did show him how much he affected me. That didn't stop me from leaning down and touching my mouth to his before pulling back enough to search his eyes. They were warm and soft like my own. Before I grabbed him and did things no little girl should see, I grinned and walked from the room after I kissed a happy Nevaeh on the forehead.

The shower was a quick one. I hadn't really wanted one but workin' in a garage fixing cars and shit made me want one every night so I could slide into bed clean.

By the time I made it back out into the living room in loose-fitting shorts, Jay had Nevaeh undressed and ready for her own bath. He picked her up from the change table and faced me. "Did the water change when I filled her tub?"

All good. Need a hand?

"Just gonna give her a quick one," he said. Her tub sat in the corner of the room, near the kitchen. She wasn't yet in the bath since Jay thought it'd be gross if we sat her arse on the floor our feet stood in. Actually, he was thinking of redoing the bathroom or getting a waterproof mat we could take in and out for when she did have a bath. I'd voted for a mat; we just hadn't gotten around to gettin' one. As Jay made his way over, I couldn't help but admire his form.

I froze.

We hadn't checked the mail when we'd got home. Fuck, our results could be sitting in there and the night could possibly get way better.

Jay suddenly spun towards me and held Nevaeh out in front of him like he was allergic to her. "Help," I read on his lips and started forward. Fuck was she choking?

But then I saw it.

And stopped.

A fine line of piss streamed out from between her legs down to the floor.

"Fuck, help. What do I do?" He waved her around, and the piss went all over the place. Vin barked at the action. She'd never done this before. I'd heard of Koda doing it a few times, but Nevaeh hadn't slipped up and peed on her dad. "She's not stoppin'. Hell, baby, did you save it all up for this second?" he cried.

I couldn't help it. I threw my head back and laughed my arse off. The fearful look on his face, the way he stepped towards the kitchen, then retreated to her change table only to shift back to her bath, cracked me the hell up.

"Shit, shit, shit," he chanted as he stepped my way and placed Nevaeh in my arms. I gladly took her since she wasn't peein' any longer. "You're her daddy also, so you gotta help your man out and bathe her. I'll clean this up before I clean myself up."

I was her daddy also.

He just fuckin' said that.

Ka-fuckin'-boom. There went my heart as my emotions swamped me.

And if he didn't have pee all over him, I would have claimed his lips right then and there. Christ, I fuckin' felt like sobbing, his words had meant that much to me.

Jay must have read my feelin's from my face. His hand came up to my cheek. "Yeah, Maddox. I ain't doing this without you now. We're a family. You, me, and our girl."

Fuck me.

I gulped down the thickness in my throat and nodded. Jay's smile was warm, his eyes soft. He knew I was feeling too much, so he let me get myself under control and turned to start the cleaning.

My heart slammed into my ribs as I watched where I was goin' and stepped over to the tub. I kissed Nevaeh's cheek before I placed her in the water. She loved her bath time. Thankfully after her first one, we'd learned to place a waterproof mat under her tub so it was a quick ease mop up and she could then splash the hell outta the water. And it was lucky I was only in shorts, so all I had to do was wipe myself down after it.

As I held and watched Nevaeh, my daughter—holy Christ, I wasn't sure I'd ever get used to that—I was in the position to see Jay clean up all the mess. Still couldn't get over what a great dad he was.

Never thought Jay "Knife" Conger would turn into a family man, yet there he was.

Fuckin' grateful I was the one seein' it and got to be a part of it.

He was definitely it for me. Fuck, he'd been my fantasy for so goddamn long, and now I had him. He was mine. Living under my roof and sleepin' in my bed. We cooked together, we rode together, we fought together, and we'd soon be fuckin' each other.

Knew it'd take time for me to have his arse, but he'd be worth the wait.

Jay was mine.

Nevaeh was mine.

We were a family.

He glanced over at me and smirked as if he knew what I'd been thinking.

Fuck, I loved that man.

JAY HAD ONLY JUST WALKED from Nevaeh's room and into the living room when I'd finally remembered my thought from earlier. We hadn't checked the mail. I was up and outta my seat then out the front door within seconds. I lifted the lid and peered down at the letters in my hand in the dark.

Fuck, I couldn't see properly.

My steps ate up the pavement as I made my way back inside. Once in the house, I kicked the door closed and then winced, glancing to Jay to see if I'd woken Nevaeh. He had a smug smile on his face, no doubt understanding what I was searchin' for. When he shook his head to indicate I hadn't stirred *our* girl from her sleep, I sighed and went back to the envelopes in my hand. Sure, it had to be the day we got all the fuckin' bills.

I threw the phone, electricity, gas, water, and land rates to the floor, only stopping when I came to two slips I didn't recognise. One was addressed to Jay, something I'd told him to do a while ago, for his mail to be redirected to my house, and one was addressed to me.

It had to be them.

I pushed Jay's envelope into his stomach. He grabbed it in time before I stepped around him and tore mine open. I pulled the paper out and read it.

Negative for everything.

Spinning, I faced Jay. He waved his paper in front of him, smiling big. I grabbed it and passed him mine.

Negative for everything.

Slowly, I raised my gaze to his.

We crashed into each other. Our hands ran everywhere as our mouths nipped and licked at each other. I pulled his tee from his body and dropped it to the floor before our mouths connected again. The kissing was hot and heavy, but the way we tugged and undressed each other was an urgent frenzy of desire.

My heart thumped in my chest. I was finding it hard to catch my breath, and my hands shook, but I ignored it all.

I wanted, no, *needed* Jay more than anything.

My back hit the wall as I stepped outta my shorts Jay had already pushed down my legs. He palmed my cock while I undid his jeans and pushed them over his arse where I cupped his cheeks, dragging his body against mine.

His hand slipped free from my dick, and he pulled back to order, "Bedroom."

Nodding, I took his hand in mine and practically dragged him down the hall and into our room. It hadn't been just my room for a long time and each time I thought of it, my body warmed. Vin slipped past me on a jog and sat on his bed just inside the door.

Jay tugged me around to face him, his hands sliding to my neck. "Wanted inside you for a fuckin' long time. Now it's here, need to make sure it's good for you."

Anything you do will be good for me. It's you, Jay. Nothin' you do I'll hate, 'cause you're the one…. Crap, I couldn't do it. Heat hit my cheeks and Jay saw it.

"Tell me," he ordered, with a gentle shake around my neck. "Goddamn tell me," he said, and then pressed his lips against mine softly.

When he shifted back, I signed the words I'd been too scared to sign in case they made me lose the man I never wanted to lose.

I love you.

His smile brightened his whole fuckin' face and caused my heart to leap over a beat. "Known it for a while." I rolled my eyes. He smirked. "Still, I understood why you wouldn't share those words with me when I fucked us up in the first place. Thing is though, you're it for me, Maddox Lawson. No one would compare to you because I fuckin' love you too. Hell, I wouldn't give my daughter another dad if I didn't. You're my family along with our girl."

Fuck me.

Fuck, fuck me.

You sure? I signed without really thinkin', not really understanding how a man who was all about pussy could love a guy like me.

He chuckled. "Fuck yeah, I'm sure, and if you ask me that again, I'll hit you."

You want me.

"More than anything," Jay replied.

Then take me.

CHAPTER TWENTY-NINE

KNIFE

Seein' Maddox sign I love you… fuck, it shot me right in the heart and dick. Hell, I was already rockin' an erection, but watchin' his hands move over "I love you" made my cock throb along with the tremor that raked over my body. Ignorin' my reaction, I told him exactly how I felt. His gaze was intense, the whole moment was, but he needed to know I wasn't just messin' with him any longer. Like I said, this was it for me.

He was it.

I fuckin' loved the man I was crashin' into so hard that he stumbled back. I loved the man whose lips I was claimin'. Loved him in each and every fuckin' way.

Forcin' him backwards as I still kissed him hard, we stopped when his legs hit the mattress. His hand slid between us, and I broke the kiss to look down as he circled around both our cocks and jerked us off at the same time. If I wasn't in such a mood to take what was mine, I would have asked for a sword fight. Instead, I'd save that for another playful day, because right then, it definitely wasn't time to be playful.

Glancing up, I found Maddox already lookin' at me. "I fuckin' love seein' our bodies naked together. You're so goddamn hot," I told him. It was something I'd wanted to tell him for a while. Shit, I'd lost count of the times I got hard seeing his abs, his tats, his chest, and most of all, his dick.

He slid his arms around me, our cocks rubbin' together when he pressed his hands into my arse and glided his body up and down against mine. I didn't need words. I didn't need him to sign because I knew how he felt about whatever I was sayin'. He showed me with his actions.

"Turn around," I ordered, my hands on his hips pushing him away. He smiled, his eyes heating with passion, and I knew my own eyes would read the same.

Fuck, I needed to be inside of him.

He shifted around, bent over for me, his hands moving to the bed so his arse was in full view. I fuckin' liked what I saw. His puckered hole.

Quickly, I took the steps to the bedside drawer and pulled it open, grabbing the tube of lube before kicking it closed and standing back, right behind him. Not ready for the lube yet, I threw it on the bed beside him and placed my hands on his arse cheeks. I ran them over each globe and then slapped. His body jutted forward, not expecting it, and he looked over his shoulder at me, his hooded eyes showing me what he wanted.

I slapped each cheek again and then ran my hands over them to lessen the sting. He groaned and pushed back. Leaning down, I did something I never had before. I wanted to; it was a part of Maddox's body. I wanted to taste all of him.

With a firm tongue, I licked his ring, ripping a grunted moan from him. He tasted of soap from the shower, yet there was a lingering saltiness to him. Running my tongue up and then down, I made sure I left enough saliva around his hole before I stood up and teased it with my finger. He pushed back again. I knew he wanted more, but fuck, I wanted him lost with desire and nearly burstin' to come because once I got inside of him, I knew I wouldn't be lastin' long. I was so goddamn hard and leaking pre-cum already. My balls were seconds away from drawin' up ready to squirt my release. I teased his hole again and again before sliding a finger inside. Then another joined the first, stretching him, gettin' him ready for me.

When Maddox looked back again, I told him, "Lay on the bed, on your back." He did, his movements fast and eager. As he settled in the middle of the mattress, I climbed on and knelt between his legs. Just the sight of him before me had me wanting to wank until I came all over his stomach and chest. A claim all on its own.

He was mine.

Instead, I was about to claim his arse, like I had his mind and heart. Reaching out, I spread his legs wider and ran my finger over his hole again.

"This mine?" I asked on a growl. My body hummed, my dick throbbed, and my heart went crazy waiting for his response.

Yes.

"All mine?" I demanded.

Yes. His hands shook as he signed.

243

"Good. Because I'm all yours. You ready for me, babe?"

Christ, yes.

Leanin' back, I grabbed the lube and slathered it over my cock first and then over his hole while Maddox looked on with a clenched jaw, probably wantin' me to hurry the fuck up. But I didn't. I played with his hole some more, watchin' him drown in desire, his mouth opening and closing, sometimes with a groan and sometimes silent. His cock leaked all over his stomach, and I wanted that on my tongue, so I leaned down and sucked the tip of his dick into my mouth, runnin' my tongue all over it.

Fuck. I had to have him.

Removin' my finger, I moved until my upper body loomed over him, and my slicked cock nudged his entrance. "You want me?"

More than anything.

"Fuck, babe," I bit out through clenched teeth as I edged the tip of my dick inside. With the amount of lube I'd applied and with how tight he was, my dick slipped away from where I wanted it to go. I rested my weight on one hand and took hold of my dick, then leaned back a bit so I could see my hand guiding myself back to his hole and slightly inside.

"Christ, fuck, you're tight," I mumbled. Yeah, I wasn't gonna last long. His arse surrounded the end of my dick like a vice.

Maddox's hands touched my chest. I brought my eyes to his before he glided his fingers to my shoulders and applied pressure there for me to come down. I did, our chests touching. I went to my knees more and pressed my cock in further.

His hands came up above his head to sign, *All the way.*

Shakin' my head, I said, "I don't want to hurt you."

"*Fuck*," he mouthed, his head digging back into the bed. He signed again. *All the way.*

"Not yet."

He brought his hands down to slap my arse with such force my hips thrust forward along with my cock, right inside of him. "Fuck, fuck, fuck," I chanted. "You okay?"

He opened his eyes enough to see my question and grinned. His hands went above his head again. *Oh yeah. Fuck me, babe.*

Lifting back up on my straight arms, I glided my dick out and then thrust back in. Maddox groaned loudly. I looked down between us to watch my dick entering him over and over. All while mumbling to myself about how hot, slick, and tight he was. I could have even said I wanted my dick to live inside of him. I wasn't sure because I was lost in the pleasure of it all.

My pace picked up as I slid my eyes all over him, taking in our first time, memorising it. Maddox's hands tightened around my wrists. Christ, his face was pinched, eyes screwed tightly, but it was in a look of ecstasy. He fuckin' loved me being inside of him as much as I did.

His cock was leakin' a hell'va a lot more than before. His balls were already up inside his body. I groaned at the sight and felt my own balls draw up. Too close... I didn't want it to end.

I needed his mouth when I came. I went low, and his eyes opened. He lifted his head to meet my mouth and grunted against my lips as I felt his release squirt between our bodies. Our tongues tangled, and still he kept coming. He tore his mouth from mine, breathin' heavily and then, fuck me, *fuck me*, he growled out low, "Jay."

He spoke.

He fuckin' spoke. I was frozen for all of a second until he urged me forward and back with his hands at my hips, and the pleasure of a near release took over.

I moved back to have his eyes. "Gonna come." He nodded. "Fuck, gonna come in your arse. You want my cum?"

"Yes," he said. His deep and raspy voice had me losing my load.

"Fuck, yes," I grunted and kissed him until I lost the last drop right inside his arse. Still pumpin' my dick very slowly inside of him, I got to my arms, and once I had his eyes, I said, "You talk."

He nodded, then shrugged.

Holding still, with my dick all the way in, I said again, "You spoke."

His hand came up. He cupped the side of my face and then ran his thumb along my bottom lip.

You gonna take yourself outta me? He questioned with his hands, a raised brow and a small smirk on his lips.

"Nope." I shook my head. "Like it too much." He chuckled, causing his arse to clench around my dick. I close my eyes and groaned.

A flick to my nose. *Move out.*

"You sore?"

A little.

"Fuck, sorry." I slowly withdrew my cock from its happy place and then leaned in to kiss his chest, his shoulder and then his lips, before climbing off him to sit on the bed beside him. We were gonna have to have a shower; we'd made a mess with the lube and his cum. Mine was probably leakin' from his arse too, which made me want to spread him and look.

Fuck, just the thought of my cum inside of him perked my dick up to manage a little bob. However, there was something I wanted even more. His hand landed on my thigh and squeezed. I lazily ran my fingers around his nipple, up over his shoulder, neck and across his lips.

Having his eyes, I mentioned again, "You talk."

He sat up. *Could always speak, never wanted to. There's something wrong with the way I talk. My brain doesn't match up with my mouth. Words get muddled. There's some big fancy name for what I have. Doesn't matter any which way. The end is still the same. My brain is fucked.*

Jesus Christ.

He could talk. Why hadn't he said anything, even the smallest word around me?

His fingers caught my chin, and he lifted until he had my gaze before he dropped his hands to sign. *The only person I spoke in front of was Memphis, and that was because he was like a father to me. Never tried in front of you because I didn't want the man I was in love with to think I was stupid. Jay, been in love with you for a fuckin' long time. Didn't want you to think less of me.*

"Don't you think if I took you with no talkin' at all I could take you any way you came? Fuck, Maddox, hearin' my name come outta your mouth... goddamn beautiful."

Jay, I can't—

Grabbin' his hands in mine, I shook my head. "I don't want you uncomfortable, ever, and I can already see from your look and tense body that talkin' about you speakin' makes you feel that way. I ain't asking for you to, shit, I don't know, give me full sentences. But... Maddox, you're here, in this home, with me and Nevaeh, just us. I want you to feel you can be just you in front of us and not think we'll judge you any differently."

His eyes lowered. I watched them flick over the bed while his mind ran around with thoughts. I honestly didn't give two shits how he spoke. I just wanted him to trust me that he could do and be whatever and not feel self-conscious about it.

This was our home.

Our life.

And our little family unit where there should always be trust and love.

Would he come to the same conclusion?

Finally, he raised his head. His eyes went straight to mine where he smiled softly, even shyly and… Jesus, he said, "'Kay," and nodded.

My whole body warmed; my face near cracked with the huge smile I gave back. Rockin' to my knees, I got in his face, kissed him once, and said, "'Kay."

EPILOGUE

KNIFE

A month of pure fuckin' awesomeness since it *was* Maddox and myself. Yeah, we had random fights over little shit. We were bikers; we were bound to butt heads every now and then. At least the make-up sex was outta this world. So, hell, even if all the moments weren't pure bliss, I was still so goddamn happy because Maddox Lawson was mine.

We were sitting at Pick and Billy's bar, in a booth off to the side with other brothers. Nevaeh was at my ma's having a girls' night. Ma loved her time with my girl, just as much as Nevaeh loved getting spoilt by her grandma.

Although we'd had the night off, I wasn't really feelin' it being at the bar. I'd come to love the nights at home just lazin' around with Nevaeh and Maddox. Then also the time Maddox and I had after she'd gone to bed. Buried inside of him was something I wished I could do all the goddamn time, but I'd been wonderin' lately why he hadn't been pushing to want to take me in the same way. Hell, I got off on havin' his fingers, but I wanted more, and I'd picked that night to push to get what I wanted.

I was watchin' Maddox sign to Billy about some car he was fixin' when I felt the booth compress beside me. Turning my head, I saw a woman in her early twenties had slid in to sit next to me.

"Hi." She smiled.

"Hey, sugar. What you needin'?"

"My friend over there." She pointed to a blonde with a pixie cut who stood at the bar. "Mentioned you might be able to help us out tonight."

"Yeah?" I asked with a raised brow, and after takin' a sip of my beer, I added, "With what?" I could feel Maddox's attention on us and from the way he'd stiffened at my side, he knew, as I did, where the woman was gonna lead the conversation.

She got close to whisper in my ear. "Heard how good you are in bed, honey. We'd like to see just how good."

When I threw my head back and laughed, she shifted back, confusion written all over her face. She was stunnin', so was her friend, but that didn't matter. Not any longer.

Shaking my head, I said with humour lacing my voice, "Sorry, sugar, but you got the wrong equipment to get anything from me."

She bit her bottom lip, her head tilted to the side. "What do you mean?"

"See the fella next to me?" I gestured with my chin to Maddox, who was indeed watchin' our exchange. "He's the only one who's gonna get any action from me." Leanin' in, I said and signed, "Because I love his cock."

Brothers chuckled around us.

The woman smiled. "We won't mind sharing or watching."

Maddox snorted. He leaned over me and bit out low, "Mine." Then signed, with Billy relayin' what he said, "Ain't no one elses." Over the past month, Maddox had opened more to sayin' small things, not only in front of me but some of the brothers and especially if he really wanted to get what he meant across, like layin' a claim to me. Of course, the brothers had been shocked, but like a lot of things, they dealt with it quickly.

She frowned, nodded, and exited the booth.

Glancin' to Maddox with a smile, I asked, "Wanna get outta here?"

Some of the brothers groaned around us. Fucked if I cared they knew I wanted him. Maddox nodded. I was just about to yell a farewell when Della, who had only arrived two weeks ago with Melissa, Dallas's women, yelled, "You can't tell me what to do, Handle."

She had been walkin' past our booth when she yelled it, only to come to an abrupt stop when Handle grabbed her wrist and spun her to face him.

"I can when it's a stupid fuckin' idea. You ain't doin' it, Della."

She got close, right in his face. Handle let go of her arm and crossed his arms over his chest. She glared into his hard eyes, and said, "No man, never again, has a right to tell me what I can and can't do. Get it through your thick head." She spun around and stormed off. Melissa came to Handle's side and said, "I'll talk to her."

"You'd better and get her to change her fuckin' mind, or I'll lose it."

She searched his face, a small smile played on her lips before she nodded and raced after her friend.

Didn't know what the situation was between our brother Handle and Della, but it wasn't our place to get involved, unless asked to. What *was* our place was the shit still happenin' with the strippers getting beaten. Only a couple of days ago one had gone missin' and the sick bastard was gettin' closer and closer to our joints. It was more messed-up shit, only it was something we were gonna fix. As soon as we had our hands on the fucker.

BEAST

On the drive home, I let the scene at the bar play in my mind one last time. Seein' Jay talk with that woman, one who I knew was his type, had fuckin' fury rising deep inside me. However, like so many other times, my man blew me away when he'd admitted in front of the brothers and her, I was the only one getting any action from him. Christ, my chest puffed out when he'd put her in her place, only to get pissed when she didn't back off straight away. That was until I butted in. Small words were fine for me to get outta my mouth before my brain stuffed it all up, and I was usin' them more often. Jay gave me the confidence to do so. Hell, he'd changed my life, and it'd always be for the better.

Walkin' inside the house, Vin came running up for a greetin'. I hadn't taken him with me because I had Jay. The man who'd just walked past me and Vin after shutting and lockin' the front door. Lifting my head, I watched him as he strolled down the hall and right into the bathroom. Seconds later the floor vibrated a little from the pipes running water through them in the bathroom.

With a final pat, I stood, took off my club vest and placed it on the couch before I started down the hall and ordered Vin to his bed in our room. I entered the bathroom to find Jay in the shower. I pulled back the curtain to see him washing his abs with soap.

Fuckin' hell. I loved his body. Couldn't get enough of seein' him naked.

Under my watchful eyes, I witnessed his cock grow from half-mast to a full erection. My man wanted some, and I was, like always, more than willin' to give it.

The feel of his cock sliding in and out of my arse was…. Christ, I didn't have enough or the right words to describe just how much I loved it. We'd had our days of fast and hard and then there were days where he took his time, went slowly, sensually. If I could say anything, I'd call it makin' love with the way he took me in those moments.

Jay's wet hands on my tee where he roughly jerked me forward, where I had to step in or fall on my face, brought me outta my thoughts.

"Need you to kiss me."

Chuckling, I signed, *Could've just told me to get undressed beforehand.*

His eyes were wild, hungry. "Need it now."

I'd do anything for Jay, so I did. I took his mouth with mine. It wasn't a gentle kiss, a press of the lips. No, we went at it. Teeth, tongues, and lips were sucking, nippin', and sliding over each other.

Jay lifted my tee. I shifted back enough so he could pull it over my head and throw it to the shower floor. His hand came to my jeans; the button popped open under his fingers, and then he slid the zipper down. I trailed my fingers over his body and down to his arse to grip it tightly in each palm. Dreamed of his arse. Fuckin' loved his arse and wanted to take his arse, but I wasn't sure he was ready for it. Even when I knew he got off hard from my fingers, it was different when it was a cock slidin' in. So I'd wait, even if it killed me. I'd wait until he told me or showed me he wanted it.

Jay's fingers hooked into the sides of my jeans and tugged them down. I eased back to help him. Since they were wet, it was a little harder.

"Fuck," I gritted, when I stumbled back a few steps and nearly fell on my arse until Jay took hold of my arm to steady me. Once I had my legs free, I went to grab Jay, only to find him laughin'. *What?*

"Next time I try and seduce you, make sure it ain't in the shower where you nearly fall and could probably cut your head open or get a concussion."

My lips twitched. *Why you trying to seduce anyway? You know you can have me any time you want.*

He shrugged, his hands coming to my hips to tug me forward. "Want you to know you can have me also."

My jaw clenched, my body reacted in a way where it sent a shiver over me. Fuck, my blood rushed right to my cock. I needed to make sure I'd read him right. *You want me to have you?*

"Christ yes."

"Have. You?" I asked in a whisper.

"Fuck me, Maddox."

Blindly, I reached out and shut off the water, all while keepin' his gaze. I arched back and snagged a towel, roughly dryin' him and then me with it.

My teeth ached with how hard I clamped down on them from the adrenaline pumpin' through my body. *Won't be able to have much restraint,* I admitted. *I'll fuckin' try, but need you to get in the bedroom and on the bed. On your hands and knees for me.*

His smile was sultry. "Anythin', babe." He lay a gentle kiss to my lips before he shifted around me and outta the shower.

He was givin' me all of him. I knew he loved me, he proved it time and again, but this, what we were about to do... fuck, it was everythin'.

Droppin' the towel to the floor of the shower, I stepped out and slowly made my way into the bedroom. My breathin' became erratic when I saw him, as I'd ordered, on his hands and knees on the bed. Only he was lookin' over his shoulder, his eyes running all over my body. He saw how hard I was, could probably even see the pre-cum leakin' outta my tip as I made my way closer.

I went to the drawer, pulled it open and snagged one of the lubes. Didn't bother closing it before I placed my hands on the bed, near Jay's shoulder, only to lift one off and grip the back of his hair to drag his head back so I could kiss him. He moaned into my mouth. Lettin' go of his hair, I ran a hand up and down his back and then to his arse, and back up, over and over while we kissed. With my other hand, I undid the tube. I broke the kiss enough to squirt some lube onto my fingers before I claimed his mouth with mine again. Using my slicked fingers, I played and teased his puckered ring. At first, he tensed, only to then relax, and when he did, I slid two fingers right inside. He gasped against my mouth and then sighed when I hit his prostate.

I finger-fucked his tight-as-hell hole and stretched him as I did it, needing him ready for me.

Jay ripped his mouth from mine and groaned when I pressed in and up. He was breathin' heavily and rockin' back on my fingers. He caught my eyes. "Fuck. Want you, give me you." There was no way to deny that demand, especially when my whole body was cravin' just that. Slippin' my fingers free, I rested my hand against his hip as I got on the bed behind him. His feet spread wider, and without me guiding him, he pressed his chest down into the bed. I bent, kissed his arse cheek, grabbed the lube and spread it over my throbbing cock and then shuffled forward on my knees, takin' my cock in hand.

I touched the tip of it to his entrance. His body shuddered, and he took a deep breath before relaxing back against me, pushing himself down on me.

I moaned. He was so fuckin' tight and yet he still pushed back, easing himself onto my dick. The head of my cock was in before he stopped and took another lungful of air. I rubbed his back and glanced at his face; it was screwed up.

Christ, I didn't want to hurt him.

Pullin' back, my dick bounced free. Jay got to his hands and glared over his shoulder at me. Smilin' in a reassuring way that we weren't stopping, I lay on the bed next to him and patted at his leg. "Straddle," I said.

Nodding, he climbed over me. I applied more lube to my cock and to his arse while he was up on his knees over me.

I would have loved to have had control and taken him.

But not for his first time.

His hand went between his legs where he took hold of my cock and placed it at his ring. When he had the tip back in, his hands went to my chest. I held his hips tightly as he slowly lowered himself at his own pace down on my dick.

Fuck me. It was heaven. Fuckin' heaven bein' inside of him.

Bringing my gaze up, I caught his eyes as he slid past the tightness and then all the way down. His eyes closed, his mouth opened, and even without hearing it, I knew a sound must have escaped.

"Hell," fell from his lips as he pushed his arse up off me and then back down again. "Yes." He opened his eyes as he rode my cock slowly. "Fuckin', fuck. No wonder you like it so much. You feel so good in there."

"Yeah?"

"Christ, yes." His rhythm picked up. He couldn't get enough as he pumped his arse up and down on me hard.

He was driving me crazy. My control slipped. I reached up and grabbed his shoulder, his neck and then tugged him roughly down. While diggin' my feet into the bed, I lifted my hips up and fucked his arse as I planted my mouth over his, causing us both to groan.

I drilled his arse hard and fast. I couldn't stop. I wanted my cum inside of him. He broke the kiss. "Fuck me, I'm gonna come soon. Yes, just there, fuck, yes, more, like that." One of his hands slid to my neck, his fingers and palm digging in as his fiery eyes met mine. "Tell me."

"Jay?" I asked, not fully understanding, I was too close to releasing in his tight little hole.

"Fuck. Tell me, now."

"Love you."

It was what he wanted. I knew it when I watched his lips move around the word, "Yes." Then his mouth touched down on mine, and I felt his hot sperm hit my stomach between us, he found his release with me just fuckin' him. Takin' him.

My cock soon exploded deep inside of him. I gripped his hips and kept the fast pace right until the end. Another slide down, up and down where the last of my cum shot deep.

He settled all his weight on me. It was harder to breathe, but I didn't care. I wrapped my arms around him, and while I eased my own rapid breathing, I kissed his shoulder again and again.

His hands going to each side of my head, he leaned back and kissed my lips.

His gaze roaming my face, his mouth grew wider in a smile. "So fuckin' glad I dry humped your arse in my sleep in Sydney, since it led me to you, and to findin' love I never thought possible."

Snorting out a laugh at his dry-humping comment, I grinned up at him. My heart was warm and felt so fuckin' huge in my chest from the amount of love I had for the man above me. *You're my goddamn forever.*

"I sure bloody am." He winked and kissed me again.

SNEAK PEEK — BREAK OUT

HAWKS MC: CAROLINE SPRINGS CHARTER: 5.5

PROLOGUE

HANDLE

Loss was something a person could never get over. It played in your mind each and every fucking day. What made some loss worse was how your friend or family member died. Mine would burn bright because of the betrayal my blood brother, Slit, put me through. He'd gotten heavy into shit he shouldn't have, and I had to have his back, but in doing so, it brought attention to my old lady. In turn, the ones who corrupted my brother tried to control my brother through me by taking her.

Feeling that loss, the way it happened, it still sliced at me each and every goddamn day. They'd killed her because of my motherfucking blood brother. It was why I'd snitched to the Hawks MC about Slit. We'd both been members, but Slit had been screwing them over too, dealing out information he shouldn't have. As soon as I'd got that painful call, I'd handed my brother over and ripped open another wound. Only one that healed quickly... his betrayal made it so. I'd known they'd kill him. Shit, I even watched it happen, but I did nothing to help him. He deserved *nothing*.

Loss was also something Della would feel for a while.

Della.

Fuck. It'd been two years since my old lady was torn from my life and in those years, not once had another woman turned my head.

Not until Della.

How-fucking-ever, it was fine to look. I just didn't want anything to happen between us. I never wanted a relationship again. Besides, she was messed up, which was understandable after the shit she'd been through. Hell, she was feeling her own loss from her sister's death, and then the loss of her freedom when she'd tried to bring the man to justice, only to sink into his fest-pool of darkness. She'd been caught. He used and abused her in ways no woman should ever experience. Not that he ever laid a hand on her. Instead, he had his high paying members at his strip clubs do it. And then, *fucking then*, her parents pretty much chewed her up and spat her out, wanting nothing to do with her.

Her life was shit. Her memories and messed-up thoughts controlled every action she made.

Running a hand over my face, I sighed loudly and slapped my hand on the bed I was lying on. It wasn't my own bed. Actually, it was, but only for a few months longer. My president of Hawks MC ordered me to stay in Sydney after the hell that recently went down. At first, we'd been there to help Melissa, to get her out from under Jimmy's scrutiny because

Dallas had a claim over her. Then Melissa told us about Della, and there was no way we'd leave a woman, any woman, to stay in that nightmare each day.

Jimmy was dead, by our hands. His men the same. The women were safe, but they had to stay in Sydney too. Since Jimmy was publicly known in the business world, his death was televised, and as Melissa had been forced to marry him, she was fresh news for the vultures to swarm.

I had to stay until the shit had been cleared, until Melissa was old news and she could finally move back to Melbourne, to her man, one of my brothers, Dallas.

I didn't mind the break, but seeing, being around, and even scenting Della all the goddamn time made it hard. I wanted more than anything to slide into her. My thoughts even went as far as wanting to protect her with everything I had... but I also didn't want her to drown once again in hell.

I was sullied. Everything and anyone I knew was in jeopardy. Hell, it had happened to Jenny; it could happen again to Della.

The door to the bedroom opened. I turned my head as Della slipped in, closing it to lean against it.

"You good?" I asked. Melissa and I had found a therapist who did house visits. We'd organised for her to come over so Della could talk. This was after her parents turned their backs on her, causing Della to shut down completely. Some would have thought she would have shut down mentally after being abused in every way. Jimmy had put her through the ringer. Still, she hadn't. Actually, that wasn't true. No person would be the same after what happened to her. She'd been angry, hurt, and had lost some of herself. But it was her parents who knocked her over the edge. Having the people you loved the most turn their backs on you could definitely do that to a person.

Bringing in Elina was the right choice. Della had told us after Elina, the therapist, had left, she wasn't pissed at us for organising the counselling. Since talking with Elina, she could breathe easier. Still, I wasn't sure how long that'd last. Hell, if it were me, I'd be murderous if someone tried to step into my business.

"I am, at the moment," she admitted.

Snorting, I placed my folded hands under my head while I watched her. It was the first time she'd been in my room, and I wondered why she sought me out. "What you need, darlin'?"

Her eyes closed slowly, and I watched her chest rise and fall rapidly. Something was bothering her, and I needed to know what. I didn't move from my position. I lay waiting for her to open up to me and tell me what was on her mind. We weren't close. In fact, I swore she hated me, and if it wasn't for her hot body and the pain she felt that echoed with my own, in some fucked-up kindred way, I wouldn't have given her the time of day. I wasn't looking for a commitment, and that was what Della would need after being handled by too many men in the wrong way.

At least that was what I thought. I knew I was lying to myself. Since seeing her, I'd wanted her, and then her next words rocked me to my core.

Her eyes opened, and in them I saw... shit, determination for some reason. "One night."

Could she mean what I thought she did?

Christ, I wasn't sure I was strong enough to deny her what I thought she was asking.

"One night for what?" I asked, my whole body tense from those two words rolling in my head.

She straightened. I saw her hands at her sides fist, but not before I caught them trembling. "I-I want control."

"Darlin'?"

She shook her head, at what I wasn't sure. "Will you let me have control, of your body?"

Yeah, that's what I thought she was trying to say. I didn't let my eyes widen. I tried to control my heart beating hard in my chest, but I couldn't, but at least she couldn't see it.

Fuck.

Was I going to let her have what she wanted?

Me?

It could screw with my head, but goddamn it, I wanted to give it to her for my own selfish reason, to get my own fill of her, and then maybe she wouldn't be on my mind all the time. I also wanted *her* to feel she had control over a man, especially when so many had taken her control from her.

"Forget it," she snapped and went to turn until I called her name. I didn't like the thought of her leaving after it took a lot of guts to reach out to me. I was screwed. I knew I said I didn't want commitment, a relationship, but deep down, I could see myself settling again with the woman before me, and that was bloody scary.

"I'm yours for the night. For whatever you need."

It was messed up. We both were. But maybe in some bloody way, being with each other could help us both. At least that was what I told my aroused self.

Her shoulders dropped. She nodded and then spun slowly back around to face me. She mumbled something, which I thought was thank you, and then picked up the bottom of her tee, pulling it up and over her head.

Christ. She had no bra covering her sweet-as-fuck tits. As soon as I saw those beauties bounce, as she threw her top to the floor, my dick went from half-mast to hard in seconds.

Both our eyes were haunted, but desire was also firing away in them. Della popped the top button of her jeans and slid the zipper down. She bit her bottom lip, before releasing it and asking, "You... please, let me just touch you?"

She wanted total power over the situation.

And I'd give it to her.

Nodding, I crunched up enough to rid myself of my own tee, grabbed a condom from my wallet that sat on the bedside table, and placed it on the bed beside me. I then lay back. My hands went once again behind my head. She walked to the side of the bed, her eyes sliding over my body. With shaking hands, she pushed her jeans and panties down her long legs while keeping her gaze on the bulge behind my jeans. Yeah, she could see I wanted what she was offering.

Her eyes didn't meet mine when she knelt on the side of the bed and then scooted closer. Her hands came to my jeans and undid the button, then slid the zipper down. I lifted my arse up enough to help when she gripped the sides and shoved my jeans and boxers down. My dick sprang free and slapped against my stomach. Della watched it.

It gutted me there was no expression on her face. If I didn't see the desire burning in her eyes, I would have told her to get out, but I did see it. It flickered away in the depths of her eyes, and I was sure it only ever did so for me. The thought made my gut clench and my balls draw up in antic-ipation.

She left my jeans at my knees and straddled my thighs. After she'd donned my cock with the rubber, she placed one hand on my chest. Leaning up on her knees, her free hand came between us and gripped my cock. I clenched my jaw at her touch.

Fuck, it felt too good.

Della finally lifted her gaze to mine as she glided my knob over her slick entrance. Fear may consume parts of her but her desire, her body spoke the truth. She wanted this. Me. Her mouth moved as if she wanted to say something, but she didn't. Instead, she sat back down, gasping as I filled her wet pussy.

My hands itched to touch her, to pull her down and claim her mouth while I thrust up inside her, but I didn't. Still, with my hands behind my head, I watched and enjoyed the show above me.

She lifted herself up and then down again. Her other hand joined the first on my chest. Her eyes slammed closed, her back arched, and she threw her head backwards. A moan slipped from her mouth, and I hadn't seen anything more fuckin' perfect before. Her pulse ticked rapidly in her neck; she was scared, yet she was strong enough to continue riding me, taking back some part of herself.

Hell, I was already close. Just watching her fuck me, use me, ride me, take me into herself was more than I thought it would be. Shit, if I wasn't careful, I'd want it again and again. But I couldn't. It would be a one-time thing, and I had to accept that.

When her head came down, her eyes opened. Pain. In the depths her pain burned, soul deep and devastating. Raw emotions spilled forth as her tears brimmed.

"Take it," I ordered roughly. "Take back the power. This is you, your life, your control, and no one can take that from you again."

"Handle," she whispered. "I'm sorry," she said, only she didn't stop fucking me, my body.

"I'm not."

"It's wrong—"

"Fuck that. If this is what you need, then fuckin' take it. Finish it."

Her bottom lip trembled. "Please."

"What?"

"T-touch me. I'm cold, so cold."

Reaching up, I wrapped my arms around her and dragged her down. My mouth met hers. There was no sweetness. It was hot and heavy, but not forceful. I took my time with her mouth as I spread my legs a little and dug my heels in to lift up and grind my dick into her. She cried out against my mouth, and I ate it down. Her pussy clenched around me. She whimpered, and soon, I was joining her own climax with a grunted groan.

I relaxed back into the bed, and she sagged over me. All too soon her mind caught up with her, and she was climbing off me and the bed quickly.

"Del?"

She shook her head and scrambled for her clothes, slipping into them. Her voice shook as she said, "That... I'm sorry. I shouldn't have—"

"Don't," I demanded. "I knew what it was."

She nodded, stood straight, and got herself under control before she stated, "It can't happen again."

A stabbing pain shot through to my heart from her words.

Still, I didn't say anything. She waited for a beat of a moment for me to reply, but I didn't have the right words to give her. Her sigh was audible as she made her way to the door and, without looking back, she quietly exited the room, closing the door after her.

"Fuck," I clipped, running a hand over my face. Sitting, I dropped my feet to the floor and got rid of the condom in a tissue and then dropped it. I rubbed the back of my neck. "Christ."

Shaking my head, I stood and went to have a shower in the joining bathroom.

I'd just made the biggest mistake. I wanted her again already.

That moment between us was beautiful, yet so fucking devastating.

CHAPTER ONE

DELLA

Melissa, who I preferred to call Lissa, and I had been living in Melbourne for only a few weeks, and I was starting to get itchy feet. Not in a sense that I wanted to leave. So far I was enjoying Lissa's friends and living there, but I needed to fill my time with something else instead of reading. I needed a job. I also needed to find myself a place to live. Lissa's house was amazing, but her walls were thin, and each time Dallas stayed, I heard way too much going on in their room. Thank God for audio books and head phones.

A job could also help fill my mind with other things rather than the rough man who seemed to occupy it all the time.

Back in Sydney a couple of months ago, I'd made the wrong choice by trying to fill a void. But it had been more than that. I'd been attempting to gain back my control through Handle. It was wrong, especially since I was already attracted to the guy, even though I acted like I wasn't. Men like him were hard to come by, and I never thought after everything I'd been through that I'd want to be touched. But I had, and I wasn't sure if that was wrong or not after I'd dealt with sick monsters who'd raped and beat me.

Yet the night with Handle was everything a woman could hope for. He was gentle, sweet, and just plain amazing. Being around him made me feel safe, and that night I'd felt wanted and in control. Being with someone *I* wanted to be, where nothing was expected in return, had been empowering. I'd cowered away from those feelings, hadn't touched on them in a long time.

Still, I had to move on, discover who I was before everything had happened. As each day passed, I was slowly coming back to me. A smile or a laugh here and there helped, though night-time was the hardest, especially when I found myself wishing a certain biker was next to me instead of the cold spot on the mattress.

It was at night I also missed my sister the most. She'd been such a loving soul. She'd had a beautiful outlook, not only on life, but on people as well. Ashley had trusted too much, and it was the one thing I'd warned her about that got her killed.

God. My sister was gone from the earth, and it wasn't fair. She died too young. There was rarely a day that passed that I didn't wish it had been me instead of her light disappearing forever.

But I was trying, truly trying to make a difference in my life. I was finally doing something I knew she would want me to do.

I was going to live.

Ending my life had once been a common thought every day, but no more. I was going to live since she couldn't. And I could only hope she would be happy with how I lived my life.

Ashley was the main reason I kept going. I would find my happy medium and cherish each day as it came.

"Yo, Del," Dallas called. "Want another drink?"

Shaking my head, I said, "No thanks."

Lissa and I sat in the corner of Pick and Billy's bar with Dallas and some of his other biker brothers. We were having a quiet drink and enjoying each other's company. It was also the first chance we'd had to have a drink to celebrate our arrival in Melbourne. When we'd first arrived, we'd been busy with moving things in, changing addresses and such, and learning the lay of the land.

"So I was thinking, you know how you mentioned you wanted a job?" Lissa asked, and then took a sip of her bourbon and Coke.

"Yes." I nodded. Since Lissa was a computer whiz, she was already working for the Hawks MC, redoing their websites and such for all their businesses, plus providing support for their other business in Sydney.

"Mena's starting a day care at the compound for all the rug rats. She mentioned the other day needing some help."

My eyes widened. Me and kids? That was a no go. Children and I didn't mix. I was certain they knew I was scared to be around them. It was like a dog sensing when a person was frightened and got off by scaring them even more. Kids did the same with me.

I wasn't sure what exactly it was about children that had me backing away quickly if they got close. Although, it could have something to do with snotty noses, smelly butts, and grubby hands. Hell, anyone would think after what I went through, I wouldn't be so scared of little humans, but I was.

In fact, just the thought of being around them all day, every day had me swallowing hard.

Letting a nervous laugh free, I said, "Thank you, but no. I'd rather go back to stripping than work with kids." I winced at my stupid joke. God, I wasn't even sure why I'd said it. It just popped out and from the looks I was getting, everyone thought I'd lost it. Maybe I had.

"I'm not sure stripping would be a good idea right now with everything going on," Lissa commented dryly.

That was true. There'd been a news article about the trouble happening at strip clubs around town. What I would call, from what I'd seen on the news, a madman was beating strippers as they left work. One had even been kidnapped, beaten, and then left for dead.

I certainly didn't need or want to put myself in harm's way again. Regret for letting the silly slip of my tongue filled me, causing my cheeks to heat.

"You ain't strippin'" was bit out low behind me. My damn belly quivered from that voice.

However, I clenched my jaw. I hardly saw Handle, yet he apparently thought he could pop up unannounced and tell me what to do. It ticked me how I enjoyed it so much, hearing his voice, having him near. I'd assumed from him staying away from me that he was done having anything to do with me. I wasn't ready to fully admit to myself how much that hurt. It was why I immediately took the offensive, so he didn't see what I was feeling. Turning my head slightly, so I could just see him, I glared and snapped, "I will if I want to."

He leaned down. His warm breath fanned the side of my face causing me to swallow hard and school my features. He snarled, "It's a stupid thought. Don't think it again, 'cause you won't ever strip."

My heart was frantic in my chest. I wanted to slap him, kiss him, and punch him all at the same time.

"Brother," Dallas started, but I saw Handle's hand come up and then heard Dallas sigh.

"You think it won't bring up bad shit in your mind? You think—"

Standing abruptly, I turned to face him with my hands on my hips. He slowly ran his eyes up my body as he straightened.

"Handle, back the fuck off," Lissa called from behind me.

Jabbing my finger in his chest, I said, "Yes, you need to shut the hell up, Handle."

He crossed his arms over his chest. "You got nothin' to be ashamed of with what happened to you. Everyone here knows what went on. We all know you gotta be smart, and the thought of you strippin' isn't a good move."

Fuck him. Who the hell did he think he was presuming to know anything about what I felt, what I went through. And to do it in front of everyone…. My fists vibrated in anger. I was aware they all knew *everything*. It pained me how they knew what I went through, but only because I didn't want their pity. They'd saved me, helped me out of a messed-up situation. Still, it wasn't right speaking about it in front of strangers.

My hands landed on his chest, and I pushed. Only he didn't move. I lasered my eyes into his, hoping he'd suddenly combust. When he didn't, I let out a growl, pulled up my hands, slapped them to his chest and shoved. The prick didn't move an inch. So I growled again in frustration and stormed past him, shoulder checking him along the way. Only I was sure it hurt me more than him when once again his body didn't move.

I made it halfway across the floor and chose to yell, "You can't tell me what to do, Handle." Next, my arm was gripped, and I was spun to find a fuming Handle in my face.

"I can when it's a stupid fuckin' idea. You ain't doin' it, Della."

Stepping closer, our noses only inches apart, I felt Handle release my arm to once again take on the I-am-man-you-listen-or-else position by crossing his arms over his bulky chest. Glaring, I snapped, "No man, never again, has a right to tell me what I can and can't do. Get it through your thick head."

Before he could say or grab me again, I quickly spun and stalked off, right out the front door. It was there I ran to Lissa's car. When I realised I didn't have the keys, I kicked the tyre then threw my head back and screamed into the night. *Jesus, Ashley, who does he think he is? Can you help me work out the fool because I can't?*

He had no right.

No right to tell me what I could or couldn't do.

Shit.

Tears prickled my eyes. I wasn't going to cry. God, why did I want to cry?

That man turned me crazy.

I should have just told him I'd already come to the conclusion I wasn't going to strip, but I didn't. Instead, I snapped and ranted in his face. He deserved it, but I didn't want to be that person.

Grumbling to myself again, I kicked at the dirt, throwing my hands to my hips.

Why did he have to be a dick and say that stuff in front of everyone? Or even say anything at all. He had no damn right.

"Del," Lissa called. I looked her way to see her walking towards me. Dallas stood on the front steps to the bar, watching her every move. He didn't like to let her out of his sight when they weren't either in the compound, house, or outside of the bar. Unless there was another brother around who he trusted completely.

Why couldn't I find someone like that? Of course Handle popped into my head. There was a time I'd thought he'd be it for me, but since we'd moved and I hadn't seen him, I was second-guessing my choice.

I scoffed to myself. I didn't need anyone right then anyway.

Hell, he'd probably be like Handle and try and tell me what to do. Then again, Dallas seemed to do the same to Lissa, only she told him where to go after it.

Melissa stopped in front of me, and before she could say anything, I got there first. "I'm sorry."

Her brows rose. "Why?"

"We're here to celebrate. I shouldn't have ruined the night by letting him get to me."

She shrugged, hopping up onto the hood of her car, patting the spot next to her. Once I was seated, she bumped my shoulder and quietly said, "I think you scared him."

A laugh left me unexpectedly. "Scared? Handle? Why would he be scared?"

"I think the thought of you stripping when there's been trouble around scared him."

Scared Handle? No... what? Could he? Maybe?

Oh shit, there went my heart flourishing with hope that Handle did care and not in a protective guard type of way.

"It wasn't like I actually said I was going to do it." I shook my head. "He didn't have to go off like that in front of everyone."

"I know."

"He's such a... pain in the arse."

"A good-looking one at that."

Snorting, I shrugged, acting nonchalant. "He's not my type. There's also the fact I never want to get involved with another man anyway."

She bumped my shoulder again. "At least not yet."

Smiling, I admitted, "At least not yet."

"You want to come back in? I'm sure he regrets how he acted by now."

"No, thanks. I think I'll head back and get some sleep." I smirked. "Before you and Dallas get in and start rocking the walls."

I also needed to get away from Handle before he drove me crazier, to a point where I'd end up jumping him to just shut him up.

Lissa busted out laughing. "I promise once I've renovated

the master bedroom and we've moved into it, you won't be able to hear a thing."

"Praise the Lord."

She sobered as she studied me. I knew what was about to come out of her mouth before she even opened it. "You okay?"

That question.

That *damn* question. I was tired of hearing it or getting asked it every day. I knew she, even Julian and Dallas, asked me all the time because they worried, and for that, it warmed me, but I was over it. I could only pray if they saw more smiles, laughs from me, with time that question wouldn't pass their lips again.

When I eventually found a blissful life.

Sighing, I realised I might have to move away to someplace new to not hear the question. I was sure bliss and I didn't, and never would, know each other.

Nodding to Lissa, I told her, "I'm okay, but eventually, one day I'll be more than okay for the rest of my life."

"Damn right you will."

I smiled at her confidence, and I hoped I hadn't just made a liar out of myself.

ACKNOWLEDGEMENTS

Thank you to Lindsey Lawson, who read *Hear Me Out* as I wrote it and also helped me through the process of figuring so many things out for Beast. Working with you as I went along really helped. These guys are as much yours as they are mine. xx

Becky Johnson, you always amaze me. The process of writing and publishing isn't easy, but what helps is when an author has an editor like you.

Wander and Andrey, thank you for always being so helpful. Wander, your photos are brilliant!

ALSO BY LILA ROSE

Hawks MC: Ballarat Charter

Holding Out (FREE) Zara and Talon

Climbing Out: Griz and Deanna

Finding Out (novella) Killer and Ivy

Black Out: Blue and Clarinda

No Way Out: Stoke and Malinda

Coming Out (novella) Mattie and Julia

Hawks MC: Caroline Springs Charter

The Secret's Out: Pick, Billy and Josie

Hiding Out: Dodge and Willow

Down and Out: Dive and Mena

Living Without: Vicious and Nary

Walkout (novella) Dallas and Melissa

Hear Me Out: Beast and Knife

Breakout (novella) Handle and Della

Fallout: Fang and Poppy

Standalones related to the Hawks MC

Out of the Blue (Lan, Easton, and Parker's story)

Out Gamed (novella) (Nancy and Gamer's story)

Outplayed (novella) (Violet and Travis's story)

CONNECT WITH LILA ROSE

Webpage: www.lilarosebooks.com

Facebook: http://bit.ly/2du0taO

Instagram: www.instagram.com/lilarose78/

Goodreads:

www.goodreads.com/author/show/7236200.Lila_Rose

www.ingramcontent.com/pod-product-compliance
Lightning Source LLC
Chambersburg PA
CBHW071547110726
47908CB00007B/2021